REMEMBER
TO RECYCLE

TANTRA BENSKO

Sign up for the newsletter to keep up with the series, be alerted to discounts, receive gifts, enter raffles, learn the background, and more at http://www.insubordinatebooks.com/

"Mystery and conspiracy lovers rejoice! Standout author Tantra Bensko is back with another incredible mystery/adventure featuring Nancy and the nefarious forces of the Nevermind...This is a twist-a-minute narrative that switches adeptly between three points-of-view...To sum up, this five-star sequel to the author's acclaimed debut novel, *Glossolalia*, will leave you breathless and wanting more. What's next for the Agents of the Nevermind? We can't wait." — Publishers Daily Reviews

What readers say about Glossolalia: Psychological Suspense, the first book in The Agents of the Nevermind series
Glossolalia: http://flameflower.wix.com/glossolalia-suspense

Each paragraph from a different review

Professional Reviews

This reader is definitely ready for the next installment down Bensko's imaginative rabbit hole of creativity!
Hollywood BookR Reviews
The unreliable narrator motif adds to the overall success of the novel, and as far out as the plot ventures, the actions of herself and those around her never feel out of place.
Indie Reader
It follows in the literary footsteps of Tom Robbins rather than that of Thomas Harris, which provides the likable, if odd, flavor.
Portland Book Reviews
Never boring, the book takes us on a whirlwind tour of LSD projects, conspiracies, a love story, fugue states, mind control including drugs, the occult, the Mob, psychosis, fascist drug lords, glossolalia, sex, multiple personality disorder/dissociative identity disorder (MPD/DID), wars and arming various groups to overthrow politicians who are against U.S. government policies.
US Review of Books
It is this kind of skillful foreshadowing that elevates **Glossolalia** *far above any other ordinary examination of what the bad guys in our own government might be doing to us - or, rather, what they HAVE been doing for decades.* — *Publishers Daily Reviews/Midwest Book Review*
Amazon Customer Reviews

The book that didn't stop surprising me it would seem. Was not expecting the action-packed adventure that Tantra Bensko had laid out before me with my new favorite characters, Nancy and co.

Tantra Bensko's novel, **Glossolalia**, is a complex and most compelling read that I have ever laid eyes upon...the book consists of several different genres and combinations that make it a powerfully engaging read.

It's a story that is impossible to categorize and quite possibly the most unique book I've ever read.

The novel offers a bleak, but redeeming picture of ignorance vs. knowledge, bravery vs. cowardice, and fact vs. fiction. Bensko's **Glossolalia** thrills from the first page to the last, answering some questions and leaving others for the audience to ponder for a long time.

Glossolalia is a very unique story that highlights lots of modern dilemmas. It's a very fast paced story that keeps you entertained through all of it.

Fights, chases, edgy sex, power to the people, twists and turns, secret rooms, missing time, and bold truth rarely found in novels until now.

If you want to read a book that transcends the norm, and gives you something to think about long after you've finished it, you need to read this one.

High octane story with a great heroine! Imagine my surprise to find myself on a roller-coaster of action and intrigue! It felt a lot like watching an action movie, with car chases and knife fights and deadly poisons.

Psychological is definitely an apt description of this yarn beautifully spun by Tantra Bensko. Of course, I would love to read more!

It's a story that is impossible to categorize and quite possibly the most unique book I've ever read.

Echos of Brave New World and George Orwell's 1984 reverberate in this modern thriller that once you start reading, you will not want to put this book down. Read it, and then ask for more.

I very much enjoyed this book. If you are ready to go on a journey into the complexities of personality, enjoy strong characters who mightily deal with the difficulties of managing good and evil, and at the same time enjoy a suspenseful and intriguing story then you will love **Glossolalia**! *I'm looking forward to more in the series!*

If you like roller coasters at all, it's going to be absolutely mind-blowing to ride this thing – **Glossolalia:** *Psychological Suspense by Tantra Bensko. The book has a lively story line and I anxiously returned to its reading after putting it down for a while.*

This was one of the most suspenseful novels I've ever read. I was drawn in right from the beginning and couldn't stop turning the pages. I had to tear myself away from it and ended up reading it mostly all in just two sittings.

Caught up in Nancy's fugue consciousness and the mysteries that all the Jolly Wests in the world are committed to burying, we follow closely behind her thoughts and courageous acts to learn what it means to be shattered and what it takes to put Humpty Dumpty together again.

A great book to read if you like suspense books!

She fights for her freedom on both levels, in a twisted and fast-paced plot.

It is this kind of skillful foreshadowing that elevates Glossolalia far above any other ordinary examination of what the bad guys in our own government might be doing to us - or, rather, what they HAVE been doing for decades.

It was intriguing and hard to put down. I highly recommend this book as a must-read.

I'm a big fan of Nelson DeMille, and the suspense is on par with his work. Looking forward to the next volume.

The plot, in itself, is as intriguing and engaging as it gets, compelling the reader to read on and turn those pages one after the other through its beautifully woven plot.

I understand that this is but the first in a series of novels in which Ms Bensko explores and exposes a "fictitious" network of deceit she entitles "the agents of the Nevermind." I hope that is so because I would love to learn more and more about this "Nevermind" as she conceives it. What a concept! Just let it work in your imagination for a moment. Of what might the "Nevermind" consist, of what not? It is a whole complex of the misunderstandings, lies, machinations by which we have been manipulated since... well, when? These agents and the term Nevermind" are only the most recent incarnation. It involves everything from accepted religion, the mythologies behind such, the bureaucratic workings of Globalism, the individual enslavement of individuals and families. It is fascinating, absolutely, and, alas, a metaphor for a network of greed and deceit I fear is all too real.

This unique book engaged me from the opening scene when Nancy, an otherwise skittish and awkward person, courageously follows a truck she believes is dumping illegal toxins.

Filled with car chases, cults, sex scandal and nail biting suspense, this book will please anyone who loves a good mystery, or who is interested in the bigger mysteries that all of us must face.

Glossolalia is a fast-paced, quirky book that lives up to its tagline of being a "psychological suspense thriller" while also being extremely fun to read.

Most of all, Nancy is a character you'll be rooting for, in a world you don't' want to inhabit, in a setting that looks suspiciously like your own neighborhood. Is that Tim Burton enough for you? The book is probably closer to an experimental spy thriller...if Alice's Lewis Carrol had written in for modern times. Edgy and fun, dark and disturbing, high octane and low blows—this reader is definitely ready for the next installment down Bensko's imaginative rabbit hole of creativity!

GLOSSOLALIA is a suspense novel like I've never read before. Usually with suspense novels, and perhaps because I've read so many, its usually same s*** different faces - NOT HERE!

Perhaps the author will guide us into some background as the books come out - I can only imagine she will. For a first taster of the ideas the author wanted to relay, I love that she jumped right in and shared the twisted, convoluted, corrupt dealings that go unseen, but are perhaps very real.

In **Glossolalia** nothing seems to make sense for a very good part of the book, but then...it happens. You start finding meaning in the little details, putting two and two together, seeing the connections between it all. And before you know it, you have it right in front of you: an intricate story where nothing is left to chance, filled with complex characters and with the most disturbing explanation. A plot where everyone plays their part and no one seems to be on Nancy's side.

I haven't finished reading this enthralling novel but it draws in mind the sort of off-the-wall characters and situations that have long attracted me to the writing of Tom Robbins, Kurt Vonnegut and Douglas Adams. (Yeah, I know: I have a rather limited interest in literature). The initial blast of context on the first page took me by surprise (I don't know what I *was expecting) and as I have been reading, I find I am turning each page with "WTF will happen next ?" puzzlement and anticipation.*

The plot simply has everything: suspense, twists, fantasy, politics, brain-washing and even a bit of romance. It is a rich mixture of genres, difficult to typecast, and it honors each one of them. Hand in hand with our protagonist, we discover bit by bit the odd things that are part of her life, and we feel her struggle with herself, we suffer the frustration she suffers.

The movement in the novel went fast. I felt like I was watching Raiders of the Lost Ark, every scene action packed with very little rest.

Sex! Murder! Conspiracies! This novel has it all, and it comes at the reader non-stop. There's no chance to catch your breath and it's hard to put down. So there's that. Social engineering is an interesting topic, especially in today's crazed socio-political climate. The protagonist is a kickass lady who doesn't take shit from anyone.

I want to read it again because of how it made me feel! Incredibly well written and very different at the same time, I highly recommend **Glossolalia** *to anyone wanting something different in all the best ways, and enjoys a book that can be reread rather than just get to the end and stick on a shelf or get rid of it.*

Bensko is a consummate wordsmith.

Bloggers
It's a story that's impossible to categorize and quite possibly the most unique book I have ever read.
Lindley Reviews
What is really interesting about **Glossolalia** *is its underlying message about the importance of critical thinking. Nancy starts off as naïve and not knowing much about the world, and she's jealous of people who have more*

knowledge than her. But then she learns to not just accept things at face value and instead she decides to investigate until she figures out the truth. Even if the truth turns out to be terrifying and turns her world upside down.

Muses and Marvels

Tantra Bensko's novel, **Glossolalia**, is a complex and most compelling read that I have ever laid eyes upon...the book consists of several different genres and combinations that make it a powerfully engaging read. Suspenseful, check. Conspiracy, check. Political thriller, check. Science fiction fantasy double-check. Alternate universe double checked. Readers worldwide can find a little of everything within this stunning novel. This tale is full of action and intrigue from page one to the last page. Mind control, murder, and sex. All of these interesting things woven into a surprising story that will blow readers' minds away. I just finished reading this and now, I am looking forward to the next brilliant adventure by the talented writer.

Urban Book Reviews

While Spy Thriller type books of the past somewhat simplistically placed intelligence agents in the role of saviors and protectors of all that is good, readers are becoming more capable of increasing complexity regarding the CIA, NSA, FBI, and other agencies. The success of books by Barry Eisler, for example, shows the trend toward more realistic portrayal of foreign policy is widely welcomed.

A Cheeky Book Addict

Websites to delve further into The Nevermind

Read all about *Glossolalia* at
http://flameflower.wixsite.com/glossolalia-suspense
Read quickly about the series at
http://flameflower.wixsite.com/agentsofthenevermind
Read about each book in the series, at Insubordinate Books at
http://www.insubordinatebooks.com/

This book dedicated to these heroes who exposed topics referenced in this novel

Vanessa Beeley
Eva Bartlett
Cynthia McKinney
George Webb
James Corbett
Ole Dammegard
Sibel Edmonds
Nancy Scheper-Hughes
Kathryn Bolkovac

Contents

Chapter One

The Crack

Sunday

Nancy's shoulder pressed against the window, steaming it up, as she leaned back against the thick plank. She put her feet up on the footstool, her boots clunking against it, her toes tingling from cold. The smoke from the wood stove in the living room sucked back in through the space in her doorway, tickling her nose. The woman she rented the closed-in porch from was gone, in the city with her boyfriend. Nancy could leave off her medical burn-mask and curly straw-blond wig for the night.

Her face was unscarred, other than for the tiniest slices from a quick nose job to hide her appearance from facial recognition software. Her naturally strawberry blond hair was dyed dark brown and rough-cut extremely short. Her skin wasn't as pristine and translucently glowing as it had been before she escaped the Nevermind.

The house was far enough from the road that she didn't worry about her naked face being spotted in the candlelit evening, especially considering the low hedge and the fog.

An owl hooted in the thick trees. One of Nancy's piano students, who lived the next house down, was practicing the Mozart assignment. The tinkly optimistic piano refrain of the tiny ice cream truck trudged up the hill. Nancy chuckled. It finished out its inevitably, surreal cyclical broadcast: a middle-aged woman's voice scolding, "HeLLO!" with a stereotypical New York Jewish meets Valley Girl sarcasm. As in, "Are you stupid or something, why are you not here buying ice cream cones, get with

1

the program!" And after that, a bizarre "haw haw" laugh that was so creepy it was funny. She'd never seen any brand on the van.

She had never heard children running out to stop the truck and clamor for treats in the many months she'd lived there. She imagined laughing about the ice cream "truck," a van actually, with a friend, any friend, sharing the wordless joke. Well, other than the woman she rented from, her only friend was Becky, a young woman down in the city. Nancy's place was too high up in the hills, with steps, even, for Becky to handle visiting it.

A shocking BANG right beside her head. At first the window held tight, glass cracking like a spider web around the point of impact, the white spot quickly disrupting the center. The window shattered against her, nicking her eyelid, and glass crunched under her when she leaped away, grabbing the mace like a master as she rolled under the desk. She hunkered and remained motionless, breathing quietly. Only the piano trill of the ice cream van broke the silence outside, receding slowly.

She crouched low, moving toward the window, holding up the footstool as a shield, as she reached up for her mask and wig. She put them on haphazardly, and raised her head slowly to peer out the window, kneeling in the shards, bleeding through her jeans. The strong wind gusted against her forehead and she ducked. She lifted to peer again. Nothing unusual. She caught a whiff of a subtle smell from the outhouse. A crow lifted off the tree branches, its wings flapping in front of the moon.

She stood on the footstool but couldn't see past the shrubbery to tell if anything — or anyone — was down there. The twigs brushed back and forth against the wood. Her wig almost blew off, and she grabbed it, peering into the distance. She went outside her door, down the narrow steps, and leapt toward trees, rolling into their shadows, and grabbing them to peer from behind.

She turned her back on the yard finally to look inside the bushes beneath her window. She put on thin gloves from her pocket, pulled the branches back, and reached down into it, feeling around. Something rounded. Cold. Wet. Why wet? There was no ice, or snow outside.

She bent her face to the ground and reached in between the dense trunks. Her hand closed around it. She pulled it out. A snow ball.

It was a huge ball, densely packed, looked to have been melted a bit and refrozen so it became icier, sharper on one side. And too heavy. She set it down in a pan in the sink. She pressed the button on the cooler of water her landlady drove up from the city, running a trickle onto the snow ball, but she didn't want to waste too much. The water was for dishwashing and cleaning up the kitchen, as well as drinking and bathing with. It would melt soon enough.

She tried to laugh in thanks for the extra water, dirty as it was, but her mouth went sideways under the rubbery, thin medical mask. Had someone figured out who she was?

She moved it to the top of the wood stove. She wadded up the newspaper. The crumpled headline announced FIGHTING TERRORISM. Bits of text were visible: "to both the U.S. State and Defense departments . . . president signed a new order to deliver unlimited arms and support . . . waives any arms export control restrictions on providing military aid to any and all 'foreign forces,' extremist . . . as well as thousands of U.S.-trained and equipped moderate opposition waiting in camp." *Moderate, my ass. Moderate mercenary Terrorists.* She forcefully threw the paper wads into the oven. *Moderate Terrorists? Working hand-in-hand with the acknowledged terrorists — which we're also supporting.* She made a tent of twigs and pieces of bark, and sticks, and struck a match against the rusty iron stove. *Good riddance to media lies. May they burn in peace.*

The icy ball dripped a hefty puddle into the shallow pan, and Nancy smelled chocolate. Cherries. Bananas. Inside the outer ring was ice cream. It was the ice cream woman. Ice cream man. Whatever it was.

True, she was hungry. It looked tasty and she was tempted to eat it, but she didn't relish the possibility of poison. Chocking on a cherry bomb. She stayed back.

The pink and brown, yellow and white whirled their liquid colors together. Beneath the soft colors emerged vivid crimson and indigo, shining paint in an emerald green that overlapped the others here and there, and then she saw it: a smooth stone painstakingly painted with a translucent wash, liquid showing it off at its most beautiful.

She grabbed it with a serving spoon and washed it off, then set it down on the cutting board. She rolled it over and saw the image: two women gazing at each other. One thin, buff tomboy, the other with long dark hair. Behind them, a giant monster mouth, looking as if it would swallow them both whole. Behind the open vaguely shark-like mouth peered eyes, glistening, intense, white space around the irises. It made her heart beat faster.

Why the hell would the ice cream seller do that? She'd heard the truck go by often since she'd moved there from across states.

She felt herself begin to break into action. She'd started hitchhiking some nights when she just couldn't take the restlessness, throwing herself upon the whiskey city. Waking, forgetting from so much intensity. She could feel a hitch down the mountain coming on that night. A chance for adventure, where anything could happen. Some knowledge was growing in her, and she didn't know why, or what it was. But whatever it was meant business.

She looked around in the woman's shed beside the house. Mice scampered off, and a rat waddled away. She found a tarp and heavy tape, and held them against the wind bursts; the crinkling of the material bothered her ears, sensitized by the bang.

The other woman painted on the rock made her think of Becky. She felt testosterone pumping. She wanted to protect her friend from the monster. Being close to Becky had become a mysterious mission for Nancy. That's why she'd moved across states to begin with. She'd been still recuperating from her nose surgery when she'd been sent the anonymous tip: Nancy: *Befriend Becky Lowensly Bronvonowich.*

She'd looked up the name. Only one in the country. She'd tracked her down. She'd managed to "happened to meet" her at the health food store.

She felt that feeling again that had grown familiar since she'd met Becky: a sense of urgency bubbling up underneath her perception. All she knew was that someone was playing window ball for no discernible purpose, with a very strange artifact. And she wasn't sticking around any longer that night.

Chapter Two

All Laid Out Around Me

Monday

A crazy-loud ice cream vendor just drove by my bridge, waking me up. Rascal. It's hardly light yet. I'll bet the driver just wants to show off. Well, I can be loud too, right back atcha! And a smelly poot too, at you, hoo hoo.

Fart smell just adds to the mix; the Bible by my nose is starting to mold. What a stench. Better get a new Biblee. Tee hee. Hard to take it seriously when it's called that, isn't it? Wonder if anyone guesses that I keep the Good Book next to me when I'm sleeping under the bridge so no one kicks me in the head! They probably feel sorry for me instead, for being so stupid as to believe that squirty shit.

Still a little wet and gravelly on my face, but could be worse. The water on the concrete has dried around me overnight. Not so bad being awake early, really; I can roll off the wet spot now, and let my back dry. Hey, the spot is shaped *just* like my body. It's like my shadow staying there. What's the matter, shadow, buddy, too beat to get up?

Makes me want to put clothes on the wet spot. Maybe mix and match Haley's pumps and Connors' fedora. Tell it to get to work and make some people smile.

That's always fun.

I'm glad I can still fit into the costumes. I'd miss Haley and the rest of the characters if I couldn't.

I feel sorry for people who just have one kind of clothes. They aren't actors like me. Sort of mundane, they are. Need to get out of themselves more. Get another life.

Today, I want my day to be dry. Maybe practice my Latvian accent. Make my workout twice as long as usual. These rocks feel so good under my hands.

Lunges and twists, curls and punches.

Ugh! Connors' outfit is starting to mildew, too. Goddamn it, why does the rain always find a way to soak my shit, even under the bridge? Fucking rain! I was hoping to have time to get in a little more sleep. Stay in today.

But no. *Now*, I definitely need to find a new Connors shirt in a free box today. Will take the 63rd street route. The neighbors there always put the best stuff on the sidewalk. Even boxers. Nothing makes ya feel loved like someone else's used underwear soaked in the rain.

It seems like I always have too much to do. I've hardly had time to read all the neighborhood's mail lately. I do read almost all their mail, though. For *her*. Hell, people in those houses don't even notice I exist. They look right past *all* the guys who are in front of their faces, going through their bins. Handy. As you know, I take my time. I know how many bottles of beer they drank that week. How many chocolate bars, usually in some inverse relation to how many tissue boxes they went through.

Their old summons, receipts, jury duty notices, printouts of speeches, divorce requests, scrawled dreams. They write notes to plan out arguments with their boyfriends. Work schedules, postcards from their favorite aunts meant to be kept forever, printouts of Craigslist personals favorites, speech revisions, lists affirming they're worth it and good-looking. I read all those things.

Just wish they put out umbrellas for a change. Even one that doesn't work is better than nothing. I better get started, so bug off. Oh, by the way.

People in the houses assume we don't pay attention. Sometimes we know more about their lives than they do.

Like who is going to die.

Chapter Three

Mysteries at Home

Alone in her apartment, Becky fed breakfast to her cat, Maiden Reverse, who matched the young artist's long brown hair. "I'm sorry, girly, it's the cheap canned food mixed in with that dumb dry stuff. Don't you want it anyway?" She raised the big bag of dry food toward the nearly empty top cabinet, smirking about trying, yet again, to see if she could reach it without freaking out over the height. Other people wouldn't realize how brave she had to be to push beyond her panic, that composition of her life that kept her within the dark frame of spatial limitations.

She pulled up the step stool, which she and Nancy, of the most passionate friendship, had painted one day, inside a dusty sunbeam coming in from the window through the filmy gauze of the curtains, the wind waving chiffon designs on the painted surface. The stool displayed a surreal landscape of winking octopi, wild with baskets filled with elaborate indigo letter eights.

She wished for Nancy, wanted to hold onto her hand for balance, like she did during monthly Phobia Nights. Nancy was so strong. She never shared her own problems with Becky, even at Phobia Night, whereas Becky always shared intimate issues in her life with her. Nancy was such a good listener. Becky told herself at that moment she'd be more like Nancy. Silent. Tough. Proactive. No victim-mentality there, even though Nancy had to wear that mask on her face. The burning must have been incredibly painful. And Nancy must look so awful, she'd never be able to find a man.

Becky didn't want to hold onto her victimhood. She didn't want to be a weakling. There was just something in her subconscious affecting her so strongly, her life presented her with a nightmarish perception of heights. Though Becky regularly forced herself to make progress and face her fear of heights, her phobia had yet to improve. Instead, it haunted her dreams with shattered images of falling toward something beyond her brain's ability to conceive. A kind of populated blackness. A sound that meant the death of love. A shock of ugly composition to humanity she didn't want to see.

Instead, she willfully turned her head resolutely toward beauty. She was so tender, her slender artist's fingers seemed like a force of nature, plants underwater, glowing, sending ripples of goodness all the way to the shore.

She flexed her muscles extra hard, while she put the cat food bag on a high rung and stepped on the bottom step, holding on, grabbing tighter and gasping as it jiggled. She held her breath. She held the stool with one hand while she picked up the heavy bag with the other, steadying her legs, raising it to a higher rung. It started to wobble sideways and she reached to catch it. Her blood left the surface of her skin. Her palms oozed so much moisture her hands slid on the stool. She panted. Licking her lips, her tongue felt the jab of sudden rough.

She slowly moved her left arm toward the cabinet and steadied herself, as she closed her eyes and went up to the second step. Her face tightened. She raised the bag up to a higher rung and set it down. She held onto the cabinet with one hand, opened it with the other, then as she grasped, she unsteadily lifted the bag toward the shelf with her free hand.

Her burnt-orange short skirt rose along her toned thighs, and Maiden reached up and batted at exposed fringe. Becky lost her balance and the bag dropped. Morsels fell everywhere around her in a dry brown shower as she screamed and bent to clasp onto the step stool. Hyperventilating, she grew so light-headed she bent and put her head down against a rung as she merged with the stool. The sharp metal pressed into her forehead; the coolness made her shiver more.

She didn't even try to get down off the ladder for several minutes. The floor might have been miles away. She thought of throwing herself off onto the floor to get it over with, the same way she had the impulse to jump off a cliff if she mistakenly found herself in an edgy location. She was shaking, growing weaker, adrenaline taking her down. She slowly climbed down to the floor and lay on top of the rough kibble. It smelled like Chinatown.

She closed her eyes as she lay there sprawled out on the emerald green tile. She couldn't even pay attention to the TV that was droning on. She just had to recuperate from her phobia reactions. *Oh, God, I'm such a wuss!* She imagined laughing about that moment with Nancy. Would she get on the floor and show her what it had been like? Would she throw herself down as exaggerated and over-the-top as she could? Was it worth the risk of banging herself up? The cat's tail went across her nose and she sneezed. The tail went back the other way, fur entering her nostrils, bits of it sticking inside, and she wiggled and slapped her face, blowing outward. Maiden leapt up and ran backwards with her spine hunched in the air, lifting her front paws off the floor. She disappeared through the doorway, behind the couch, Becky unable to stop laughing weakly.

After ten minutes, she arose. Trying to ignore her trembling, she swept up what food Maiden hadn't devoured. "Hey, what are you smiling about?" Becky noticed the little catnip bag on the second to the top shelf had much less in it than she remembered. "You pig! Did *you* do that?"

The fluffiness turned away.

"One day, I'll be able to buy you the healthier stuff. Lots of fancy wet food. You'll be rolling in catnip, baby! Just you wait and see. I have a feeling Stan is going to ask me to marry him in a few days. Don't look at me like that. He has plenty of money he doesn't know what else to do with. He wants to spend on a wife. That's how he was brought up. I guess it makes him feel successful. He said he'd be there for me, if I ever need him. Can you imagine someone being so nice? He's like an angel, an answer to my prayers. Or was it *your* prayers for more wet food?" She reached down and rubbed Maidy back and forth quickly and roughly, as she teased in her silly cat-voice, "I'll bet it was! I'll bet it was!"

The plump cat turned her head back over her shoulder, narrowed her eyes, and then faced the wall.

"Don't look at me that way."

Maiden turned around and blinked.

"Come on, kitty, you know I had to drop out of school. Stairs. Hills. What can I do? The Frame Job no doubt pays less than any regular art gallery in the city. It's a block from the one soup kitchen in the country that will feed felons. But every other gallery has two stories, a basement, or steps to get up to it. Just awful. Face it. I need a man if I'm going to . . ." She looked at the cat, who meowed. "You know — not *die*." She bent over, twirling around, squealing, flailing, then lowered her head suddenly with a sly grin at the cat.

Maiden pressed up against Becky's bare legs, shedding onto her skin. Becky bent down to wipe the hairs off, saying, "Thanks for making a mess. Maybe I'll have a *real* maid soon. Someone to clean up your mess so I could spend my time after work making art. I want people to talk about my the profound greatness of my art after I'm gone. Oh, you don't know what I'm talking about, do you, fur ball?"

The TV caught her attention with a clip of the British Foreign Secretary praising, "The incredible, selfless bravery of the Rescuers who pick up injured and dead bodies who have been bombed and executed." Becky loved British accents, especially for men. The Foreign Secretary was handsome, and she liked how his hair was blown over his forehead by the wind in that shot, making him look a little like a rock star.

The scene on the morning news switched to a dark-skinned leader of the "neutral humanitarian group," the Rescuers, speaking about how they camped in rebel-held territory and all day long, every day, rushed in and saved 100,000 lives after bombs were dropped on them by their country's president. "We can't bring the dead back to life. But we can give them a decent burial."

Becky was touched by his courage, and felt sorry for the people killed by their leader. She planned to donate the sales of her next three pieces of art so she could give the Rescuers more money. A week prior, she'd sold the mahogany dresser and the walnut roll-top desk that she'd saved from her childhood home, for her latest gift to them. She just hoped none of the Rescuers got killed while carrying out their services. So far, there had been no reports of that happening, and many people were claiming it was because of the protective prayers of everyone in the NATO countries. *People making up those stupid stories about the Rescuers looting from bombed buildings, stealing from injured citizens, and injecting their children with lead to kill them, are just mean,* she thought, but tried to forgive them. *It's obvious the Rescuers are honest heroes. Why can't those people see that?* She remembered the indie journalist interviewing a citizen as he said, "They only pull people out of the rubble when the camera is on them. After the camera was off, they told us to pull the people out ourselves."

She shook out her tense muscles, concerned about the effects of the looming chance of a third World War within the week. She knew that meant she, and millions of people, might not have long to live, and the borders of nations would change. But she was ready for it if it meant keeping that Balkanized country's leader from killing his people. He'd even been reported to regularly drop sarin gas on them, and she was revolted by that, imagining how they must have felt being burned. She found herself wondering if her friend Nancy's face had been burned by chemicals or fire. She, like many, had become focused more on the news recently, with this impending war. She hadn't spent much time looking into military issues in other countries over the years, as they usually seemed more or less the same, lots of violence far away, with religious fanatics going after each other. She wished everyone could patch up their differences.

She wanted to save up money to mail off her huge paintings to a gallery in New York that wanted to show her work. They were waiting on her. She couldn't wait to see Stan's face. Patron of the arts. The thing was, she didn't know if she wanted a maid. She didn't like being waited on or treated like something special. She felt squirmy about the idea of being watched in her own home by anyone she wasn't prepared to open up to fully. But Stan, well, she's sure opened up to him fully lately. So deeply it scared her. Bound and gagged and spread.

She found some tape in the closet and put it over her laptop's camera. She knew perverts watched through people's laptops. Extortionists would blackmail powerful people with what they recorded on their webcams. She would be blind not to have some suspicion of how intensely beautiful she was, with her round features and deep-set shadowed eyes and pouty lips. Who wouldn't want to watch her? Even the neighbors stared. But it didn't really matter to her other than if her beauty of appearance as well as her art paid Stan back, making herself worthy of his generous love.

She didn't have much in the way of neighbors, however, as all the houses across from her were empty, owned by the huge church on the corner, apparently too expensive for them to fix. The roof directly in front of her living room had provided ample joke material for guests, as it dipped down lower year after year. The house next to it had a window broken out, and another boarded up. The one next to that wasn't in bad shape, just very small, maybe not worth fixing up, with the church opening it up to occasional guests.

As she gazed out at the empty guest house, she noticed a man wearing an obvious toupee, and a woman wearing a burka on the doorstep. Was the man even wearing a fake mustache? It looked like a totally different color than his hair. A standing joke with her visitors. They sometimes saw people walk in that house. But *never* saw them *leave*. Obviously the secret entry to the center of the earth!

She remembered a dream she'd had about being watched during the night. One of those men from the dream she'd actually

14

seen leering at her during the last couple weeks, giving her knowing looks. Even police were looking at her weird lately. And the red-headed minister at the church on the corner, Reverend Red, they called him. He was the worst. He'd always ignored her before but now it was like he was looking right through her clothes. She grasped under the bottom of her light green chiffon skirt and lifted it up to the light to see if she could see her hand through it. She realized she'd just flashed her neighbor and dropped it. She tried to look casual as she closed the layers of the curtain, blushing.

In the dream, a gawking man had been as big as the sky. He could see her from everywhere. He knew something she didn't. And it was choking her. The clouds bled. A noise was taking over the landscape, clanging, banging, the sound of doom. Her dream scream had woken her just as the recycling truck was outside her window sliding the bottles and cans crashing inside itself. She held onto the counter as the wave of clammy nausea overtook her. No, she'd get past her fears. That nightmare was the next on the agenda she'd go over with Nancy on Phobia Night. They made those monthly nights as fun as possible, with music, wine, brightly colored clothing, and animated play-acting.

She searched online through the galleries and frame shops in the city, since the Frame Job combined both skills. She found a new gallery. She clicked through the website pages until she found a shot of the building. Steps. As always. Impossible.

She took photos of her paintings in the morning light and compared them to the ones she'd taken before. She cleaned them up on the computer, countering the inevitable glare on the glinting surfaces. It was inevitable. She couldn't afford to get good slides made by professionals, so Stan had said he'd do it for her. He hadn't gotten around to it yet and she had deadlines. She fidgeted.

She picked up the flash drive with her paintings and put it in her pocket. She'd gotten great reviews on the depth of her art in magazines. During her free time at work, she was going to pick out the frames that would most set off her tear sheets she'd been sent from a glossy magazine featuring her paintings. She was going to frame her Artist's Statement too that day, and hang all those alongside the paintings at her solo show, whenever it happened.

As she swept the taupe kitchen floor, some fur spun up and landed in the oatmeal as she lifted the lid off the pot. She reached in to take it out. "But I'll take you on our honeymoon to Florida. You'd love getting to spend time outside there. You've never even *been* outside; it's amazing." Maidy chased the broom, swiping at it. She padded to the sandbox.

"In Florida you could see what real sand is all about. It gets warm from the sun. Mmm."

Maiden Reverse ran across the slick floor, sliding toward the wall and doing a flip. Becky laughed. "You need so much more room than this to run around in, don't you? I'm sorry to say so, but you're putting on a bit of the pudge. I don't know how, as little as I feed you, Maidy. It's truly a mystery."

Becky pulled down the ironing board for a quick press of the thin jacket to wear to work. She hummed a Sibelius melody from a symphony while she ironed until she stopped mid-note. She bent down to inspect a stain on the jacket that had transferred from a big sticky blob on the board. She stood there, soft lips open, trying to figure out how that blob of black goo got on the material. She searched her memory for how she could have possibly done that the last time she ironed a few weeks before. It didn't seem like Stan to break out the ironing board when she wasn't looking. She felt a wave of sweat. This was beyond anything she'd noticed before. The other little inconsistencies around the apartment could be explained away. Sort of.

She couldn't stand it. Her eyes stung, and her nose got stuffy. She didn't want to cry. She wanted to beat up something.

No, maybe one of her friends could have done it — though she was sure none would have broken in. She held her breath, trying not to cry. Maybe on a night when a few were visiting, one had snuck off and used the ironing board and spilled something on it, without realizing. But why? She imagined her friends all one at a time secretly getting obsessed by wrinkles in the backs of their shirts. They spun around like dogs trying to bite their tails.

That was better.

The best thing was not to think too hard about it, and just be a good sport about mystification. When she got too serious about trying to figure out a mystery like that, and there had been a few of them recently in her home, she had an even harder time sleeping during the rare quiet periods in her neighborhood. With all the recyclers going to every house in shifts, one person, then another going through her things, waking her up all through the night, she was having trouble getting rested enough to make rational choices. She could barely think straight.

She talked to Maidy as she continued getting ready for work. "I think Stan will go to Florida. I just wish he'd talk about the future more. He gets that handsome grin and turns away. I think he's shy. Maybe we could go on vacations to the country once we're married. You could see bees and butterflies and mice." She repeated her soon-to-be name, Becky Marks, Becky Marks, Becky Marks.

She turned on the TV to learn the news of the escalating conflict that could lead to a world war the next week if Russia retaliated against the covert destabilization of surrounding countries. A news anchor was wearing goggles, standing in front of a crashing, dirty, burning city, saying: "I'm the first reporter coming to you live from the front line at the eastern half of the city, the Old City, where moderate rebels, brave freedom fighters, battle against both the terrorists and the pro-government forces. The national army has just forced the rebels out of twenty percent of the Old City by the national army. A tragedy leading to the deaths of more children. We expect the neutral activists, the gentle, unarmed heroes, the Rescuers, to come in and save as many of the wounded as they can, and give them warm clothes, new houses, toys, and hot meals. Your donations have made this possible."

Strange, it seems like all the relatives would be lining up to see their families they haven't been able to contact all this time that the rebels have held the Old City. The legal government has made it accessible to them again. Where are they?

The reporter stood in the street full of buildings previously held by the "moderate opposition," which had their fronts blasted off. Becky peered inside the buildings. *Where are the unused missiles and launchers?*

Behind the reporter, Rescuers were reaching into the ground, into holes littering the ground conveniently each a yard apart, lifting out cute children and holding them in the air. The camera zoomed into the children's fresh, rosy faces smiling at the humanitarians. The children's eyes were so deep and soulful, Becky wanted to gather them all up and sing them to sleep so they could go into a better world for a little while. No holes contained adults the rubble had fallen onto for some reason. No corpses. Only unharmed attractive girls and boys, and a couple babies. *Where were their parents when this happened?*

A storm was blowing the dust everywhere in the landscape. Everything behind him was filling up with shifting sand that stuck to everything, and drifted. Strangely, the wind was blowing his hair in the opposite direction of everything else. She puzzled, and watched more closely. Not one speck of dust touched him. *How was this possible?*

Then she remembered green screens. The projection behind the news anchor to give the impression he was on location, to totally fool the viewers. Some people she'd overheard had been laughing about how that technique had led to some embarrassing gaffes recently. *Saves them money, I guess. A reasonable business practice for our modern age.* As she continued to watch, she noticed how odd one obscure man's behavior was along the side of the main action. He'd been standing in the distance, mostly out of the frame, until, as if on cue, he'd begun dragging himself and screaming. Like a strange dream. She didn't think any more about it other than to just shake her head over how surreal the day was becoming.

When she took a glass out of the cabinet and turned on the faucet, she noticed a grimy lip mark on it. Stan had given it to her

18

only a couple weeks before, as a test to see if she liked it. She did. So, that style of glass could go on the wedding gift register he was putting together. So sweet. She sometimes didn't wash glasses well enough if she was tired, and left lipstick stains. But this wasn't pink. This was more like grease, with crusty old food.

The lips left prints wider than hers. Whose lips had been drinking from her glass? She shivered and rubbed it off hard, feeling a twinge of nausea.

She flashed on a memory from the night, a dream; she tried to remember every one. She pulled a sheet of paper from the printer and wrote it in her barely legible scrawl. "Was with Stan, him shooting the videos of me in the bedroom."

Videos involving white ropes and black scarves had been their normal activity for the last weeks. She hoped he'd get over his sadomasochist obsession with putting her in peculiarly odd poses and get to the nice new house in the flats. With lavender walls.

She'd keep up her gym and yoga practice, pushing her muscles to get in outrageous positions. She could never do The Tree Pose, though; her ankles were weak and unsteady. Since meeting him, she'd stretched herself into new parts of her sensual psyche. Or that's what she told herself. When he strapped her in those odd positions, she tried to play with all the directions her limbs could go in, all the twists of her neck, the curls of her loins. She just wasn't into the pain. She continued scribbling her dream. "Then, he bent me so far back I split just a little bit. I started shining. Something bright. I don't know."

She'd typed it up for her dream records, and threw the note paper into the recycling bin. She finally took a deep breath. She was learning to be submissive, because she saw how much he enjoyed it. He'd go quiet, catlike in his movements, focused on her through the lens in the red spotlight. She felt proud in her chest that she could bend her will to his, if that's what being a good lover was about. She had to trust him, to open up all ocean like that, even though she still felt her ligaments twitch all along her groin, near to breaking.

Didn't all women take a chance in love? She traipsed around the room, flitting her dress. She stumbled from the cramping in her upper thigh. Had she sprained her vagina? She limped around making breakfast. Buddha-hands, bright yellow fingers, so many fingers, like lemons but not so sour. She cut some of the tips of the citrus fingers off and mixed them with honey in warm water. Delicious. Alive. Sunny. She longed for something sunnier with Stan. Something yellow instead of black, black, black. Still, did glamorous models ever wear yellow? No, they wore black.

She'd been woken out of her dream by men going through recycling again. The recycling truck came so early, most people put the bins out the day before. The guys who gathered the recycling were out in waves, one at a time per bin. One person would get the best stuff. The next person would get the less lucrative. Later, others would come along, digging deeper, throwing everything out on the sidewalk to get to the bottom, flinging the lids back, which sounded like gunshot. Or maybe that's what it was.

She lived on a corner so the truck came on a different day on the perpendicular street. She heard the sounds of the men going through the glass on those days, too. The trucks were loud as they picked up the bins. Whatever broken glass was left inside slid, crashing down. Her heartbeat had become irregular. She'd tried every kind of cheap earplug on the market. She was too sleepy during the day to remember well. She tried napping, but the guys going through the recycling woke her. Her stomach's eyes were wide open. Her startle reflex was triggered.

When she pushed Maiden off the bathroom sink and brushed her teeth, she noticed the bristles were slightly moist. She hadn't brushed her teeth the night before! She'd been too tired. Right? It was a foggy day. She knew ambient moisture prevented her brushes from drying out overnight sometimes. But twenty-four hours? She ran her fingers over it. Was the humidity *that* high? Maybe.

What was she going to do, call the police and say her toothbrush was sometimes staying wet too long, or that it seemed like the cat got into the food bag while she was at work and then closed it back? Was she going to tell them to look into Stan's life because she thought her own boyfriend might be a stalker? What if he found out and dumped her?

The stain on the ironing board, the stain on the glass, the toothbrush. That was too much! Someone was breaking into her apartment and doing weird things! How could anyone be expected to just go on about her business? She threw her phone. It crashed into a cabinet, and broke into pieces.

One more expense. Well, too bad. She'd just have to do without. *Who needs a phone, anyway?*

She had too much on her mind: her paintings, her wedding. Florida. Beach, sun, sand, Maidy outside, paintings inspired by the sea. She picked up her paper bag, which sat by the door, full of scrawled dreams, letters, memos, receipts, books she'd spilt coffee on, empty wine bottles, and her work schedule for the week. She carried it to the recycling bin.

She found herself embarrassed for the struggling men going through the bin to see her expensive lip plumper box, and the anti-aging cream using essence of caviar to make her neck look tauter. She tore the boxes up in pieces so they wouldn't see what they were, just random pieces of skin tone, with images of fish eggs abstracted by the white frayed edges.

She walked quickly to the bus stop and headed to Frame Job. She prepared herself emotionally to walk past the soup kitchen next to it, the only one in the city felons were allowed to attend. Saturdays were the most trafficked, so she prepared herself for hours of detailed focus. She had to make herself stop going over in her mind all the strange things she'd discovered in her house that day.

Had she locked the door, with her new set of keys? She could have locked it wrong. She hoped it was just Stan but if he was lying to her about that, what if he was lying about being single? No, no. If she didn't ask, it would be OK.

She would buy a security camera to put in her apartment right away.

Her confusion was transported by a floral scent. Looking toward the wind, she saw a blond man planting flowers in a box along the sidewalk in the distance. She breathed in deeply, and smiled.

She passed by a shrub and bent to smell it. She picked a flower and stuck it behind her ear. She couldn't stand it, and walked back a few yards. Had she locked the door? She waved at Maiden, sitting in the window sill.

She was stopped before she could make it back to her door to check the lock. An elderly woman wearing an official button was collecting donations for the Rescuers. "Help them provide aid, darlin'? You know we're all called to austerities by the people on TV. Do you have a heart or not?" Her words got a little louder by the second as Becky tried to ignore her, and Becky felt guiltier with each rise in decibel. She reached into her purse to give her five dollars. She'd donated nearly every day to someone collecting for the Rescuers of the foreign country, a name that didn't come easily to her mind. She couldn't stand not doing so, after all the stories about them on the news. Unfortunate people. Maidy would just have to wait for that wet food. And she hated to admit it, but one day, she'd have to buy another phone.

When Becky heard the bus coming, she ran back to the stop, ready to be taken inside its metal maw.

Chapter Four

Subconscious

Nancy dreamed at the oddest times. She'd never established a normal sleep schedule in her life. Lately, dreaming was different from what it had been like before, back when her dreams had been controlled by her handlers in the Agency, switching her life around in the craziest ways. So surreal. But she still thought it was a little weird.

At the moment, she wasn't thinking, but was sort of dreaming. Becky seemed to be hugging her. Becky bent her face close to Nancy's and whispered. The words were sing-song: "And you're my best friend ever. And you're my best friend ever." Becky was singing a melody strangely out of tune into Nancy's ear. At first, Nancy thought it was something Becky was making up, not even trying to get the melody right, as she faltered trying to figure out the lyrics. Nancy couldn't tell what the words were at all at first, and then a word or two came through, always surprising her, knocking her off the conclusions about the nature of the song. It was repetitive in an annoying key. Off-key, more like it.

She then wondered if Becky had joined a cult. No song like that could exist unless it was made to deify some dead Baba from India. It was like a chant that wasn't supposed to be music, surely. It was almost like having a mosquito buzz in her ear. Nancy wanted to swat her. But she was a guest at Becky's house, over for dinner. The dinner was getting cold. She wanted to eat it. But Becky's singing was getting more and more circular, almost like the song was trapping her, squeezing her.

The notes slid around without ever hitting the proper frequencies. Each one seemed to be inside a glass jar, and they were too dirty for the sound to come through nicely. Some parts were dirtier than others, thick, thick dirt, with black mold growing on it. The sound couldn't come out correctly through that so it made it wave around. Each note was worthless as a note, but as a fact, it was somehow meaningful. A frequency signifying something. She tried to read the labels on them but she couldn't make them out. She'd heard people couldn't read in dreams. She wondered for a second if she were dreaming, and had attained some kind of spiritually advanced state from chanting to a guru who played a flute to a dancing snake.

She tried to file away the endless facts about Becky she was learning from the vibrations of the muffled, droning song. She didn't like it. Becky needed to back off. Or maybe Nancy just needed to push her away.

I sort of do like it, though. Friends do cuddle sometimes. I guess this is what friends do.

Becky's singing circled tighter around her, a snake of sound full of facts in glass jars that lived in the wounds underneath the scales. She was trapped inside a cobra, and so she waited patiently. The cobra was sort of Becky's song, but sort of something else too. Like Nancy was inside something dark. But full of brilliant, animated dreams inside dreams that were like a Bosch painting.

Becky leaned up against her, holding her. She whispered in her ear, the coil tightening around Nancy even more. *Am I having a Kundalini experience? If so, why is everything murky?* Nancy looked around in the dim light, with so few details, yet so many.

Facts were stacked along the walls of the snake, which had encompassed her and then expanded. Each level of the infinite snake coil contained a fact within each scale. Somehow this made sense to Nancy, as if she'd known it all along, and this was dejavu. She'd been studying those facts hidden behind the scales for months. She knew if she lifted up one of the scales, it would break off, and the fact-powder would fall out into her face. She knew the

24

powder would be pale, off-white with a tad of olive mixed with chartreuse. But if she broke a scale off, it would wound the Cobra badly.

The potential wound disturbed her. Poor snake. She couldn't do that to it.

She longed for the facts that encircled her. She wanted to become them. To free them without killing the snake. At least, not until it was time. Was she supposed to kill it later? Poor snake. She didn't want to. She wanted to pet it and pet it until it shown.

Chapter Five

All in a Day's Work

I guess Becky's not so smart as all that; according to her diary here, she thinks a stud named Stan is going to pay up her whole life, just to be able to poke her in the rear. I guess a lot of women are like that.

This diary is such a pretty little book. I like the feel of the edges of the hand-torn art paper against my thumbs. So soft. This feels good, too, flipping the pages against my cheek. It's so much nicer than paper that's just been chopped.

I watched her make the diary in the park down the street from her apartment one day. She sat there on the grass tearing the pages. I could tell she put her whole self into every little direction of the tear, so it wasn't just boring and straight. The tears were art. There was a little breeze just starting a little bit, you see, so I took a chance on what I could foretell would be blown around in the wind. I dashed off to my bridge and changed into my Pete Zelite outfit. It uses up my hair grease whenever I make myself into that guy, but it's always worth it. I was so glad she was still there when I got back.

I sat on the bench, even though I'm not a fan of how that metal shit feels to sit on. What's up with that? But the thing is, it was downwind from Becky. Teehee! God, I love me, sometimes. I'm so damn smart. So, I looked away from her just right so I could keep up with those loose pages out of the corner of my eye. I was a little nervous, tell you the truth, when she was poking holes in the paper, getting ready to put ribbons through them and tie the book together. It was hard to keep my leg from bouncing around, but that's not suave.

But it was perfect. Just in time, love came through for me. Love Conquers All. When the wind picked up all gusty, I was *on* it! I was such the gentleman, catching all the papers flying in my direction. I did a killer leap and spin. When I winked when I came down and bowed, presenting the pages to her, she was blushing. I want to say her smile was cute, but that's not very respectful to a great artist. Her smile was — well, I'm sorry. If you'd seen it you'd get it.

If you saw her smile, can you give me a signal? Maybe touch my balls? Waiting. Hah, no? How do I know where you even are? Your face could be an inch from my po hole and you could be latherin'. You could be taking a nap for all I know. Could be writing all my thoughts down to turn them into some asylum or give them to invading aliens or something, for all I know. I've got a lot of trust in you, baby. You and me, we're a team, Sir or Madam Interrogator.

Oh, look at that. Wet spots in her diary. Is Stan making her cry again? Or is she longing for Pete Zelite? Heh, I would be if I was her.

I like it how Becky washes jars by hand before she puts them in the recycling. Check these out. She even takes the labels off. That's a real woman. I've seen her doing it through her window. She gets even the gunkiest food off completely. Can you imagine how much that would make me love her?

And she stores her food in jars instead of plastic. Some of them would fetch some money. I almost start to empty one out, and take it, but I can't do that to her. She's never used this shit so she never will. It'll just sit here on her shelf until she throws it out. But that's for her to decide. I'm not a meddler. I have my limits. I'm an honorable man.

Ahhh, interesting, she has a doctor's appointment. She's got tinnitus. Good, I can use that fact. I'll chug it in my memory hole.

Some of these socks don't have matches. I better fold them together, the ones in pairs, so it's easier to see she needs to do something about these one-offs. I wish I'd brought some pairs. One of the free boxes today had socks in it she would have liked. Damn. There might not be a next time.

Is that thong Stan's? Cause it sure ain't Becky's style. One more bit of evidence that Stan is gay. I knew it.

Ever since she left her key in the door, I been crazy busy with her.

I already knew from her recycling what kinds of books she liked, what bra size. I knew how much she had in her bank account. Hell, I know that kind of stuff about everyone in the whole neighborhood. Except that Al guy who doesn't recycle. What sort of a jerk does that? Doesn't he care about the Earth?

The little girl who lives on 939 Franklin Street — she's so sweet. I hope she gets the main birthday present she wants. I know she can't get them all But maybe the top five on her list. Number six is just silly. Who needs a candy giraffe who makes big old stinkies? At least the little girl will get number three on her old list. Tee hee, I know, because I stuck number three in her mailbox once I read the list last week. I had to sell a lot of cans to buy that little Rescuer doll, but it was worth it. It made me prouder than anything else I've ever done. I'm going to do it more. Recycling isn't going to make me enough for that on its own, but no worries.

All that time watching Becky go in and out of her house, while I was going through her recycling right in front of her, paid off. She's like the others around here, looking away when they walk past us. Never try to see our faces inside our hoods. I'll never forget how excited I was that day she left her keys in the door. I had the keys before she was back for them two minutes later, haha! I swear, I got the fastest hands in the neighborhood.

Of course, we know I'm no dummy; I'm wearing a pair of the gloves I use for digging in the recycling bins outside people's houses. Not sure if I ever mentioned that. There's so much to talk about to you. You know? And I'm wearing the little plastic bag over my hair and bags over my shoes. Whenever I go into her apartment, there ain't no prints and no hairs to identify me. That's nothing unusual around here. Some of my best friends don't have shoes. I give them bags, and rubber bands to hold them on their feet.

People don't even look at me funny when I'm dressed like this. The bags I wear are dirty, so they just blend in to the grit all around us and us cyclers. Listen, cyclers are all around the block, going at it big time right now. No one looks at anyone else around here; they don't want to see.

Sigh. Yep, I have to admit, I want to drink some of Becky's chocolate milk. Staring at it in the fridge. Why would a grown woman drink chocolate milk? I guess the question is, why would a grown man want to drink it? Well, that's different. I wouldn't buy it. But if it's right there with you, that's different. You know how it is.

The light's too bright in there. I turn the temperature setting down for her. Some of her food's getting frozen hard around the edges. She'd never know the difference if I took a swig of milk. But I'd get all foggy-headed. I wouldn't be able to remember all these new deets. I take a hell of a lot of pictures with this five-dollar camera, even though my memory is like a steel maze: just some things for the scrapbook. This Single-Use camera is amazing. I've taken hundreds of pictures with it. I haven't seen any of them yet, but it's going to be great.

Mostly I like to take real things instead of taking pictures of her stuff. And I'm a nice guy, right? I mostly take her recycling. I don't want to take too much stuff from her apartment; I care about her. Why else would I wash her fruit? I doubt she'd ever know it was me, but you never know. Well, if you're listening to this, you do know. If you're not listening to this, well, well, well.

I do wear my persona costumes a lot when I'm out and about in her neighborhood. Well, our neighborhood. I mean, my bridge is just a few streets away. I walk around. One time, I cut the shrub outside her door. I'm perfect that way. I've got those skills.

I asked to talk to her, one time, standing outside her door. "Have you heard the good news about the Lord?" That was good times. She talked with me for a long time. And I made her laugh. That whole lying down of the lions and the lambs thing makes me laugh, too. All those lions getting fat with no reason to run any more.

My favorite characters to be are: Connors, ol' Haley, and the Latvian. Yep, Pete Zelite! He's too much, that guy. Such a heartbreaker.

Oh, God, I love it. Even her neighbors wouldn't know all these guys hanging out around her place are all me. I just use the key she left in the lock. See, I was just standing there, at the bin one day, reading her grocery receipt while I was slowly putting it in my bag. I wish you could see where I hang my bags off my cart. I made it all of wood and bike tires and shit. So there I was, on that epic day. The day she left her keys in the lock.

It's funny, I talked to her later, as Pete Zelite, outside her door when she ran back to check. Her cheeks were pink and her mouth was open while she breathed. I could smell her. She was looking all over for the keys, and she yelled to her upstairs neighbor to ask about them. She said, "I probably dropped them somewhere, anyway. No one would know what they go to." The way she looked at me, her eyes wide and such a deep, moist dark. Wondering about my opinion. And waiting on my accent to deliver it in just the right way that made her move her hips a little more loose.

Anyway, so back to the now. I know you like that, Baba Interrogator. Live in the now. Stay linear. Forget about whatever the hell I did in the dark ages. So. I carry the bags and I putee them on my shoesees as soon as I slipie insie.

I wipe up anything I track into her house real good. Really, she owes me for that, keeping her entranceway cleaner than it was before. I wonder if she's noticed yet.

And now, you'll like this. I'm giving a little bit of the chocolate milk to her cat, in a lid from one of her empty spice bottles. Cat doesn't seem to like it, but she knows I care about her, anyway. She's butting right up against my knee. Sweet little thang.

Time to pull down the ironing board and iron Connors. Just have to iron around that glob of goo. Pete Zelite got into the iron last time, and man did he make a mess. No more of that for him!

I wish I hadn't ironed her clothes for her last time. I just wanted to save her time. Wanted her things to be neat. Like when I take her clothes out and lay them on the bed, like she's dressed and lying down, I put them back on the hangers better. I smooth them, you know, balance them on the hangers, and put an even distance between each hanger. She just jams them all up together willy-nilly and the shirts are hanging off one side, herself.

I'm putting a towel around the iron now that it's cooled down just a little, and putting it on the floor for Maidy to cuddle up next to for a while. "There you go, kitty. Feels good, doesn't it, little one?"

I'm giving her catnip from the bag next to the dry food, and she rolls around on the floor upside down. I get down and roll around with her! It's fun. It's like Becky and I have a baby together, a white-brown one.

Hold on, just gotta sweep up the residual catnip and drop it out the window onto the sidewalk. Fun watching the specks fly around in the breeze, catching the sunlight. Homeless cats will love it. Becky will never miss it. OK, hold your tongue. I'm making a call from Becky's landline to Horn's Pizza. That's what first got me into having good times with characters. I can be anyone when I call Horn's and tell them I'll pay when I pick it up.

Then, when no sexy Pete Zelite from Latvia, or Connors Bronner, who can't pronounce his n's, or geriatric wheezing Haley Potter, shows up to pick up the pizza and they put it outside to throw away, I'm waiting, dressed like one of the other characters, and so they don't think: *oh, look, there's that coyote Dave again, prowling.*

One time I covered myself in my army blanket and pretended to be asleep in the alley until they brought out the box to the dumpster. Then, nom nom. I'm kind of an actor. Not just the pizza personalities, either. I dream about these characters I make up. I live them. I *own* them on the streets. Sometimes the streets talk to me about them. Sometimes the streets love me. How do I know? Because sometimes the Free Boxes on the sidewalks of Los Angeles have just the clothes I need to be the person required for whatever I'm up to that day. It's like they're set out for me special. Muah!

What's that thing on her dresser? Oh, I can't believe Becky tells so many people she doesn't have change to give them when they ask on the street. She does, too! And would have more if she didn't buy those jars of anti-aging cream. Ew, with caviar in it! Little Missy's secret. Well, it's safe with me. I could tell all my recycling buds about it, and they'd never stop asking her for a handout. But I love her. I'll be her pal. Still, I might take a bigger swig of that chocolate milk, after all. Serves her right.

Now I have all the information I need.

Productive morning. Onward. Bye, Becky's apartment. Hope to see you again sometime on entirely other terms. Shh . . . Don't tell Becky then that you know me, eh? Not a peepedoodle.

Now I can check through the Goodwill down the street to kill time before they throw the pizza out.

This is my favorite time of year here. All the Halloween costumes. The skull art. The Day of the Dead. All of it. I wish you could see me, ol' Interrogator m'boy. But you'll have to make do with listening to my thought reports. Do you hate being invisible?

Wait, don't answer that.

Haha. Like you ever have answered *anything*.

Oh, *yeah*! I just found a new shirt for Connors. Yip yip! Bless those neighbors who put these clothes in a box; probably into making their mark on society, probably like to eat Chinese, I'd say, from the look of the little red sauce stain on the arm. They probably sit against a couch a lot, considering that wear on the fabric along the back where he'd lean up against it and watch TV. I'll bet they like sitcoms.

I like to take extra time when going through the recycling of some of the people who put out clothes perfect for the characters I'm working on. I want to know what was in their minds when they decided they didn't need that shirt. What made them walk down their stairs, find a box, write FREE on it, and give me Haley Potter on a platter?

To do the pizza thing, you have to dress the part to do the voice right even though it's just on the phone. Even though they never see you. You have to really feel it from the inside out. You don't want them to catch on you're faking it. Then they get annoyed. I hate it when people don't like me, but it's not so bad if I'm Pete Zelite. Insults just roll off his back. Like duck mincemeat. Or, whatever.

The people I make myself up to be, like Haley, don't just fade away. Once I do a character, I have that one forever.

Goodwill is more crowded than usual. See, man, I'm not the only guy who likes to get decked out for Halloween and stuff. Oh, hell yeah. This is THE costume! It's that one guy. The famous guy NATO sent to save the victims, the Rescuer hero. . . What's his name? Dayan! That's it. Gotta try him on. I'll bet it feels great to be him. Nothing holding you back from what you want to do. Just going for it. What a dream. All those people's dirt-smudged faces smiling at you, in gratitude for the toys. Toys that look like you. God, what could be better?

I see his story on the news a lot. Not as much as I want to, though. I mean, it's not like I spend a lot of time watching a TV. I don't know if I've mentioned, I do stop by and watch Becky work out at the gym. The windows are huge there and it's so well-lit even at night. I see the thingies, whatever they're called. White words going across the news, cause it's turned down to make way for pop songs that make Becky go, go, go on that exercise bike. Funny how she likes that one right in the center of the row. I know that about her. I love her so much.

You can't help but hear about the toy guy everywhere. They even announced news about him in the toy stores when I got the girl her presents that she put on her list and then threw out, poor thing. I wish I could have afforded one of the Rescuer dolls for her. But they're so damn expensive.

I know it's a good cause, though. I don't blame them charging that much, cause the money all goes to some organization. And they send it on to the people the Rescuers save from the rubble. I never knew rubble was such a thing, before. It's like — *everything* over there. See, Dayan gives toys to the kids in that poor country bombed by its evil dictator. Even I donated to his cause. That was a lot of recycling to pay for that one, I tell you what. A lot of days' work. And each day, man, that's a lot of hours of grabbing glasses. But to hand over cash to the guy collecting donations outside the grocery store? That was my proudest moment. I feel like I was made for that. The Rescuers are out there saving some kids because of me. Not that I think I should have a statue or anything.

Damn, Dayan looks good on me. I think. Hard to see exactly what I look like in mirrors. Is it that way with you, too, Mr./Mrs. Interrogator? I can see in my mind, no problem. I'm thin as shit. Never could grow a beard. Little short. But you hardly notice when I'm dressed up as Dayan.

"Hey, everybody, I'm Dayan! Look, I'm Dayan! Hey, did you know I gave him money? He's risking his life, to give the kids toys that *I* bought. I like to donate toys to kids, too. Did you donate to Dayan yet?"

I don't know what he's looking at me like that for. Pussy kid.

There's a younger boy in the same costume as mine. It looks so much cuter on him. Haha, I remember when I was that age, going Trick or Treating. Costumes were the best thing, ever. "Oh, hey, there. You're Dayan, too! I deem you a co-hero! We're all in this together, right? Rescuers gotta help out everyone after the meanies bombed the shit out of them."

The boy down there is actually puffing out his chest at at me. Haha, what is it, little man? Noah, he just said, "No, we didn't donate to them. My mommy said it's all a crock. She said the Rescuers are crap."

"What!" I can't believe he just said that. What an awful mother. There should be an agency to take him away from her. I think there is. He's got that thing. Confrontation Disorder or whatever.

"She says the Rescuers and the moderates are really the terrorists that nating is paying for. Whatever nating is. They're the ones doing the torturing and stuff."

"Because they give *toys* to *kids*?" That does it. Sorry, I gotta pick up that crazy boy and shake him in the air. How dare he say something like that about those guys out there risking their lives to help people in a godforsaken country where people don't even look like us?

I feel big hands on my shoulder. "Hey, you don't have to rip the costume. Jesus Christ! OK, OK, I'm going. What are you selling the costumes for if you don't . . . Ow! Let go of me."

Some friend you are, Interrogator Dildo, standing by while these guys have at me. This store security lets that kid say evil things about the Rescuers? Kid should be locked up. I hope there are some surveillance recordings around here that caught that.

"Oh, Jeez, Sorry to bump into you. Hey, man. Didn't you hear what the kid said? Are you going to let him get away with that? Look, man, I have as much right as anyone else to be in here." Ouch, why are these guys dragging me out. Are they security?

"No, I didn't hear what the kid said. And no, you don't have a right to be here. So, listen. Am I going to have to call the police? Huh?"

"Sure, go ahead. I'm sure they'd be on my side. I'm an American. Seriously, the kid is not patriotic. Where's his mother? It's her fault; apparently she *doesn't have a TV*! Watch the news, lady! Watch the Rescuers movie! That'll learn you a thing or two. Get our enemies and our allies straight, *OK*!" Some people!

Chapter Six
A Muffled Voice

Becky grabbed a tall chair at the Frame Job and pulled it next to her, holding on. Becky didn't let go as she balanced precariously on the footstool along the back wall of the gallery. The floor was a long way down. Her breath hastened. Her grip tightened. She felt a darkness around her and the abyss before her, a whooshing inside it, cold muscles, hard ligaments, like pieces of sweating ice, pinpoints of vision around her, and she slowly let go of the chair.

She slowly balanced, straightened up, and reached her arm up. Her heart leapt toward her chin. She was as high up as a treetop. She was about to die. She was spread out into her death already, and she held on again, her lips quivering, her palm made of ocean.

She adjusted the artist's name plate along the top of the painting. Sighing, glad to be still alive, she stepped down, shaking.

She sneaked a small amount of red wine from one of the open bottles in the kitchen, pouring it into a small paper cup. She wanted a whole glass of wine, maybe even two, for lunch. She wanted to talk with Stan while she drank, laughing over the wine with a smart, educated man who wanted to be with her always. She wanted to be giddy.

True, he didn't laugh as much as she liked, but wine did help bring out his playful side. And he liked to buy quality bottles of Pinot Noir, not the cheap stuff that gave her headaches, like the bottle she splurged on each week from the corner store for three dollars.

She called Stan on the gallery owner's phone, asking him if he'd like to meet her for lunch at their favorite restaurant between

Frame Job and his house where he always shot his side projects on weekends.

His voice was hurried, saying, "No, not a good time. But I'll see you tonight; so what's the rush? Can't get enough of me, hey, baby?"

She wiggled because that was true. She felt addicted to him, his black hair and intense voice from those lips sometimes distant, thin, and taciturn, but which she could tease into more fullness.

He said something she couldn't make out. It seemed as if he had his hand over the phone.

"What?"

"Just, I need to go, sorry, Becko. See you tonight."

Becky heard the sound of a muffled female voice on his end, behind him. She instantly wondered who the woman was, if he was having an affair. The voice seemed like a moan. As if her mouth was covered, and could not say words.

"Who's that?"

"Oh, just a photography client."

"For Weddings Galore?"

The moan sounded more urgent.

"Is she OK?"

"She's fine. Get back to work. I'll bring some roses by soon, how's that? Some very special roses."

Becky wondered if it was going to be *the* night. Proposal time. He'd been hinting overtly about asking her, though his answers seemed perfunctory when she brought up children. She hoped she could get him to embrace the idea more enthusiastically once he realized the joy. But she thought he was planning to ask when they were going to do the video soon at the Reverend Red's church, on Oct. 31st. That would not be long now.

After she hung up, as she went back to the desk, a couple walked into the shop, no doubt to ask about getting some cheesy "art" framed, and they did what they all do first, walk around pretending to be interested in the art on the walls. Typical. She couldn't bring herself to talk to them. She stayed in the kitchen.

She couldn't help but wonder if Stan was seeing someone else. She'd never seen his house. She'd been glad not to have to even think about riding up the roads winding around the hills and go up the staircase to get in. Gave her the willies.

Life was closing in. The impending war. Already so many drones, so many bombs. She wasn't sure why so many people were alright with supporting the rebels to get rid of their legitimately elected leader. Someone was talking the other day about how his people liked him well enough. If something was not broken, why fix it? Hadn't the thing about him not actually gassing his own people meant supporting them should be revised? There were lots of things the news had mistakenly said about him that had come out, but most people seemed to get mad for some reason if she brought up where those bad things were debunked, so she just stopped paying attention. She had to concentrate anyway on the impending marriage and moving to a new house together. She needed to concentrate getting her solo show together, trying to find a theme for her paintings that made a difference to the world, a message she could get behind. Meanwhile, she was distracted by some creep breaking into her house and doing weird things. And people in the gallery were trying to get their kid's doodle of Mickey Mouse framed. *Give me a break.*

Stan had said he would never go to her place when she was at work. But he had the key for emergencies. Was he a liar? Who else would it be going in and moving things, ironing, and using her toothbrush? Still, she couldn't bring herself to ask him such a ridiculous question. It sounded ridiculous. And she just wasn't the confrontational type. She didn't want to risk him getting mad at her and blowing the proposal.

She put her hand over her heart. Best case scenario: he loved her so much he couldn't get enough of her. He wanted to be that close to her. To even break into her house. To move her clothes around. Maybe he dressed up like her, to understand her better. Studied her clothes to prepare to give her what she wanted. Soon they'd be living in the same house together somewhere, as close to each other as they could be all the time.

Becky couldn't call Nancy. She was used to that, and now, she didn't have a phone herself. But she knew where Nancy usually lately was on Mondays at noon. The health food store down the street from Frame Job. Managing to eat her day's worth of minuscule calories by trying out their samples, after taking her weekly shower at the Y. Becky admired her for living off the grid. But this time of year the water at Nancy's place was getting pretty cold. It wasn't quite as feral and romantic that Nancy took showers at the Y now instead of only pouring the water in the bucket from the big jug her housemate always filled up. But Nancy still seemed pretty rugged and independent.

Becky found her at the store. Nancy was wearing a red striped dress. Becky took a sample of chips and cheese. She put it in her mouth as she stood behind Nancy. She bent forward and chewed it loudly right next to Nancy's ear. Nancy turned around and when she saw Becky, they both broke out laughing.

Becky took her to a real lunch across the street.

She kissed Nancy on the cheek of her burn-mask. They sang to the waiter, turning their orders of roasted beet salads into song in an improvised duet. Nancy said, "Would you like to try some of this?" holding a round slice of beet on her fork and reaching it toward the other woman's mouth.

"Oh, yes, try some of mine?" asked Becky, and fed Nancy a slice of beet from her plate. As they ate, they leaned forward across the little table to chew in each other's ears. Becky got a red stain on her dress, but she decided not to care.

Becky said, "You know, I once shot an avant-garde short film, where I slid along the branch of a tree with the camera. Hardest thing I ever shot, making the movement smooth. But the branch was amazing, so twisty and long and all kinds of pastel colors. And then I spliced in a close-up scene where I chopped a beet with a hatchet. Bam! Hatchet lifts and there's the deep red behind it. That was synced to the crescendo of the music."

Becky was happy with Nancy's admiring response.

As they ate their salads, Becky pointed at the jumble of strangely juxtaposed taxidermy, surreal furniture, thrift store art, and masks in the display windows of the stores across the street. "This is my favorite block in the city. Last one to stand up to gentrification."

"Yeah, like you're an expert on the city. I don't know how you stand it, hardly going anywhere because of the heights thing."

"I know. But still, I love how they jam all those totally different things in that store in such crazy ways. Like that statue of a bear with wings next to the table made out of bones."

"And the Egyptian costume on the knight," Nancy added.

"And the petrified snake, I think that is, next to the clock that runs backwards." Becky watched Nancy's face carefully for her reaction. She'd noticed snakes did something to Nancy she didn't understand. Nancy looked down in silence.

Becky jerked her head toward a man sitting at a nearby table and said, "I think that's Reverend Red. From the church catty cornered from my apartment."

"The minister you're pretty sure is going to marry you guys, right? Listen, I don't want to meddle or anything, but sister, are you really sure you want to spend your life with Stan?"

"Stan gave me a wedding gown. He says, get this, it's just for a sexy video. Rich!"

Becky looked down, hesitated, took a deep breath and said, "I could trade you my major art pieces for you to spy on Stan for me. You know I can't handle the heights, myself. He's always home, and I can't go there. I heard someone with him today when I called. It makes me wonder if he's cheating."

"Anything to help out, honey bunny."

"And you could watch outside my house when I'm not around, too, if you get around to it. I'd give you more art. The paintings should be worth a lot before too long. If you can do it soon, that would be nice. Because I know it's probably my fear of being watched causing me to make up things, but I got the idea today that someone had been in there. Maybe Stan. Maybe not."

Reverend Red laid his money out on the table, and as it started to blow across the surface, he laid his steak knife on top of it. Then, he grinned and smirked mysteriously. As he held Becky's eyes, he slowly, by increments, turned the knife to point at her. He folded his napkin with overly enthusiastic precision.

Nancy's fingers stiffly relaxed from their pose. "Don't you need to get back to Frame Job?"

"Let's talk more about it on Phobia Night. Want to push that to tomorrow instead of next week?" Nancy awkwardly grabbed her money quickly and they got up to walk out.

"Deal."

Chapter Seven

Purple Dolphins

Take note of my day, Mr. Sir or Madam Interrogator. Want to guess why? Because it's *copy shop* time! Oh, come on, you know, the one on the corner by Random. Around from Becky's. The thing is, I totally know how to use a computer to get online and download some free art. I'm piecing together a flyer advertising my *utmost* psychic skills.

Becky likes dolphins. You know how spiritual chicks are. I'm so good. The purple dolphins go on the bottom of the flyer. Right there. Should I call myself Blow Hole Billy? No, heh, she might get the wrong idea. I haven't decided if I'm going to be a woman or a man psychic. I thought maybe I'd be Connors, but that'd be weird. Maybe he should be the getaway guy instead. Trick of Fate? Trixie of Fate. I like the sound of that. Trixie I am, then. All in big. Bold. Cursive font.

Becky likes Florida, so . . . I'm grabbing some pictures of octopuses. . . Hmm. Maybe not. That doesn't quite fit the mood she'd like. Palm trees? Flip flops sitting next to the dolphins. Looks like so much fun. How could she say no?

Let me work, here, dude. Looking good: *Professional Clairvoyant. Special in Your Area, Half Price This Week.* And then, in smaller letters, *Will He Marry You? Will You Get the Job? Will Your Cat Join You in Heaven?* All questions I know she has. She'll be so excited.

OK, here I go, do de do, leaving the copy shop, walking along.

I'm thinking about cannibalizing Haley's outfit. Her scarf would work for Trixie's, too. But that would be just — not right. It's wrong to mix up different characters. They need to have their boundaries honored.

So, I'm just dressed like me, scouring the neighborhood, looking in the FREE boxes. I wonder what neighbor ladies are thinking about right now, and who is throwing out a useful New Age dress this minute. Blue floral and gold glitter would be perfect, ladies. And obviously *purple*. Always purple. Come on, trick me out. Trixie me up and at'em.

Hmm. This box isn't labeled, and the stuff is wet. But yeehaw. A purple shiny dress. Hell yeah. My size. And hella hallelujah, pink tights. Miss Trixie is in bixness.

Well, I give up on finding any wigs. Hardly happens any more. I don't buy no second-hand wigs. No. So, I'm on my way to the Beauty Outlet. They've got everything around here. Becky and I are so lucky. There are some tall, shiny buildings and there are regular houses. It's such a mishmash. Stores and churches, abandoned houses, and ah, here we are.

Well, well, well, so the owner of Beauty Outlet, the owner, well, he looks at me like he doesn't too much like me.

He must think I'm making fun of him, buying those blonde wigs for black women there. But I like his prices and variety. And since he's right next door to the Nit Pickers Lice Removal, they take it seriously about wearing plastic when trying them on. I'm not about to get bugs, not me. I've seen what they do to people. Nasty, nasty bugs.

Haha, I wish you could see this. I'm getting one of those plastic caps. And, I can do it: trying on a rainbow colored fro.

Oh, God, no! I can't look. Haha, so horrible! Oh, my God.

But then, I always get a little freaked out by mirrors. Does everybody? They're so distorted and fuzzy. Why can't they make better mirrors, where you can actually see how you look? I never look as manly as I want, my posture sometimes looks fucking ridiculous. I don't know, I just hate mirrors, I guess. Fucking mirrors. I guess only rich people get good ones that show the truth. We get the ones that make us feel bonkers.

I should probably drink more tonight so I don't remember my dreams after that goddamn spooky fro. That sounds like a reasonable plan. Luckily, I brought my flask.

Oh, yes. This blue wig, haha, it matches the dolphin on the flyer. Perfect.

OK, here I go, off jauntifying on my merry way down the wonder-lane to my bridge for my nighty-nights.

See ya later, 'gator.

This drinking whiskey idea is pretty nifty, but I have to say, sometimes it's mighty strange waking up some random place, not even sure where I am or how I got there. Does everyone who drinks as much as me get missing time? I tell ya, it seems like a lot of people can get away with way more booze before they black out. Guess being a lightweight saves my good ol' liver. Liver giver. Liver my timber. Liver river. Nah, that one's no good. Liver quiver! Haha, liver quiver is the best. Tee hee!

Oh, are you still spying on me? What is it you want to learn? You have to follow me all the way from the copy shop to the bridge? Well, I'll just pass up the porn mag at the bridge, then. Heh, heh, just kidding. I'm such a kidder. Want a nip? Oh, sorry, I *forgot*! You can't *drink* with no *mouth*, can you?

Anyway, so yeah, walkin' along . . . and now, I'm taking out Pete's outfit and laying it out on the concrete. Oh, yeah, right, I'm at my bridge by now if I didn't already tell you. But the rain is still coming down and around and dripping on me.

45

I'm putting his arms out to the sides. Why not? I like them that way.

"And here you are, Haley." And, yes, oh Interrogator, my love, I *am* taking out the Haley costume and putting her clothes down on top of Pete's — face down.

The characters gotta like that. You bet they do. Uh huh. Git it!

I'll just let ol' Connors stay crumpled up flat in the corner. Haha. He has to hate that. You know he does. Haha. *Connors.*

At the bottom of the box are the shoes I've been saving. They're pink. They clash with the shade of the pink tights, I tell you what. Like they exist in two different worlds. The tights are pastel, the shoes are neon. It makes me shudder, but Becky's not going to look down at my feet. She's going to stare under the table at my feet while I'm answering her questions about Stan marrying her? Come on, you think I'm stupid? No way.

I hope not, anyway, because one shoe has a buckle, and the other doesn't. I can't figure out if I lost it, or if it's a different model of shoe, and that drives me nuts not to know. I think about it too much. Thinking is shit.

Besides, I've never been crazy about my feet. They're kind of narrow. But, wearing big shoes to make them look bigger gave me blisters, so what are ya gonna do?

I put on the Trixie outfit, ta Da! I do look loverly. Like can read dolphin's minds and wave my arms and ascension spews out like spider webs. Check out my bootie patootie!

OK. Scooping up the other characters off the concrete. Now, stuffing them on top of poor Connors. Haha. Conners. Haha, OK, OK, give him a break, guys. Come on up, that's enough, now.

I wonder if ol' Connors remembers when I introduced myself to Stan that day I was dressin' up as him. I know how to make Stan trust me and open up. He shook my hand that time. He even gave me his card, with his name, address, and a phone number and the word DISCRETE, when I said we should get together one day and talk about this insider stock trade I could get for him.

I can't decide who I like pretending to be best. But Connors, man, he's a delight. Pure dee-light.

Oh, Jeez. Interrogator. No, please, why do you get like this? Where are you taking me this time? Why does everything always get so gray?

Chapter Eight

Mystery Friends

Tuesday

Nancy saw someone she thought maybe she recognized from her days of Nevermind intrigue. Was that a man she'd been instructed to trade international secrets with? Had she slipped him tips on how to take down a dictator by enticing him with his favorite forbidden pleasures, which she could provide? All it took was dressing up in a dream and a slinky black dress.

She ducked around a corner, pulling her wig forward to keep the driving rain out of her eyes, which were not covered by the medical mask. That made her feel paradoxically vulnerable, when her eyes were the only part of her head exposed. She'd stopped wearing mascara when she'd escaped the intelligence Agency, but still, her lashes were getting matted and she could hardly see through them as she squinted in the cold wind.

She hid there — not a place she'd have stood otherwise, with the downpour concentrated in the gutter draining in full force on her shoulders. She'd woven metallic threads into her clothes when she moved there, to reflect thermal radiation, so she could trick the overhead thermal surveillance. She had to say, it also gave her a little extra protection against the cold wind and rain. The silkscreened faces all over her jacket, to further throw off surveillance cameras and facial recognition software, however, just cried.

Nancy made it to the stop for a bus going toward Becky's part of the city. If that man she'd seen was her secret Agent compatriot, he hadn't recognized her. She was always on the lookout, and she never took chances. She'd even purposefully learned to change her gait from the way it had been in the past, to throw off the Agents. She now kept her knees bent, loping, and coming up on the balls of her feet with each step. The gait was a good choice, casting optimism over everything. Being bouncy made her smile.

A little boy was asking people around Nancy for donations at the bus stop, dressed up in the popular thin neon blue and red nylon Halloween costume representing one of the Rescuer heroes, and wearing the official ribbon given to people officially collecting for the "humanitarian aid" group. The President of the Balkanized country in question had protected his citizens from deadly medical, pesticide and agricultural chemicals, had given them free education, health care, and maternity leave. Supposedly, as reported on U.S. mainstream news, he was also counterintuitively chemical-bombing heavily populated areas in his own country from time to time. Of course, that was proven false. The CIA had done it to set it up to look like it was him, and the Nevermind covered it up nicely using fake video. Anyone who brought it up in the cool crowd didn't get laid.

The media's job, to carry out for the Nevermind Intelligence Agency, was to demonize that country's leader. The reasons were complicated. One was to gain support to destroy as many people as it took to score pipeline access and destabilize the last stronghold in an area surrounding Russia. Thus, WWIII was about to begin in a week and the masses were all for it. Those poor darling children the Rescuers featured in their videos, set to wrenching music in their hearts. Something had to be done. Of course it did.

While ninety-five percent of the U.S. population couldn't point on a map to the Balkanized country in which the Rescuers were supposedly risking their lives to help the victims, they dreamed at night about the poor children there, being pulled from the rubble, comforted with blankets with Rescuer cartoons, and given their first meal in days. The masses had good intentions. There were people who saw through the ploy. The awake people just weren't represented — in academia, for example. They followed the indie articles detailing how the Rescuers deter any unhealthy civilians trying to get aid from the hospital. The hospital was only available to the terrorists, and to the healthy civilians, primarily the children, for organ harvesting.

Individual children were sponsored by donations to the Rescuers. One girl's wide-eyed pictures were spread all over social media. She'd been shown in different Rescuers' arms being pulled from rubble at different locations, all posed beautifully for the cameras. The Rescuers always held her with their hands on her crotch, spreading her legs open. The photos always caught her full lips open in what looked like a sensual expression. Potential sponsors paid increasingly high amounts of money in auctions to adopt her. She supposedly had a social media channel that was obviously written by an adult, and photos of her were splashed across the page, showing her with her mouth open to receive a spoonful of food, her eyes closed, head tilted back, hair teased and sprayed.

The morphing of the perceived role of the terrorists had been a bizarre experience for anyone truly watching. First, the most famous terrorist groups were covertly funded, trained, and armed by the US to be the supposed enemy to fight against, but most people willfully ignored that fact. The U.S. pretended they were fighting them at first. They used them to create coups, taking down other countries and installing U.S. puppet dictators. They'd destroyed all the countries surrounding Russia. Meanwhile, the U.S. overtly supported the Rescuers to clean up the mess after the terrorists' slaughters. After many years of pretending the terrorists had arisen spontaneously in a civil war, newscasters like the handsome, virile Tom Tellen, had suddenly portrayed the terrorists as the good guys to feel sorry for when Russia was taking them down. Instead of liberating the country, the ending of the war was portrayed as genocide, and the terrorists were presented as the victims. Most TV viewers didn't notice. Human interest stories got them emotional enough critical thinking went out the window.

Russia had to be reviled, for whatever reason the media could make up, because they were working to move away from the U.S. dollar as a reserve currency. They'd been invited into the Balkanized country to help it get rid of the NATO-sponsored terrorists. And, said country was also one of the few nations left with a state-owned central bank, and the IMF was not happy about that independence. So, stories had to be created about their president's security team theoretically killing protesters, and an uprising supposedly in reaction to the killing of the protestors was staged by the U.S. and NATO — long before the protesters were killed, engineered by the CIA for regime change, with weapons stockpiled at a mosque. During the protests, their president had given orders for the police to carry no weapons, and protesters killed many of them with weapons smuggled in by the CIA ratline from the previous countries they'd illegally overthrown. CIA snipers killed protesters to push the narrative about the president being brutal, in need of being overthrown with help from the U.S. Weapons were given to mercenaries streaming in from several countries and a no-fly-zone was created, which killed more civilians.

Indie videos poured out using forensics on the Rescuers's clips, showing endless inconsistencies. Partisans who only got their news from college radio shows, comedians touting the party line, mainstream news, and social media updates by people averse to research paid no attention to how the videos showed the same boy, with hair, clothing and smudges in exactly the same state, being "rescued" by one Rescuer, then, pulled out of rubble by a different one, then a different one, then killed by the first one who rescued him, while the man was wearing different clothing, dressed as himself in a militant outfit of terrorists who had been the strategically created enemy of the U.S. for years. People were tracked if they watched the breakdowns of the videos, and were put on a no-fly list. Numbers of views on the videos were set repeatedly to zero, the videos didn't show up in search engines, couldn't be monetized. Creators of the channels had begun disappearing.

Anyone who didn't praise the Rescuers in his social media status updates was considered a callous, sexist, patriarchal, white supremacist racist, was unfollowed, unfriended, insulted, and certainly not invited to parties. Each day of the week was devoted to a different child supposedly pulled from the rubble by the Rescuers, with weekends being devoted to individual Rescuer heroes who had "saved her" in the clips shown obsessively on the news. The most commonly watched news anchor in the country, Tom Tellen, spoke of little else. The brave Rescuers, he said, were "unarmed and neutral" and the world's best role models. No mention was made of how they harvested the organs of the children the Rescuers brought to the hospital.

Nancy weighed the risks of following the faked videos more closely. Even researching how to do that was dangerous. She'd been trained by the Nevermind how to be a honeypot, how to do occult rituals, and how to kill, not how to be an expert in avoiding their own surveillance. She was thinking about these things because she'd heard some words faintly coming from next to her. She looked over the shoulder of a woman waiting for the bus; she was listening to a Brandon video on her device. Staying completely untraceable, with no internet history or IP address, Nancy was limited to gaining precious factual information by spying on people as they tracked where the underground alternative new stations would pop up again here and there after being censored, like Whack-a-Mole.

Nancy half-reconsidered the decision to have no computer. She'd been firm on that self-protective policy since she went underground and moved across the states to befriend Becky. It was easy, living in the porch, off the grid. They had no internet at home. The woman she rented from had no desire for it, which was perfect. But if Nancy had some kind of device, she could take it into a coffee shop, go into the Deep Web, not talk to anyone, browse anonymously, only ration her email to contact the indie-video sensation Brandon again with vital information if there wasn't enough time to mail a letter.

But still, the surveillers always paid the most attention to people using encryption. Agents targeted them to find out what they were doing, to infiltrate, pretend to be their friends, and steal their privacy using agency privilege. It would draw attention to that emergency email she'd have to use to log in. She'd be on camera using the device at that location, and with zoom, what she wrote would be visible on the recording. Computers now came with iris scanning. There was — everything. There would always evolve more ways of finding a person's internet footprint.

Free information was put out constantly by the major companies, all basically intertwined with the Nevermind as public relations, while it tracked every aspect of viewers' lives. Social media sites, YouTube, and search engines tracked everything they did, even when they weren't logged in. They'd recently censored out of existence the majority of the sites she'd want to see, anyway. Mostly, the only thing left was propaganda. But not completely. Hungry for knowledge, Nancy would sit in bars, wearing her mask, until no one was around interested in watching the ball games, and she'd change the channel briefly to see what the news said. She'd reason from that the truth of the matter, always opposite of what the anchors said. She'd listen in on conversations of people interested in conspiracies, and try to gauge what was accurate and what was far-flung. She used her understanding of how the Nevermind put a spin on things, and manipulated emotions, to deduce what was behind the images they showed on the front pages of newspapers in the stands, and the comedy skits on during prime time.

The dark-skinned woman standing next to Nancy wore a scarf around her neck that partially covered a tattoo of a pug in a top hat. Nancy's eyes wandered to her throat, curious for any slight movements to reveal more of the intriguing design. Nancy prepared to tell her she was only looking at the tattoo, if the woman caught her eye and hid her device. But instead, the woman moved the device closer to Nancy when she noticed her peering. Nancy must have had honest body-language, as the woman had no chance to see her face. The woman had found Brandon in the newest incarnation of his beleaguered site. He wasn't visible — he never was, hiding his appearance, which was noticeable especially because of his gigantism. Instead, there were slides. He was talking about how, "There is no proof the president has ever chemical-bombed his citizens at all. There is also no proof he had used sarin gas on his people. There is, however, plenty proof the U.S.-sponsored terrorists did it themselves on orders you can see here. The U.S. has to win the pipeline war with Russia so we can supply Western Europe with oil. Doesn't matter how many Islamic people in the Middle East have to die for that to happen, right? But let's just forget about that and talk about how racist, Islamophobic, and insensitive people are that we don't like, shall we? Meanwhile, the Rescuer branch of the terrorists act out scenes of rescue, to get funding from Turkey, the U.S., Europe, and the Gulf Kingdom. From your friends, and family. They are thieves who steal everything the citizens have. If the women are wearing ear rings, the Rescuers cut off the ears to get at the ear rings fast. See this photo of a man taking a happy selfie with the child-beheaders? And here he is in this photo, accusing the national army of killing his little girl — the same girl as in the other photo. Check out this man. He set up micro financing in their country at such exorbitant rates, hell, some people are forced to sell their kidneys to pay the interest, at the hospital they set up, saying there's a cholera epidemic. There is no cholera. It's a cover story."

That sounded to Nancy like an intelligence ploy the Nevermind Agency specialized in propagandizing: making sure the media put out whatever spin they wanted them to, to manipulate people's emotions toward whatever war and laws they desired with narratives worthy of award-winning cinema. She was deeply ashamed she'd been involved in the Agency in the past, even though she'd had no choice. She couldn't help crying as she sat on the bus, learning about the organ harvesting.

The plump little boy in the Rescuer costume held his mother's hand, as he asked Nancy for donations to the Rescuers. The Rescuers supposedly needed to bring Rescuer-brand candy to the children for Halloween, though most people there had probably never heard of such a holiday. Nancy wanted to keep watching Brandon's video, but didn't want to be rude. She listened to his story, rather than interrupt him.

Three others standing around handed him money to put inside the donation Jack O'lantern, which the smiling, androgynous young curly-haired donation collector had put a funny rain hat on. He lifted the hat up gently, peering up at her sideways, as water slid down it onto the money.

She said no.

He said, "Fine, turn your back on me now, woman!"

The bus was crowded, standing-room only, pressed next to pushy people. Someone smelled of peanut butter. The man next to her looked at her, flattened his thin lips, as if he thought the smell came from her. She tried to make a subtle expression suggesting it wasn't her, but that was impossible while wearing the burn mask. She wiggled her eyebrows, and he looked stunned and turned away. She'd apparently conveyed the wrong message.

She had finally freed herself from the image in which the Agency had made her. She'd pieced the shards of herself back together in a new pattern. She'd earned a chance to live like other people, focusing on being happy, relaxing, working, not keeping up with the news if she didn't want to, not trying to fix everything wrong with the world. After her escape, she wanted to live a normal life, make friends, develop a community of like-minded souls. *Sure, I'm holding back my identity from my only close friend. And lying about why I'm lying about it.*

Phobia Night made her eyes twitch. But she'd never have *any* friends if she told the truth. And the mysterious message she'd gotten about how she should befriend Becky made her toes tingle in her shoes, made her want to tap her feet together and explore whatever adventure awaited from the friendship. Even if it meant walking into a diabolical trap. It would be worth it to have a community of at least one.

She grabbed a seat once enough people got off the bus. She sat next to a bony woman with a narrow, long nose, and severe brown hair. The woman was looking at a video on her device, which caught Nancy's attention because it was Brandon talking, finishing the broadcast she'd been watching earlier. Nancy couldn't see it, but she could hear he was asking for donations to help with his channel, because of the new levels of censorship of news that questioned the propaganda on the mainstream stations. Nancy wished she could electronically send money, but she'd used only cash since moving there. Being impossible to trace was her life.

The most popular social media and major search engines, which were known associates of the Nevermind, censored websites that put out material that sabotaged the public's perception of the prevailing military agenda, and that undercut the news stations' social engineering. Some of the sites they censored were absurd sensationalized clickbait and prank sites, though they were no more inaccurate than mainstream news, which had made many false claims leading to widespread destruction. Recently none of the list's sites, which showed evidence of their crimes, were allowed.

Brandon's hugely popular massive video site had been taken down after it ran for years. But his fans shared with each other its new iterations, as he moved from domain to domain, getting his message out, showing documents, interviewing whistleblowers, breaking apart social engineering memes. His voice was unmistakable. He changed his pseudonym each time, and dedicated listeners shared it among themselves in the bowels of the internet. Groups had formed to alert each other right away of his channel's new incarnation and discuss the topics in forums. The groups included some obsessed extremists as well as people simply hungering for news of what was going on in the world. This was especially true during the tense situation of an impending war, unless journalists like Brandon could get across to enough of the public that they were being played by both party's politicians.

Brandon talked, in his booming giant voice: "Listen, I understand that during times of crisis people don't think clearly. That's what the people orchestrating your feelings are counting on. But take a step back and do some research. Click the links below to see scenes from the journalists who are making it across the border. The Rescuers are nothing like what the media is telling you they are. They're the epitome of armed and dangerous. They're acting in the videos they send you. Your donations are not being used to help the people by these guys, you get that, right? I guarantee no humanitarian aid is being given."

His deep voice was assertive. Lots of people posted comments wondering if the rumor was true, if he really did have gigantism, induced by Human Growth Hormone during adolescence. She'd never tell. Knowing the truth was a fun little secret. She remembered how his huge arms were comforting. How he seemed too big to fail. She was glad he always wore a bullet proof vest, kept a gas mask on hand, tested food for poison, had bikers surrounding him where he went in public in his car with blackened windows. She tried not to worry for his safety. Though she didn't believe in God, she prayed for him.

He spoke on. "People! Your donations are being used to finance the interrelated terrorist groups to keep the war going and avoid peaceful settlement. The Rescuers were created with U.S. and UK funding under the supervision of a British military contractor in Turkey. Every civilian says the president is not attacking them. The NATO-led 'rebels' are. Here, we see photos of the Rescuers standing on the bodies of dead soldiers and laughing. The NATO Rescuers are a media campaign to support the regime change schemes of the U.S. and its allies, to put in fascist puppets. It was founded by a security contractor and branded by a U.S. marketing company. The Rescuers' public profile was cultivated by an advocacy group lobbying for regime change that was created by a Western P.R. firm, with the help of a British billionaire."

Nancy bowed her head and cupped her ear, straining out the voices around her.

"The persona of the group is *all* pretense," said Brandon. "All those human interest stories about the so-called civil defense group, the Rescuers, providing humanitarian aid — those are inaccurate. Do you notice in these photos here, the children being rescued are dressed in perfect new clothes, with not a bit of dirt on them, no wrinkles, nothing? How can this be, if they've been languishing under the rubble for days? How are they smiling and strong? Have you noticed they're always lushly hydrated, kissing the Rescuers in thanks?"

Nancy remembered hearing people talking about a video showing the Rescuers pulling children from the rubble, and dramatically jumping back from bombing. And then, the camera zoomed back and along the edge of the frame could be seen the edge of a smoke machine, creating the bomb effect, and next to it, a cameraman casually eating an apple, putting in ear plugs, and pushing a button to generate a bangs, smiling while signaling the Rescuers when to throw themselves onto the ground.

Nancy considered more strongly going into the Deep Web, and all the other methods of encrypted private searching. Of course, she couldn't buy a device or use a public one, without being tracked, but still, she wished she'd been trained much more extensively in communicating covertly with computers.

"Now, look at this video. Take a close look. See the little girl's necklace with her name on it? See her moles by her left eyebrow and her chin? Look at the boy. See how he didn't button his shirt right? Look at the scar on his cheek. They are identical to those children being rescued in the photos you just saw being rescued from a different part of the country last week."

A man next to Nancy shuffled away and humphed, obviously disgusted by Brandon's accusations. Nancy wished she could show him an image she'd noticed on the news when she was at Becky's house. It showed a young girl running through the rubble. It was supposedly a real action photo. However, Nancy recognized it from a video game that had gained some popularity for a short while a few years previously. She almost wanted to shove that image in the man's face. Or deck him for being so resistant to hearing what Brandon was saying. He mumbled words of hatred at Brandon, and furiously scribbled notes, most likely to write a scathing critique.

On Nancy's other side, three middle-aged women talked loudly, showing each other the streaming mainstream news. Nancy could hear the newscaster repeating the Rescuers' calls for a no-fly zone, which could only be useful to countries trying to force a regime-change. The newscaster exclaimed over the supposedly missing children. "Will the Rescuers find them before they die?"

"Rescue On!" said one of the women, in a throaty voice.

One of the others looked at her, and said, "He's my favorite too. I like how wide his shoulders are. That scruffy beard. Mmm."

"Not as hot as the actor playing him in the movie though. Right? Am I right?" The bus swerved, knocking them into each other.

The news anchor, Tom Tellen, called the Rescuers, "The spiritual giants of our age, doing this noble task out of the goodness of their hearts, helped along largely by your donations. Keep them coming, folks."

Nancy turned back to the woman listening to Brandon and looked at her, crinkling her eyes in a smile she hoped was visible through the eyes in the mask. The woman lifted her eyes quickly and shot them back down, angling her hair over her face, and covering the device subtly with one hand. She shifted slightly away when Nancy refused to divert her gaze. Nancy whispered, "Brandon's great."

The woman frowned, pulling back and searching Nancy's masked face, her eyes darting back and forth. She sighed, her collar bones moved downward. She leaned into Nancy's wig and said softly, "Yes."

59

"How refreshing," whispered Nancy. "It's good some people are aware of how it works. One country after another. Always pretty much the same. I feel so sorry for everyone killed in the wars."

"It feels awful to be taking advantage of living in a country that ruins so many people's lives in other countries, doesn't it? I can't stand the idea of so many people suffering for the sake of U.S. profit. It makes me sick."

"But, I have to say, it makes me strangely happy to meet someone else who feels sad about countries being ruined. Paradox, eh?" Nancy couldn't help smiling.

"Want to exchange numbers?" asked the woman.

"I. I wish I could," said Nancy. "I don't have a phone."

"Email?"

"No, no, sorry. I'm sorry." Nancy looked down, and tried to bite her fingernail, pressing it against her mask, before she realized what she was doing.

"Pussies," yelled a teenage boy at them. "You shut up now and move along. We don't want you on our bus. No one wants you. Haven't you noticed, you stinking cunts?" He pressed into them, his facial muscles growing harder, his breath warm against Nancy. He pushed the woman who had been listening to Brandon, her head hitting the back of the seat. He lifted her up to her feet and shouted to the bus, "This bitch is a racist! And she must like chemical-bombs. Want us to sarin you, you little dyke freaks?" The woman ran to the other side of the bus, and Nancy tripped the man when he tried to follow her.

Nancy got off a couple stops earlier than she'd planned.

Nancy couldn't get onto the library computer without an ID, but as she passed by the building, her feet veered instinctively toward it, longingly. All the internet cafes had the same rule for using their computers. Magazines and newspapers she could pick up in print were naively influenced by the official propaganda the Nevermind imposed on the mainstream news. Usually she checked it out watching Becky's but she never searched with hers, because she didn't want to give her that dangerous browsing history. She watched TV with Becky, and could extrapolate what had happened to some degree by reversing what Tom Tellen said on the nightly news.

She wanted to read more online on alternative media about the convoluted relationship between the Rescuers and the ever-shifting Jihadi factions, mercenaries, provocateurs, puppets, and of course, the most important thing, the pipeline. When too many indie reporters caught onto the facade, the factions branched off again, using different hard-to-remember names, keeping alliances while pretending when to be competing. Some called themselves "moderates." It all became too confusing for most people to keep track of, too messy. She couldn't keep up with it, herself, from the little snippets of information she gleaned. She certainly couldn't learn the truth about the situation from the Rescuers video game.

She'd read on someone's laptop at a coffee shop, the internet headlines about the P.R. firm Bell Pottinger being outed as one of the companies working with the Nevermind in England to cover up how the U.S. was covertly arming, funding, and training the terrorists. Of course, mainstream media didn't cover this. In fact, Tellen was outspoken against what they called "fake media," which covered Tellen's own fake news.

And since things had gotten weird and veered off in ways people never saw coming, in the 80s, the Nevermind was born and continued the CIA's trend of coverups and recruitments, with an enhancement of the occult practices, instigated by the President with gigantism. He'd claimed his height meant his ancestors obviously originated in Atlantis, as a superior Aryan root race. Imperialism was their right, according to interpretations of Theosophists like the spy Madam Blavatsky, and Edgar Cayce.

Nancy's eyes fell on the newspaper in the stand. The Rescuer movie was looking like it might become the biggest box office success yet. No surprise. The Ehroh Production company was owned by the Nevermind. And there was a lot riding on that scam. Defense contractors were chomping at the bit.

***

Nancy ran to make up for the extra distance she was traversing on foot rather than on the bus, splashing puddles as she pounded the sidewalk, and got to Becky's apartment earlier than she expected. By that time the rain was oceanic. Nancy's windbreaker wasn't serving her. She let herself into the apartment with the key Becky had given her months before.

She closed the windows where the wind was bringing in the rain, but left the others partly open. The air felt clean and enlivening. She turned off the lamp, removed her clothes and put them in the dryer. Walking around the apartment naked, she felt the beauty of being in her muscular body. She stood in front of the open window facing the sidewalk and the empty houses, the cool air making her flat breasts come to attention, her nipples happy.

She pulled back when someone got out of his car, but since he pulled his jacket up over his head against the strong rain, and was running, she stood even closer to the window; he'd never see her in the dark, especially through the storm. He entered the house, owned by the church like all the other empty houses around it, making Nancy smirk about the standing joke. She and Becky would be hanging out and notice random, rather odd-looking people go into the house. But they *never* saw them come *out. It must be the portal to hell. Haha.* She pushed her breasts against the cold glass. Almost as delicious as ice cubes. She almost wished Becky would come home at that moment and see that, must look intriguing from the other side of the glass. Maybe she'd dance with her up against the glass in the rain. Then, she moved in front of the open air, the breeze amplifying the enthralling chill.

The happy little piano melody coming closer down the street made her retreat into the darkness. The recording of strident, accusatory, condescending woman's voice, "HeLLO!" and then the inglorious "haw haw." But it *couldn't* be the same ice cream truck. No one would extend his route that far. It must be a franchise. But why was there no branding on the van? Always driving along without stopping, in weird places and times. Working in an obscure neighborhood far out of the city with no kids, and now in the deluge. What a business model.

She started to chase the van in case it was the same driver who had pummeled the window, but she stopped. How would she know if she saw her — or him? She'd barely paid attention to how the van was decorated. Not being an ice cream eater, she blended all ice cream ads into pretty much the same non-thing. Still, odd she didn't have some idea. Until she realized — she'd never seen it in the daylight. It was always foggy or rainy when it went by.

She went through Becky's closet, and found some clothes to put on while hers dried. Becky was late. Nancy started to fret. She never missed their monthly Tuesday night meeting. What could have happened to her? Had her stalker gotten her? Was the stalker Stan? A total stranger, or a twisted admirer who fell for her at Frame Up?

Nancy felt a twinge of guilt. She'd been preparing some costumes in case she was caught snooping around Stan's. But she hadn't run over to Stan's house as soon as she was hired. She did have to sleep, after all, and she was a piano teacher. She had to work. She couldn't be expected to immediately, and continually, see if Becky's beau was cheating on her. Still, she felt like a layabout. And, Jesus, what if someone saw her lurking around Stan? How stupid would she feel? "Oh, I'm just spying for a friend, really. She's giving me some original art. No, I don't know if it's worth anything at all." She would go to Stan's later that night — if the rain let up. Would be hard to see much through all that. But she had to try.

Wait. What if the stalker was *in the apartment with her*? What if he'd already attacked Becky? Nancy grabbed herself, pulling the overshirt around her tightly, and stopping humming. She picked up a kitchen knife and crept toward the bathroom. Becky, being a shy, private sort, left the door nearly closed. Nancy tried to tell herself that's all it was. Habit, even though she lived alone. She listened for any sounds, and put her hand on the knob. Her heart was beating hard.

She pushed the door quickly while jumping back around the corner into the hallway. She eased around, knife out, suddenly inside the room. She took a deep breath, tightened her mouth, and yanked back the shower curtain. No one. She imagined the whole scene sped up double time. She felt too silly to look in the closets.

A sudden sound made her nearly leap out of her skin. The latch, footsteps. The intruder? She hid in the hallway, grasping the knife more tightly. Her expert reflexes had kicked in and she was ready to go.

She was always careful not to say anything that could ever come up as incriminating evidence related to her previous identity as a rogue Agent. There were people she'd interacted with over her entire life, in her involuntary career, who might want to show up and do her in. Some memories rushed toward her. Her handler, a man sent to scare her into submission, an angry brother of a child she'd wrangled from her family.

Most of the children the Nevermind used were raised within Agency families. Some had never been registered with a birth certificate or social security number. One of those children came to her mind, too. She hated that a part of her had gone along with inducting the girl into the dark ways of the intelligence agency. She'd made the girl into an unwilling U.S. spy. Nancy liked to think of herself as the good guy. *A good girl.* That thought brought tears to her eyes, so she unthought it.

Her body tightened, her muscles remembering cowering before a handler who'd caught her reading a newspaper. Her body remembered going into a fuzzy place, dreamlike and confusing. *Everything just got sort of black and white, and sort of extra colorful, both at the same time.* She hugged herself, feeling stupid for being so emotionally reactive, like she was still a kid in the old days. Free of the Nevermind's programming for a longish time, she'd had no lapses into the worlds they'd created for her. But she felt the twinges at that moment. Her upper back curved over as she hunkered more than she needed to hide. She felt a lowered visionary field take over, creating a buffer between herself and reality, whatever it was. It was like being at home, her uncle saying things that made no sense, doing things she was supposed to ignore and excuse.

Like everyone in the world, she had to act like her role was OK, subservient to the powerful leaders working on their investments. Everyone had to go through his life pretending everything was normal, all the while knowing he was being sold out by pay-to-play corporations, organized crime, gun, human, and drug trade. It made so many people's minds curl over their chests and close them in with fog. Wisps of brown fog, curling under, brown fog of forget. *Damn, heh, I'm acting like a baby, wah wah.*

"Nancy?" Oh! Nancy almost laughed and almost cried that it was only Becky. "Sorry I'm late! I bought a motion-activated camera. It's not as expensive as I expected. Hey, did you make any ginger tea, by any chance?" Becky dripped water on the floor in a rhythm that was so good, she stood there still for a while as they listened.

Nancy hid the knife behind her back when Becky emerged. "Hey, Becko! Yeah, I could use a little warming up. Nice and spicy."

"What?"

"Look, I got spooked." She hung her head sideways, grinning, and slowly moved the knife tip around her body so Becky could see it. Nancy kept moving it, her grin turning playful.

Becky chuckled and hugged her, taking the knife and setting it down. "You're such a goofball. All these Phobia Nights and you still get spooked by the littlest things. Who did you think would be walking in? Oh, wait. My stalker. Never mind."

Becky cut up the ginger root and put it on to boil.

Nancy stretched, and realized how cold she'd gotten. She went into her karate routine. It had been too long since she'd done it regularly. She was getting a little stiff from all the working out with heavy weights she'd been doing, to make her muscles as large as she could. She flexed her pectorals. *Got to be ready for anything. Anything sometimes includes hiding*, she reminded herself.

Becky walked around the apartment with the camera. "Do you think it's better to leave it in the open, so if someone sees it, he'll just leave instead of doing anything bad?"

"I don't know. Maybe having it hidden would be better. You could see what he does when he's here. It's got to be weird, right? I mean, why would anyone go through your stuff like that? I'd want to get some idea if it were me. But then, I don't know. I see what you mean about having it out. He could be coming in to steal your identity. Set you up. Plant something. Smell your underwear."

"Gross! Nancy!" She ran over to her and punched her, laughing.

Nancy punched her back, and then leaped around the room. "'Bout a shot of spiced rum in the tea?"

Becky humored her with a sassy flourish, as she poured a shot from her one small liquor bottle into the tiny clay shot glass she'd crafted to look like a fish bowl. After she poured the shots into the mugs, which she'd also made from clay into larger fish bowls, with the fish painted on, she squeezed a lemon and dripped raw honey into it.

They raised their mugs high in the air toward each other, while bending forward. Eyes wide, faces close to each other, they opened their mouths exaggeratedly and yelled, "Phobia Night!"

Becky sidled, asking, "Before we really get started, I'm sorry, do you mind if I turn on the news for a minute? With the decision about the war coming up next week . . ."

"Oh God, please do. This impending World War thing is driving me mad."

"I don't think much of anyone can stay away from the news these days. The media war is wacky. All that fake news happening."

Nancy longed to know the ins and outs of what was going on internationally. She'd never been shown the full picture in her work as an Agent, just what she needed to know to be effective in certain operations.

On the TV, the reporter was looking smugly humbled. His brown hair parted civilly on the side had an extra sophisticated bit of wave that day. He was interviewing people lining up to donate to the Rescuers. Behind him were scenes of people standing in lines in the cold to donate. Many of them were obviously not well-off. She watched a family with children in ragged clothes. The parents looked proud. The oldest boy holding his mother's hand was looking down, and kicking the ground. The reporter on the street asked people about their love for the heroes they'd been promoting, asking which one people followed most closely. If they'd seen the movie yet. They showed a scene where children had their action figures from the movie in their hands, and when the trailer played, whenever one of the heroes would appear on the screen, the kids would hold up that action figure and shout, "Rescue On!"

There were scenes of the action figures being given out to children supposedly in the part of the country the Rescuers were operating in. The children somehow knew about the movie and squealed, jumping up and down. Music swelled in the background, and it went into full montage. Bands of children holding the dolls, dancing through the crowded rough-paved streets, their mothers looking on, beaming from the doorways. Ironically, the children were speaking English, but Becky didn't seem to notice.

Nancy recognized one of the photos displayed on the news, of a scene from that day, but in fact, it had been in a newspaper years ago, was from another country entirely.

The reporter spoke with another reporter on location outside the boundaries of the rebel-held city. The reporters spoke on each side of the split-screen. Something felt wrong with the picture. She didn't know what. Then, it sank in. A car drove by behind the reporter on the left; then within a fraction of a second, the same car drove behind the other reporter. A man was pulling a rope behind that reporter, on the right, and Nancy noticed rope being dragged along the ground behind the reporter on the left. *Oh, that'll be all over the internet soon.* Nancy wanted to point out the inconsistency to Becky. But she wanted to remain friends even more.

Nancy wanted to put her arm around Becky and calm down her idolization of the Rescuers. Nancy wasn't willing to expose her background in espionage, which qualified her to recognize war propaganda. The deadline was coming fast. Only a few days until what would most likely lead to a Third World War. That reluctance to reveal anything about herself, her supposed "fear" was what she "worked with" on Phobia Nights with Becky. Her "inability to be transparent and share my life story with people."

Nancy's escape had propelled her across states, but she'd have never landed in such a random place, many months ago, if it weren't for accepting the mission in the anonymous message with Becky's name and the admonition to befriend her. Nothing had happened from the move and the friendship so far other than compatibility and fun. Did some kind stranger simply want them to be happy and make some kind of godly friend-match?

Was the person sending the messages also breaking into Becky's apartment?

She shivered with the excitement of Becky getting some good camera feed of the intruder. That could make everything fall into place for both of them!

Becky took their empty glasses into the kitchen.

Nancy's eyes attained super focus when Becky spun around and ran across the room at her, soaring over the imposing footstool, yelling, "HaiiiiiiiiiiYA!" She landed on the couch, her legs landing crossways across Nancy's.

"Woot! You're ready to fly." Nancy was out of practice with her karate. But she leaped up and sparred with her a bit.

"That's right," she told Becky. "Angle your heel in there, kiddo." She weaved a little from the wine.

"You aren't exactly looking too masterful yourself."

They went into the hallway, and Becky climbed a stair. She turned back to wave at Nancy, smiling broadly, one side of her mouth going crooked. Nancy stepped up behind her, holding her lightly around the waist; Becky climbed another stair toward the next floor in the complex. By the third step, Nancy could feel warm dampness arising from Becky's body, and could feel her tremble beneath her palms. Becky charged back down, leaping onto the couch, laughing. They high-fived, and Nancy thought she saw Becky's throat pulsate.

Becky cocked her eyebrow, and leaned her head down. It was Nancy's turn. Ah yes, "Ye olde trust issues."

"Tell me one thing about your past. Go."

Nancy pretended to squirm. She shook her head no. Tears stung her eyes, wanting to drop.

"You could write it down and fold it over and hand the note to me. I wouldn't even have to open it. But it would be a start."

Nancy tugged on her mask.

"OK. I was home schooled. I was especially interested in Egypt."

"Excellent." Becky patted Nancy's wig and caressed her high cheek bone. "That wasn't so hard, was it? I don't judge you for that. It's just as good as public school, I think. I don't know about private school. You don't feel naked or anything, do you, with me knowing that? Oh, weird," she added, when she raised her eyes to the window. "Someone dressed like a giant spider is staring at me."

Nancy rose to look through the window and saw the spider's friends emerging behind him out of the shadows. More spiders. Black widows. Standing on the sidewalk and not moving once they were centered in front of the window. They took a step forward, all at the same time. Becky stood back and grabbed her stomach. Nancy's muscles tightened and her stance widened, her hands subtly assuming the karate position.

The giant spider people took another silent step toward them. The air in the room was electric. The costumed people suddenly broke formation and laughed loudly, running off, looking back and tapping each other. One tripped the other one, who rolled and flailed before catching up to the others.

"Oh, Jeez. Having fun with their Halloween costumes. Warming up for the big day, I guess."

Nancy asked, "Do you have anything I could wear for a costume tonight when I stalk Stan? I want to seem like I'm just goofing around like those guys."

"I wish it was flat enough there I could do it myself. Sorry about asking you to do this, Nance."

"I could say I'm hosting a kid's early Halloween party at my house in the neighborhood? Or dropping my kid off at one? I don't know."

Becky took her into her bedroom, and told her to close her eyes. She unbuttoned Nancy's shirt, dressed her in a loose blouse and draped cloth around and around her head. The silk felt luxurious against her skin.

She felt an odd sensation against her mask. She recognized the smell from childhood when she'd drawn in the bathtub with thick bright colors that washed off as soon as water touched them. Becky was drawing her a new face.

"I'll let you do this part. Here."

Nancy reached out, keeping her eyes closed. She slipped off her pants and put on the loose, long, silky skirt.

"Open!"

She grinned. The mirror showed her to be a dead gypsy extra-terrestrial.

Chapter Nine

Spying

After Nancy got off the bus, she walked the long distance to Stan's large house far up in the elegant hills on the opposite side of the city from her off-grid primitive house. These craftsman houses looked charming surrounded by exotic plants in their generous yards, along the narrow road that wound back and forth, with no railing to stop the view of sparkling lights far below.

She couldn't believe it. That sound. No!

An ice cream vendor. What? She struggled to find a few dollar bills wadded up in her purse fast enough to hold it out toward the truck as it approached and she stepped toward the middle of the lane. Was it the same driver, self-sabotaging with an absurd route? She had to know. Was it the same person who'd cracked the window at her house? That had been expensive to get fixed, but more importantly, was there any meaning to the painting on the rock inside the ice-cream snowball? Or was it random?

The van didn't slow down but sped up as she called out to it, waving her money. She bent, trying to peer inside the dark windows and saw something she thought might have been a red clown nose. "HeLLO!" scolded the familiar recording of an unpleasant woman's nasal, sneering voice. Nancy chased it and the van seemed to go even faster, — *too* fast, veering around a curve and into the other lane. Honking ahead. A large car nearly ran into the ice cream. A thud in the back of the truck. Maybe something large shifting. No doubt, something frozen and tasty which the driver was withholding from her.

Did ice cream-person not like gypsies? Maybe not if they were dead aliens.

She finally made it to Stan's. She was impressed that Stan was apparently ready to sell such a fabulous big house, landscaped, with a small fountain emerging from a statue of Adonis, to live in the flatlands with Becky. But he did seem to have the funds to support her.

The lights were on low. In the room with the largest lights, flickering candle flames made exotic shadows on the walls. The driveway was long enough Nancy could hide behind a tree and no cars would see her. She could leap out toward the road fast enough if about to be caught. She prepared herself to look casual in that case, lowering her shoulders and loosening her jaw.

She peered at the large photos on the walls. No frames, just color images, and along that wall, at least, all women wearing wedding gowns. Well, good. He was being honest about working for the Wedding Company, and working from home, as one of his various videography and photography jobs.

Nancy felt elation creep in. Her best friend was about to have a fabulous thing happen to her: marry a talented man she seemed to like. No longer have to be desperate about survival. Maybe Nancy was about to gain a new friend: Stan.

Her toe twitched. It cramped, pulling in toward the center of her foot, and she went down. Once she thought about her toe, and massaged it, it relaxed. But once the elation about Stan returned, the toe cramped up again. She sat down. Magnesium deficiency from stress, no doubt. She felt some wetness seep from the ground into the skirt, and stood up quickly, nearly tipping over. She stood like a crane, crouching over her foot, massaging her painful toe, when the door opened. She tried to scamper behind the tree, and had to grab it to keep from tripping over a root. She let herself down gently into the shadows.

What if he caught her? What could she say? "Oh, I decided to nap here while waiting for my son to get out of the party. I'm already done reading their Death Alien tarot cards. It's just so pretty, here. What a beautiful yard you have. You know?"

A tall, slender young woman, with hair blue along the fringe, stepped out of the doorway. Stan followed her. Electricity shot through Nancy's body for a second when she saw him, recognizing him from the photos she'd seen at Becky's house, her mind piecing together all the angles and lighting to adjust the composite idea of his appearance. He looked a little sharper. His hair even spikier. But he was far away.

They moved and a tall crimson bush partially obscured her view. They were talking very softly, standing close to each other.

Were they going to kiss?

Nancy got out her small camera. She huddled closer, leaning in to see more through the window. The thin curtains obscured her vision, but they weren't completely closed. She thought she could make out black silk sheets hanging up on hooks, with white ropes? Bit by bit her squinting eyes made out more details. The faces of the women in the photos on ocean spray green walls. Long hair, pleading, exquisitely seductive, at the peak of their commercial appeal. A picture of a woman in a wedding dress, looking up hopefully toward the balding red-haired minister with red cheeks who was standing prepared to perform a marriage. Some wore elaborate white fluffy wedding dresses and hopeful faces, some wore flimsy teddies and dreams, some wore nothing at all.

They started walking along the driveway that ran not too far from where she crouched. Nancy leaned up against the tree she'd crept behind, as if asleep, and angled her eyes at an increasingly uncomfortable position to watch them. He wore a tight blue-black, ribbed, sleeveless undershirt. He emanated a fiery sensation with his efficient body language, and his highly functional arms. He rubbed his hand over his crunchy black hair, spiked so hard with gel it sprang back up.

The woman got in the red car in the driveway and drove away. Hmm. Hard to say if it was an affair. Stan went back inside, without Nancy having to use any of the wild explanations going through her head just yet.

She breathed out hard. She jumped from shadow to shadow, and opened his mailbox. Strange. His name listed there was Wayne Norman. What she was doing was wrong. So wrong — legally. Doing anything wrong made her muscles in her forearms twinge. She wanted to be a good person. Do things according to the law. Not have anyone running at her telling her she was evil and that they were going to lock her up. She wanted nice old ladies to pat her on the head and tell her she was a sweetie. She wanted to smile at them, feel proud and safe and sweet. Loved.

But she watched Stan, anyway. For Becky.

She'd come prepared with long colorful gypsy gloves that would cover up any fingerprints if anything went wrong.

Were there any scented love letters with hearts drawn on them? No, there were not. There were, however, many outgoing envelopes with incorrect return addresses. Some had an unfamiliar name: Stan Franken. Others had, instead of a name, titles like Red Wedding Proposal and ApocoLips. They were being sent to CEOs of some major corporations, Honorable Judges, some Representatives, Chief of Staff, Secretary of State, and some names she wasn't familiar with.

There was one that was a fuller packet, addressed to Ehroh Productions at Lookout Mountain Labs in Laurel Canyon. Nancy remembered when she was young and Ehroh had bought the Labs, which had been used in the past for making videos about nuclear testing, war propaganda and training videos. There had been much talk about occult practices and dubious faked moon videos, murders, and an underground base. Strange stuff, hard to know whether to believe it, but she did know Ehroh was intimately connected with creating the Nevermind's feature films with a clear agenda of promoting a globalist political agenda. Still, what Hollywood feature film was allowed to stray far from propaganda any more?

A car slowed down as it approached the driveway. Nancy ducked down, sliding across the ground to another tree, a bigger one than before. She sidled around it as the shiny car drove into the pull-in, still a good distance from Stan's house. A middle-aged man got out, dressed nicely, wearing what looked to her like an obvious toupee, a scarf covering his chin, and dark glasses, even though it was night. Ah, another master of disguise. The world was certainly growing more Halloweenish by the minute. And it was still days away.

She scooted to a closer tree while he walked around his car, and then she rolled up behind the hedges so she was very close to the doorway. She didn't think it was likely this encounter would tell her much about whether Stan was cheating on Becky, but she had built-in investigative skills, and hadn't been able to get her sneak on much lately like she always used to when she was an Agent.

When Stan answered the doorbell, he hugged the man so sensually, Nancy's jaw dropped. He was cheating on Becky with a man?

"How are you doing, Congressman? I didn't expect to see you."

Neither did Nancy!

In her surprise to see this public figure there, she flashed on what she knew of him. Though there were elements of the congressman's voting record Nancy admired, she didn't care for Congressman Rawlings' perpetration of media's false portrayal of the Rescuers. He had suppressed admiration of the Rescuers in a long, impassioned speech she'd seen in a clip someone was watching at the YWCA's bathroom. Someone in the audience had shouted, "Didn't you see the video that slipped through the cracks, showing how a terrorist executed an ordinary citizen, and then the camera panned back to show Rescuers waiting to pick up the corpse, looking sad for the news clip? But the terrorist who shot the citizen was one of the Rescuers? And after they wrapped the body in the sheet and lifted it up, they thought the camera was turned off and they laughed?"

The congressman had called for the questioner to be removed, and after he was forcibly carried out of the room, the dubious report was that he committed suicide. People in the room with him had cheered when the congressman condemned the questioner. When indie journalists had shared that clip, it was spread about on social media, and it caused a stir. Most people had been convinced the "moderate rebels" were a spontaneous uprising in a civil war, rising against a dictator terrible enough to warrant intervention. The terrorists who were really dropping the bombs had their spokespersons on social media, becoming famous Tweet by Tweet, twisting the truth around entirely to shift the blame for hundreds of thousands of civilian deaths away from the terrorists. Their faithful social media followers in the U.S. didn't research the truth of their statements. However, less gullible people had sent out alerts on social media about the incident, and had called for an investigation into the safety of the questioner. Some of them had then had their accounts blocked.

The congressman standing at Stan's door said, "I can't stay. I just want to give you this in person."

"You don't want to come in for some brandy? Special batch."

"Thank you, no. Not this time."

"Well, listen, the girl is great. She's so ready to get married, you can smell it through the screen."

Nancy was hesitantly proud of Becky. She'd picked a handsome, successful man who liked to keep a record of their special sexy times. Maybe Becky wouldn't mind so much if he was cheating with a man instead of a woman. Or, was it a man and a woman?

"I know. I've been watching. I, what would you say, audio-video-bugged your house. But don't worry. Just the rooms you shoot in. I'm not a pervert, watching you . . ."

"You what!"

"You're very good at your work. Of course, I know that, from the video we did together. Mmmm, am I right?"

"What the hell?"

So, Congressman Rawlings and Stan *were* having an affair? Doing kinky sex tapes of their good times together? Was this a lover's spat?

"And I've sent raw footage off for people to watch."

OMG! A jilted lover's revenge?

"Damn!" Stan stood closer to him and whispered forcefully. "How am I supposed to make the money, then, if you people are watching for free? You know how goddamn much people pay for these videos."

"I sent them to a lawyer, a policeman, Judge Winey, a Sheriff Jowd . . ."

"Motherfucker." Stan's face went grey, the circles under his eyes getting a shade of purple darker.

So Stan had some sort of strange money-making scheme. But how exciting. The Congressman was bringing it to a close, exposing it to everyone who mattered. His voting record was starting to shine more in her mind. Nancy scrambled to find her pen and paper and wrote down the names he mentioned before she forgot. She shifted position in her crouch in the darkness, and the paper fell onto the mud just as her foot came down on that spot. The paper was ruined.

It couldn't be their sex tapes he was talking about. No one would do that. It had to be that Stan was doing something illegal in a less personal way. She was proud of the congressman for being upstanding, and trying to get him in trouble. Had he only pretended intimacy so he could enter his lair and catch him at illegal porn? A sting? Or was it some other kind of crime he had recorded? He could be doing anything in there. She forgot the names she'd written down.

Tipping his wig, holding onto the side of it at a rakish angle, the Congressman pulled up his scarf. He pulled his glasses low on his nose as he held his head down, looking up sideways. Nancy wasn't sure, but she thought she saw him wink.

Stan decked him.

Nancy didn't wait to hear the rest. She wanted to make him an ally. She took advantage of their loud fighting to roll, jump, and make it off Stan's yard and onto the street. Looking back to make sure they didn't notice her, she walked away from the driveway and waited. Stan slammed the door when he went inside.

When the disheveled Congressman Rawlings walked toward his car, she started walking toward him, casually, facing away from her.

He was twisting his wig on his head toward the front when she said, "Oh, hello. Haha, happy almost Halloween!" When the Congressman looked startled, she looked down and continued: "Yeah, I'm done performing at the neighborhood party for the kids. It was sweet. One of them, little Jimmy, well, he was crying about the other kids making fun of him for being gay. And, so I got them all to sing a catchy song about being friends with gay people, that had a dance that went with it, and by the time I was done, they were running around singing it on their own. It was like he'd done a great thing by giving the opportunity for that song." She searched his eyes for the joy of a gay-ally. Nothing forthcoming. She wanted to find inroads so she could gather info on Stan. All the ways she'd hoped she could work it in were fading, the longer he looked at her like she was just in his way, the stupider she felt, standing there staring at him, in that ridiculous get-up, after blathering on randomly about a party.

"So, have you found the neighborhood to be safe for kids? No perverts around here or anything? What a lovely house you have. I don't think I've met you before."

"I'm late for an appointment." He nodded cursorily and drove away.

Well, so much for that.

Chapter Ten

The Rug

Wednesday

Nancy hitchhiked into the city from her porch at 4:00 the next morning, after ridiculously little sleep, to start her next vigil at Stan's house. The man she got the ride from handed her an envelope as she got out of the car, and said, "Here, don't ask me no questions. See, someone jumped out in front of me while I was driving along and said I'd run across you, and to give you a ride, and give you this — and I'd get $100. So, fine, now I done it!"

She stared. *Nancy* was scrawled on the front. Inside were strings of numbers and letters, headed by FS, GD, and RES. What kind of strangeness was this?

She had been too worn out to go all the way to Becky's house the night before, wake her up, and tell her vague suspicions that Stan was involved in something illegal. Any other form of communications would be too risky. She didn't know how much she was being watched, considering the Nevermind combined the best surveillance skills of the CIA, FBI, NSA, and MI6 and other agencies.

Nancy figured she'd need to hide out in the dark in his yard for hours before he woke up, but no. As he opened the front door, Stan's voice wavered, "The series I'm about to finish up will make the agency a lot more money. It's got more universal appeal."

Nancy wondered what agency. Was it related to the photography and videography he did, such as for the Wedding Company?

A group of policemen agreed while grunting under the surprisingly heavy-looking weight they were lifting. The short policeman with an unusually upturned nose and a large mole on his cheek held onto the foot end of the thick rug.

"And be sure to make sure nothing happens to Becky for me, will you? Watch her apartment, emails, phone calls. No changing her mind about accepting the proposal with enthusiasm. I want to see my lovely lady squeal with delight on Halloween."

Oh, how sweetly obsessive. Not all criminals are heartless.

"What else have we got to do?" asked the tall policeman, sneering, as they carried the awkward rug out the door, down the three steps, and toward the car with blackened windows. "Nothing ever happens on the streets this time of year."

"Reverend Red has started helping watch her."

How could Stan afford to buy all their time to watch her just so the proposal would go well? And why was he so worried she'd back out? She liked him. Nancy knew he wanted to record the proposal on video, the last one in the video series, in which Becky was to wear the wedding gown. Seemed sort of kinky, the way Becky blushed and leered at her sideways when she hinted about it. Stan added, "Don't want to blow the finale. If we don't deliver, they'll nut out."

Wait, what?

Was the finale the proposal video? Deliver? What if he sent videos of Becky to his contacts? He was a covert pornographer?

She couldn't help but feel a rush of red rising into her face, behind her mask. This idea was a stretch. Not everyone in the world was an Agent of the Nevermind. He was probably just a run-of-the-mill videographer and photographer. But, why he was connecting with so many important people? The Agency had to fund itself in every way it could, without public scrutiny, and criminal activities paid the best. Engaging with the most powerful people meant that the deeds would never come to light. And that those powerful people were ensured a way of being controlled through their obsessive proclivities and blackmail. Was Nancy seeing Agents everywhere, like a madwoman?

Damn! If only she'd told Becky all along about the ways of the Nevermind, she'd have a way to explain the danger she might be in. Otherwise, Becky'd have no reason to listen to the wild speculations. If Nancy had told her before, she could find some way to grab her, and, with a sentence, run off together, dodging the Agents, to hide forever.

Or could she, really? How likely was it they'd catch Nancy instead, figure out who she was, and kill her? Becky was just a random woman Stan had met. But, if she knew too much, they'd take her out, too. Oh, God, that was crazy talk. She needed more sleep.

Were there other women Stan had recorded? If so, did they know the videos would be sold? Who would save them? Obviously not the police or judicial system. How could they? The Nevermind had priority. And it had its ways of enforcing.

"Well." Stan stuttered and cleared his throat. "I don't know how much these sets will fetch. Might be less than usual."

The tall policeman clapped his hands. Dust from the rug blowing into the air, and Stan was noticeably shaken.

"Congressman recorded me making the videos and set them free. And who knows what else. I still haven't found the cameras. I don't even know if he really recorded me."

Nancy crept over to peer in the window through the light gauzy curtains. She hoped the congressman would blow Stan's cover before Becky was taken out of his house in a rug. Should she scare Stan and make him think the congressman was about to expose him? Get him to get rid of everything and clean up before the law got there? But would that keep him from being arrested?

Stan went inside, and when he came back out, his sleeves were rolled up and wet, finishing stuffing a wadded up black cloth along with what sounded like a tarp inside a giant bag.

Or was old Congressman Rawlings a rogue Agent? Her mind boggled.

81

***

After they left, Nancy peered into Stan's house through the thin curtains. She could see very little through the sliver between them. She contorted her body to find the best angles, pressing her face against the glass, ducking down into the hedges when cars drove past.

She went to different sides of the house, lifting her feet as lightly as she could above the foliage. If she were caught, there was no story she could possibly tell Stan to explain it. She found another window with a little space between the curtains at the bottom. She spied Stan's large screen that was hooked up to one of his laptops. Others were open, but not facing her directly. He was not in the room.

She took out the small telescope she'd brought for that purpose, and there on the screen was the video editing program. She saw an image of Becky tied up in a bizarre position. The frame was titled by a large bold letter M. Next to it was another image, this time labeled A. While Nancy wouldn't have realized it otherwise, suddenly she saw the poses were clear depictions of the letters. Becky's eyes and mouth were covered with black cloths. The lighting was lurid, the contrast intense. Her pale body against the black cloth. White rose petals. A gold colored shovel hanging from the wall.

The name of the movie project was WILL YOU MARRY ME?

She thought back to her conversations with Becky. She'd been reticent about talking in details about their videos, which was understandable, as they were edgy intimacy. Becky had expressed that she was mystified by why he placed her in such exacting, non-human, painful positions, some of them repeating in different installments. She did apparently like the artistry, each scene with different props. And the special lights and fabrics made her feel like a movie star.

Nancy tried to imagine what the final installment might be like. Becky had been so excited waiting for it, her plans for their future together growing with each video, taking her closer to that final

82

one. Her voice had gotten lower and more confident and relaxed, yet at other times going into a high squeak.

Nancy didn't think that many people were into paying a lot of money for wedding-themed BDSM videos. But, whatever entertainment they were making in the name of the Nevermind had to be very valuable to a niche audience who would not reveal the videos to anyone the Agents couldn't trust. And the more taboo the scenes were, the more valuable. Not just in money.

Who were the target audience? And what were the bribery tactics that went beyond the videos? Whatever the Nevermind did was always a multi-tiered business, repurposing, monetizing books through classes, movies through video games, porn through live bestiality shows, hunting parties, plane rides to orgy islands, and pandering to those who enjoyed the occult side of life with dark rituals, Satanic chants, and goat heads.

She peered in closer. The arch project folder was named *Gold-Diggers Deluxe Editions*. She couldn't see anything else, and so she headed back toward her porch. Maybe she could get in a few hours more sleep before teaching piano lessons to two of the neighbors in the afternoon.

As she got into the gold-colored car that provided her ride not far from the bus stop, a realization made her shudder. The gold shovel. It was a video project about a gold digger, probably because of men's anger toward women who used them. Was the shovel also going to bury her friend? Nancy wanted to run.

She was going the wrong way. Away from Becky. Becky was being put in poses as letters that spelled out WILL YOU MARRY ME? wearing the wedding dress he told her he'd lend her just for the sake of the video. He hadn't been kidding. It wasn't a tease to make her get all wiggly and googly-eyed. It was death.

She had the image of the monster mouth looming on the painted rock the ice cream person had thrown. The image was beautiful, with rich, deepening layers of shellac. Synchronicity, the way the two tiny women painted on it had the right simple abstract hair and body shapes to remind her of herself and Becky, even though she knew she was probably reading way too much into it a random act of vandalism by a deranged unsuccessful vendor.

Chapter Eleven
Little Black Dress

Nancy had to try to warn Becky not to trust Stan. But how, if Becky and her apartment were watched and all her phone calls, written messages, and packages, were monitored and intercepted? Nancy asked people she passed on the street if she could borrow their cell phones, and after many tries, one man allowed her. She took the chance and called Frame Up and talked to the owner. "Hello, this is Ivy Hammerman. Is Becky there?"

"She's not working today."

"Can you leave her a message, please when she comes in? Tell her that her friend said to stay away from S."

"Strange. OK, will do."

She walked the long journey to the bus and headed into Becky's part of the city. She took paper and pen from her bag and wrote: *Investigation Complete. Stay Away from S.*

She pulled her hood over her face and looked down, affecting a different gait. A few streets away, she paid a man going through recycling bins to tape the note to the bin in front of Becky's complex. The chances of Becky reading it, understanding it, and acting on it, were slim, but Nancy had to try. It shouldn't be an obvious statement, and she wondered if it was too clear, in case the Reverend saw it.

She paid a different recycler to buy a can of spray paint and create graffiti near Becky's apartment, with that same message. She hoped no one watching the recyclers would even notice they existed. They were the perfect perpetrators, invisible to everyone who just looked ahead and thought about other things.

Nancy waited in a coffeehouse for the recyclers to report on whether Becky saw the warnings on her way to work. People around her were talking about the so-called attack on the Rescuers by the president of the country they were pretending to provide aid to. She could hardly stand it, living in an upside-down world. She felt empathy for the Balkanized country's president, who was blamed though he had not ordered the attack on his people. The CIA terrorists pretended the president had done it, to garner support for taking him down. They wanted no obstacle to the pipeline, which competed with Russia's pipeline. Operatives in Washington inevitably executed covert ops to sabotage a bilateral agreement. But that was not all there was to it. She was starting to put the pieces together of what her lifetime in the Agency had been about. Clarity was coming. She could feel it in her pores.

When the oil companies went into a country, human trafficking, drug and arms running, organ trafficking, and slave labor were close at hand. And employees of the Defense and security contractor for the US government, DieCorp Eye, was at the center of it all, including creating false flag "lone wolf shootings" across the world. DieCorp hired mercenaries from the ranks of former CIA officers and Special Ops graduates. One of their services was providing police officers for the UN International task force that was theoretically needed after "civil wars." However, DieCorp was protecting the NATO sex trade that was their real motive, not restoring order to war-torn countries. Ironically, instead, DieCorp made sure the traffickers were never caught in the local raids; otherwise, where would the UN police, Rescuers, and NATO military go for kicks? UN peacekeepers patrolled the buffer zone in divided countries for all those things to occur. The corporation dealt with the contracts of American officers working for the international police force and were brutal sex traffickers. When raids were allowed, to keep up appearances, the sex slaves were simply escorted elsewhere, in league with the Mafia. People had all kinds of sexual tastes, from children to elderly, from perfectly transgendered to the grotesquely deformed.

The pretext of civil terrorists in whatever resource-rich country was up next for grabs allowed the U.S. government to take over after the war, contracting with DieCorp for peacekeeping for the new puppet government. Paramilitary groups didn't protect the people but the foreign corporations, and this often required murder.

Citizen journalists were speaking out about it, analyzing the situation in great detail. She didn't need to do that, too. But she couldn't stand the frustration of remaining quietly powerless, considering her role in it all. If only the mainstream news would ever once talk about it, everyone would believe it was true. Instead, the media was doing its best to call true reporting fake news. Not so many people listened to Tom Tellen as they used to. But there were other, more insidious ways of getting everyone to ignore the people who were outspoken about the way it had worked in the Sudan, Haiti, Columbia, Bosnia, Congo, Libya, Afghanistan, and all the other countries, and with the war on drugs and war on terror.

Those people needed a voice. The people needed at least one rebellious movie that went against Hollywood and Sundance propaganda movies about the Rescuers. They needed one novel. One play. One celebrity to speak out at an awards ceremony. Something. Something to bring the people and the truth together through powerful entertainment.

Nancy bought a greeting card at the counter, along with lattes and muffins. It was a picture of a cat in a vase. That would have to do.

She saw a man in uniform. At first she worried he was military, with the UN. They certainly would do anything to stop her from spying on Stan. Nancy narrowed her eyes. Good. She was satisfied the uniform belonged to a policeman, for some reason, in riot gear. There was some hope for individuals in the local police force. Many were not corrupt and would respond honestly. The FBI were less likely to be out of the criminal ring. Should she take the chance that the policeman wasn't working with Stan? Should she risk outing her identity by calling attention to herself, telling him she was stalking Stan and she saw him with policemen, and there was a rug involved? No, really, a *suspicious* rug! Not likely.

Both recyclers came in together, saying Becky had just left the apartment, but took no notice. They got loud, and Nancy shushed them, glancing at the policeman. She gave them the lattes and muffins. She asked one to be a lookout, and the other to slip the sealed card, addressed to B., under the door to her apartment complex, making it hard for anyone watching to notice. She made it cryptic, but took a little more of a chance this time: Break it off with him completely, now, and disappear for a while.

"Make it look like you're just going through the recycling and the breeze picks it up — something paper, you know. Throw it toward her apartment complex, and then chase it down, with the envelope in your hand, under the paper. If you slide it in fast, no one will notice." It would end up in the entryway, and anyone could pick it up.

When the recyclers returned with their reports, one bent down and seemed to think he was whispering in her ear, though he was loud. She pulled her head away, while bending her head conspiratorially, hoping he'd quiet down. "The minister from the church on the corner saw me do it. He came over afterwards. I watched him. I don't think he saw me watch him. I was peeking around the corner. He broke a little stick off a tree and broke off everything. It was like a poker or something. He slid it under the gate and pulled the letter out. Sorry about that. Do I have to give back the money?"

"No, you did fabulous. Thank you, John."

***

After dutifully drinking her tea in the coffee-shop, Nancy went to the bathroom. She changed clothes, removing her medical mask, putting on make-up and a long dark wig, transforming herself into Angela Ageless. Agent of the Nevermind. Dark, sultry, legal. And a very good time. A woman known among some circles that dealt with matters of national intelligence, globalism, favors, scintillating coups.

She swayed her narrow hips in an aggressive forward motion as she delivered her cup, saucer and spoon to the opposite side of the busking bins and set them on the counter. She held her head high as she silently snarled a smile, looking down at the captivated male customers staring.

"Yeah, baby," said one, while another one shushed him, their eyes wide open, following her slinky form.

Pretending to be Angela was almost fun. She'd take what enjoyment she could get at this point. The muscles along her torso were freed. They celebrated. Her pelvis was alive. *She* might not be, for long, however, if the congressman pieced together who she was. That was a given.

She was leaping into the fire. She hoped it didn't burn her slinky costume.

***

She staked out the Congressman's house, ready if he went home after work. Pacing lithely in front of his driveway, she practiced her seductive spy-lady voice, working over her schemes of what to say, depending on contingencies. She had her "secret handshake" in tow. If he currently was working with, or had worked with, her kind of Agent, he'd have no question. Diverse elements within the government normally worked closely with the Agency on crimes beneficial to dramatically spinning public perception of their agendas regarding coups to take the resources, including human resources, of other countries with oil, poppies, gold, and beautiful children. She made the mysterious expression in her eyes match the smokey make-up, to look as if she approved of organ harvesting anyone in those countries who protested what was going on. She put the sway in her hips of a woman used to condoning forced prostitution of adolescents and blackmailing officials with sex tapes. It wasn't too hard to pull off the look. She knew it only too well. It hurt. But she sometimes enjoyed being an actress, throwing herself into evil roles.

A paper wad hit her on the top of the head. She looked around and saw no one at all. She opened it up. The paper provided an address, and below it: *Rawlings is here at cocktail party. Perfect.* She ran like a mad woman around the Rawlings' yard, peering into neighbor's yards, looking up into the trees. God damn!

There was a pattern. Was this the same person who sent the message many months ago telling her to befriend Becky? Was it a network? Was the haughty ice cream woman delivering messages that were guiding her life's mysterious mission across states? "HeLLO!" There was no ice cream truck that night. But she could almost hear the sound in her inner ears. It got stuck there, on repeat.

Or had Congressman Rawlings gotten word from someone passing by that she was hanging out on his lawn, and had the message delivered. Maybe he thought she sounded fine. Maybe he wanted to entrap her? Find out who she was. And once he knew the kind of attention she'd brought to the Agency in the past, he would — she didn't even want to think about it.

She decided to go to the party, in any case. Life or death, she was ready to pay amends for who she had once been.

***

The door opened. A man wearing long ear rings, calling Nancy "darling," made her feel at home. She hadn't been any man's darling for a long time, and it made her nostalgic. She gave him a sincere hug and entered the mansion, which was decorated in sumptuous red and black. She recognized a couple famous musicians walking past, and couldn't help being in awe of them. She was offered champagne, and accepted graciously. She'd developed a taste for the good stuff in years past, and whirled the champagne in the glass, breathing in the scent. People were doing their best to politely ignore her overly sexual appearance, which made her giggle, and flaunt it even more. *You try walking in heels this high!*

Congressman Rawlings, leaning against the kitchen counter, pulled away from a woman that Nancy intuited was probably his wife when his eyes met "Angela's." He lifted his glass to her and she lowered her chin to look a lioness on the prowl and headed toward the kitchen, leading with her pelvic bones like a runway model. Then, as she passed by him, she reversed the curve of her spine so her spare buttocks stuck out instead, to provide the best view to him. She knew how it was done.

The congressman appeared beside her. "Congressman Rawlings. I don't believe we've met."

Nancy gave him the top-secret sign, to reveal herself as an Agent, which naturally must not be revealed. "Ah, so that's how it is," he chuckled softly, breathing moistly into her ear. He looked her up and down. She set down her empty glass on a table. "Here, let me get you a drink. Are you a peat moss fan?"

"Malted whiskey, yes indeed. Mmm, that's fantastic. What brand is it?" She took out a tiny notebook from her silver purse and took out her pen microphone, clicking it to turn on the recording as she wrote down the brand. She didn't know who she would play the recording for, if she were caught that evening. No official would be willing against the Nevermind's legal power. Impersonating an Agent, even as an ex-Agent, to steal national secrets from a spy organization was not something any police would be willing to protect her for.

She could get a recording to Brandon to put up on his channel. But even he would have no impunity for something like that. It was a private conversation with no permission to record. Still, she was ready to have a recording handy, assuming Rawlings opened up to her. Maybe there was someone in his life he didn't want to find out about what he did.

"The host keeps his stash in a little room way in the back. He doesn't mind me taking a nip. Want to accompany me on a little adventure? The whiskey — it's my favorite year." He apparently did not recognize her as the dead alien gypsy.

Her gestured for her to walk in front of him down the narrow hall to the small room in the far back of the sprawling mansion. She closed the door and stood grandly, while she gestured for him to sit down. She was going to take a chance on her new, shocking theory. Stan was working with the Nevermind.

"I have orders for you, Congressman. You're to debrief me on Stan, er, Wayne Norman."

He looked at her suspiciously. "Wayne?"

She realized that was apparently not his Agent name, though it's what his mailbox had said. Maybe the last name on the envelopes he sent out was his Agent one: Stan Franken. He had so many names she couldn't keep them straight. "Yes, of course, you know, Stan Franken. We need your opinion on whether he's bringing in as much money as he could be for us with his videos. If you let us know any details about how he could be doing it better, of course, you'll be given some *special* gifts."

That seemed to do it. "Oh, special. I like the sound of that."

"Tell me what you can about his work on the gold-digger project. Is the payoff worth the risk?"

"Oh, come on, do I have to go into that now?"

"We both know how much I could do for your career. A little rung up the ladder, for you, big boy?" She lowered her fake lashes invitingly as she looked down at the sizable lump in his pants and flicked it gently. She moved up against it, rubbing herself on it. "'Big boy' doesn't begin to do you justice."

He spoke hoarsely. "Um, yes. Ritual bonding has been proven to make the experiencers remain loyal. And showing scenes of that ritual bonding in the video the subscribers are getting recreates the loyalty in them too. So, yes, it's a relatively low risk. I do approve of Stan's methods of ending several in the series of videos in the church. And having the occult fanatics watching, and believing they're imbibing the life force energy at its peak as it's given off when the women are teased at the point of murder — well, that's brilliant. Traditional, of course. But the way it's done, with nasty, disgusting gold-diggers, who are also sexy as hell, well, who could possibly ask for anything better?"

"Update on ritual bonding practices?"

"Halloween's ritual will involve some of the most elite experiencers. Some of us will be there to give it authority, authenticity, and ye olde occult flair. Not a big event this year compared to usual. Last year's theme was more inclusive. But this time, it has to seem realistic when the gold-diggers walk in. They have to think no one is in the church other than Reverend Red and their 'suitors.' Each one gets her proposal from her boyfriend separately, captured on video, with luscious music playing in the background on the pipe organ and a harp."

He started waving his arms around and pooching out his lips and sticking out his butt on the chair as he said in the falsetto of a gold-digger: "Right at the moment they are most stupid and shrill and going bonkers — 'oh, come on, baby, you really are going to marry me and take care of me, and I really don't care how you look, because I'll just be with the cute guys on the side and not tell you, and ooooh boy! Thank you so much for renting the church for this special occasion, I love my wedding gown. So weird to be in this position, but what the hell? Oooo, nooooooo, what are you dooing? Don't you want to support me all my life? Don't you want to be my daddy? AAAAAAAhhhh!'"

She hid her grimace. "What will the experiencers be doing at the time of the proposals?"

"Drawing on the gold-diggers' life force energy. The girl's life force supposedly gets real potent when the girls think they're going to be set for life, any minute, the commitment, the ring, the big pay-off for a life well-played. A reward for manipulation. Lifelong parasitism begins!" He gestured high in the air. "And at that moment, the tables are turned. The experiencers are all staring at her from the shadows, you understand, silent, breathing, peering from behind the velvet curtains, the light red. Oh my god, so sexy. They draw on her energy until the peak moment of the proposal."

"And then?" She wished she had some usable evidence of this horrendous sacrifice, to pander to the true believers, who thought they were psychic vampires. Or maybe they really were. She'd read about how blood and bone were piezoelectric, giving off a powerful charge as the adrenaline pumped. People in cultures like the Aztecs and Mayans had drunk the blood of beating hearts for the life force. Psychic vampires stood around the edges of Goth clubs to draw on the energy of the angsty dancers. Psychic defense methods were studied in all magickal groups.

The congressman angled his high cheekbones charmingly, narrowed one eye briefly, the wrinkles that had once been dimples curving fetchingly. "Got any freaky shit for me?"

"Yes. . . I'll surprise you. You'd never be able to imagine it."

"Something nasty. Disgusting. Putrid." His monstrously large erection could not be ignored.

As an answer, she sneered a promise at him in a whiskey-drunk way, laughing as decadently and conspiratorially as she could manage. He was being a good Agent, and so was she, but not good enough to touch him there. Besides, there was nothing disgusting she could think of yet. "I have a feeling your career is going to take a nice bump up soon, Congressman." As she said that, she pressed his penis. "I think I know just the officer who would have that feeling too. Because you're going to be so helpful."

"Yes. Yes. Go on."

"Tell me a story," she said, bending over away from him and lifting her tight skirt. "Are you . . . Experienced?"

"The Experience Room is hell on heaven. One time I was there for two giants. Two humongous men, their dicks the size of my arm. I mean, I'm big. But when I saw them, I knew my place. I wanted to go back to see them again, but they weren't available any more. Damn Stan. Keeping them from me." He started pleasuring himself violently.

"They were some of the people given the HGH in the 80's? Or they were born with gigantism?"

"What does it matter? Jesus Christ! Spread'em more, Angela, my Angela. Oh Ageless one."

Her legs shook. "Were they trained in the Atlantean Ascension arts? Did they do a pyramid act? I'll bet they would, for you. Just like cheerleaders." She purred and moved her buttocks around in a circle enticingly.

He raised his gruff voice. "Oh, get off it. I'm not into the mystical shit with the giants. I just disseminate it to the public. The superior root race, my fucking root chakra. The only disseminating I want from the giants is their semen. You should have seen how far it spewed across the room. Mother of Mary, cashn'carry." At that point, he groaned with ejaculation, as she shimmied. The mirrors on her silver purse caught the light, reflecting around the room. She tried to get lost in the light show and drift away for a moment. She sighed audibly, smiling while doing so, so she sounded better than she felt.

So, if he wanted to be able to access the "talent" so much, could he have found the information to allow him to do so without going through the "proper Agency channels," and without having to pay a high price per hour? Was that why Stan had been so angry with him for video-bugging the room? The congressman might have discovered in the process a method for free access to giants and who knows what other niche kinks he had? No need to pay Stan, in that case. Or for the others he shared it with to pay Stan, not only for the videos but to do their depraved deeds with the victims.

So, not only was he not turning Stan in to get him to stop, he maybe wasn't even just the usual intelligence agent liaison.

He was very possibly a rogue liaison, acting only for his own selfish desires. Not for idealogical agreement with the Agency's duty to the United States and England to keep the balance of power "correct" in the world. He was not to be trusted by the Agency. By Angela Ageless. Was he even telling her the truth?

So far, she'd seen no looks of recognition in the party, no one who looked like they might have sent her the message telling her to go there. As they walked back through the hallway, with his hand on her buttocks, they passed an elderly woman whose eyes narrowed. She turned her head to watch them as they passed, and she gave Nancy a knowing look. Had she sent it? There was no reason to think so. She looked around at the other partyers once they emerged into the open.

Others were looking at her, too. Had they all been in on getting her there? Was *she* the main course at that ritual?

At that moment, she sneezed. There was incense. Her wig of long, smooth, done-up hair slid forward. Her dark brown super short boyish cut was screaming in her mind. She bowed as if it was part of a planned performance, readjusting it while her face was downturned. She rose, with it on straight. She did more of a performance, to make it look like the wig bit was intentional.

They all must have been able to tell she'd some kind of sexytime with the married Congressman. That was all they needed to give her those looks. They surely weren't all part of a grand all along, to get her to go to that party. She had the sense that she was maybe not about to be eaten.

Congressman Rawlings looked around and stepped onto the deck, holding her hand to pull her with him. The lovers kissing against the railing went inside. Rawlings gave the man left standing there the super-duper secret sign and said, "Angela, here, needs to be debriefed. And debriefed bad." He spanked her. "Want to tell her?"

"What are you going on about?"

"The specialities. What would you recommend. Atlantean Giant Ascension, Christian Identity, Enochian Angels, Fuckin' Freak Show, Tantrik Magick, Levitating with Theosophical Masters . . . "

"Yes . . . Yes, they're beautiful. Mayans meet Crowley, and you get to drink the life force in. Madam Blavatsky sitting on a hen."

Nancy wasn't sure where to take the conversation.

"Trust me," said Rawlings.

"I couldn't possibly argue with that," said Nancy.

"Neither could I," said a woman coming up behind her and putting her hand on Nancy's shoulder.

The congressman stood up straight; his form, slim inside the sharply cut gray suit, was dapper, with a politely pointed laugh. "Ah, haha, let me introduce you to my wife. Marjorie. Angela Ageless." Nancy had guessed correctly at first glance.

"Ageless, are you? Well, so, no wisdom coming from maturity for you, then, I take it?" Marjorie looked Nancy in her eyes, holding her gaze.

Nancy looked down, her lashes covering her shame. She'd already broken her vow to be pristine in her morality. She'd gotten kinky with a married man. Yes, for the sake of uncovering sexual corruption Stan was involved in. Nancy felt her stomach fall. She felt hollow inside. A dark emptiness that reminded her what life was really like for Angela Ageless. That whore.

Somewhere in her subconscious stirred something vaguely familiar from her past habits the Nevermind Agency had taught her as a way to do their bidding, whether she liked it or not. But this was different. A somewhat recent habit she didn't understand. Her subconscious was used to taking charge, out of a sense of duty. Conscience perhaps would be the normal word for it, but twisted into something unique to her. It felt really weird. Often seemed to happen after new information came into her mind that she must need to process, like with a dream or something. It felt like dreaming underwater. And it was doing it again. Without telling her why. WTF.

Chapter Twelve

Sunshine Man

On her way to the liquor store, Becky passed by a blond man around her age, in a soil-stained tee-shirt and shorts, crouched over the small, square, bricked-in flower garden jutting into the sidewalk, holding his trowel in mid-sir, smiling at her broadly. She recognized the floral scent wafting through the air as the one that had been making her happy lately, and she smiled back doubly. She loved that flowers grew even in the fall in her city. *And* that there were such alluring men. Not that she had any right to feel that way. She tried overlapping his imagine with Stan's, and focusing on how devastatingly witty her beau could be.

As she neared the gardening man, she noticed his own smell. She loved the way the sunshine could transform skin into a kind of animal perfume. Not the same as the stink of spray-on tan on Stan's skin. Why did she have to compare them? Were all the handsome men she saw going to stand in comparison to her future-husband? Was she going to give some kind of numerical ranking system to them all in relation to him?

No, she had to be sensible. Think of a future in which she could thrive.

She greeted the fresh-faced gardener, unable to avoid giving an enticing look, though once she passed him, flirtatiousness turned to worry. How was she going to keep his glowing image from haunting her with a sense of longing?

A police car drove up to the curb. She thought about mentioning Nancy to the police, but what would she say? She hadn't heard from her friend recently. And yes, her phone was broken, so of course, she couldn't expect to hear from her. She swallowed, trying to make the lump in her throat go away. Nancy was tough. She could take care of herself. She'd disappeared sometimes. It was what she did.

The officers in the car glared at the enticing man she had just met. What the hell? Why was every person who was supposed to be nice and protective so into *glaring* lately? When she looked back she saw one of the policemen get out and stand by the open door, looking at the gardening blonde. She wondered if he was under suspicion for something, but she wasn't about to go back and ask him.

She bought a bottle of Pinot Noir from the store, to take a nip before Stan arrived, to calm her nerves. She asked for some pepper spray that they kept behind the counter. It felt good in her hands. But somehow, it didn't feel like enough. Against what, she wasn't sure.

The store was next to Random Cafe, and she saw the flyer on it, the same one she'd noticed in front of her apartment. Something about a psychic reading. Well, maybe that was the route to take for answers about Nancy and Stan. But what she wanted to ask, and of course, would not, was about the blond stranger she'd not even spoken to, but whose existence shook her to her bones. She felt like her skeleton was made of light.

Chapter Thirteen
So Psychic

Thursday

OK, gotta fill you in, I know. Been a while. Sorry. I just don't feel like narrating my life silently all the time, OK? (Not that I remember most of my life. Hell, that's one of the best perks of being fucking drunk as shit, right? Not like I'm going to spend all that money to drink and then still have to remember some obviously goddamn awful life.) Hell, no. I mean, would *you* put up with that? Earlier today, I walked back to Becky's street, and tacked up the flyer I made on Monday to the electrical pole in front of her door. No way she won't go for it. She likes to go to that cafe down the block anyway for lattes. The flyer's got the name of the place on it: *Random Cafe. Psychic Readings from 6:00 - 10:00.*

She won't be out here any earlier or later anyway. I know her schedule. Pathetically early to bed. If I know her, she'll show up this evening. And she'll pay me. Sweet.

A man with kooky hair and a flannel shirt is staring at me, holding his cell phone up. That's weird. I haven't seen him around before. It makes me nervous not to know the details about people walking around the neighborhood. Never know what people are up to if I don't know what kinds of things they buy. If you don't study their mail. Probably came from my childhood. I barely remember my past. But then, that's how I want it. Hell, I barely remember my present. The look he's giving me is just spooky.

Anyway, after that, I hung out for a while around the bridge in among the trees, practicing my voice, my walk, and re-reading the pages she tore out of notebooks where she scrawled her dreams. Sometimes she gets tipsy and writes and that's hard to decipher, too. I used to have a magnifying glass but I lost it. Life is shit without it.

But, OK, now, I'm back at the cafe. I had no trouble finding an empty seat at a table with another seat facing me. Typical this time of day. But I'll get them more business. Glad to help them out. They should give me free coffee. And one of them raspberry pastries.

I've set up the sign that says *Trixie of Fate, Tells All* on the table, and took the empty peanut butter jar out of my pocket. Becky washed that jar so well, that angel. I put it down for any tips in addition to the "half-off" price. They're going to get a great deal today, even if they tip.

A man walks in and sees me. Uh oh. Shit. He's not one of the people I've studied from recycling. What am I going to do? He doesn't live on my route, so he's kind of cheating by expecting a half-price reading from me. That's OK. I can do it, for Becky. I can do anything for that gal. Looks like he's coming toward me. Could be my first reading! I'll find out if I can even pull it off with strangers. If not, my plan might fall apart. Oh, God. If I blow this, I'll never be able to make her mine forever. Please, no.

Sweet. I know I look pretty good by the way he stares. He sits down, and smiles. "Hiya," he says. He thinks I'm hot. I'm so hot.

"What is your first question?" I nudge my customer under the table a little as if by mistake, and leave my foot barely touching his trousers. I know he can feel it. He doesn't move his leg away. This is going great.

"Which team is going to win Saturday?"

"Oh, let me explain this to you. This isn't a parlor game. This is serious. If messages come through for you, your spirit guides have come a long way to tell you something. I want you to let yourself relax into your feelings. Get in touch with your feelings, your body, and get out of your head."

I push my calf up against his.

"Whatever you tell me will be fine, babe." He puts his hand on mine.

"I can see you are a very sensual man."

"Yes!"

"And you definitely don't live near here."

"Correct."

I'm getting sweaty. I have nothing. "Your spirit guide says you must be generous to all around you. You must not be stingy or ill-tempered any more."

"I can't imagine why anyone would spend his whole life, or death, or whatever the heck it is, giving me inner messages, especially when I never listen."

To my credit, I don't hit him. In fact, I agree with him. Anyone with half a wit knows spirit guides don't exist. I do say: "Well, maybe no spirit guide cares about you either. Maybe that's why you haven't seen one. They are usually pretty good judges of character."

Damn. This isn't going to help at all with word of mouth recommendations. I need more people from this neighborhood to come in, people I've read about in their letters they've put in recycling. In their sad failed job applications, their poetry revisions. Half the time, it doesn't even rhyme.

"What's that perfume you're wearing? It's a little strong for me."

102

"Oh, I'm sorry. I'll go wash it off. Don't want to disturb the reading of a *half-price* paying customer." I go to the women's bathroom and wash up. So much better than the men's. There aren't any paper towels, so I use toilet paper. When I get back to my seat, he's gone. Good riddance. Still, what if he tells people I wasn't good? This is so scary!

I dip my dress sleeve in my water and get a spot of perfume I missed.

When the waitress brings my latte, I empty into it the contents of one of their non-dairy creamers. Free extra calories. I might be about to have no source of income if I spend all my time failing at this line of work instead of recycling.

I tip her with a coupon for a free fifteen-minute reading. I know enough about her to make it a good one. Once she threw away the draft of a love-note on a napkin, in the wastebasket in the restroom at Random. I'd been watching her write it, crossing things out, one slow night.

Poor girl. She got her heart broken. I could make a difference. I could help if she gives me a chance.

I know what it's like.

***

Becky's standing outside the coffeeshop window. I *knew* it was her night to go to the liquor store. Haha, she never fails, as many times as she makes those lists about stopping her habits to cut down on expenses.

Oh, God, I hope she comes in on her way back home. She seems undecided. What's not to like? Come on, girl, do it to it!

No! She's turning around. She's walking toward her apartment. What could she be *thinking*?

I get up and run outside. "Hello, Miss!" I follow her. She must not realize I'm talking to her. I don't want to alarm her, so I just keep following silently after that. I realize I have some toilet paper stuck to my cheek. Damn cheap trash bin razors, always dull.

She doesn't go into her door, just turns and stands staring at the flyer in front of her apartment. I try again. "Oh, hello. I see you're checking out my flyer. I'm just on a brief break, but I'll be back at Random any minute."

"I just have to make a quick purchase for my cat."

"Wait, your cat, she is brrrrown, correct?" I rolled the r's. I love doing that, heh.

"Yes, she *is*!" That's it, Becky. Now we're getting somewhere.

"Goin' downta Meow-town, honey?" I sang the advertising ditty for Meow-town, which I knew she gave the kitty on special occasions, and she smiled. "That's the brand you buy for your cat. I can *see* it is."

"You're *right*, actually. Pretty good."

I could see little flecks of green in her eyes with the sun hitting them from that angle. Nice. "Your cat wants more catnip. She sits there all day while you're at work. She's getting way too fat. She needs some excitement in her life."

"Not bad, Trixie."

Heh, heh. Trixie. "See you inside at the table in the back corner in, say, fifteen minutes?"

"Sure, works for me. I've been thinking about finding a good psychic. I have questions I need to ask, and a lot more of them that just came up today. You're looking at a gal who needs answers, all right."

"Like what?"

"Like about my best friend. I'm worried about her!"

"I *know*." I give her a jokingly wise look I know she can't refuse. I've got to steer her away from recommending me to Nancy, though, because she's not on my route. I read her notes about her. But I have no idea what to tell her about that mystery lady.

I head off to the corner store, buy an airport bottle of vodka, put it in my bag, and head back to Random fast, before they clear away my table set-up.

Don't want to get in there and some turdboy is sitting in my seat and I have to sit on him. Heh, heh, like he wasn't there. Me, doing a reading, and the clients thinking I'm farting but it's a boy trying to talk under my butt. Haha, almost makes me want to do it. Ah, I hear your spirit guide now. Do you hear him too? Haha!

I pour a little vodka in my coffee, even though it curdles the creamer, and settle into my open-hearted smile, adjusting the sign for my services so it catches the light. The lighting in Random is some of the best I've seen, nice and dim, warm colors. I feel good. Really good. I think all this studying people's recycling is going to pay off! This is going to be solid work for me once the word gets out how I know all the neighbor's secrets. I'll be able to support Becky. I don't want to stop her from getting married and not have something fair to offer her. I can't leave that sweet thing on her own to deal with life. Life is tough on people like her!

I feel even better when she walks in the door. I can't wait to tell her about Stan. I can't wait to see the expression on her face when she finds out soon she won't have to bother herself about that jerk anymore. She'll be free and ready to love me. To say yes to a true actor, someone who can be all the different personalities she wants to enjoy. All new ones of course. I'd let her suggest her fantasies to me. I could be a cowboy one night and an Indian the next.

Obviously, since she saw me as Pete Zelite, and Connors and Trixie, they will have to die. I wouldn't kill them off for anyone but her. Poor sweethearts. I hate to sacrifice them, but it's for a good cause. Love. Pure love and protection. And at least whoever is listening to my thoughts out there got the chance to watch the show, eh? Yeah, I'm talking to you.

When she sits down with her latte, I cross my legs in a lady-like way. I adjust the wig, because I feel like some of my regular hairs might be sticking out a bit on my left side. I turn my right side toward her. I know it's awkward turning my eyes sideways to see her, but I've gotta do it.

This woman's boyfriend is not who he claims to be, I promise you. That's why you need to hear this. He's an invasive species. He's like a machine. He feels no emotions big enough to appreciate the depth of her personality. Word is on the street he doesn't even let recyclers get to know him. He's got to have a shredder in there and put it in the compost. Or maybe he burns his papers. What kind of cold motherfucker does that? Doesn't he even have a sense of *community*? If she marries him, her life will be miserable. It doesn't take a psychic to see that.

"What's your question? Wait, I'll answer it before you ask it. First, I should mention, your tinnitus has been a problem lately, hasn't it? You're even seeing medical treatment now."

"Oh. Yes, it has. I am. You're spooky good!"

"Listen, sweetheart. You don't need to keep using that caviar facial cream. You're beautiful. You're still young, but even when you get old, if someone loves you, he'll love your wrinkles."

"No! How do you know?"

"Just be sure to tell all your friends how accurate I am, OK? Miss Trixie could sure use the bixness."

"I will. Especially if you predict something, and it turns out to be true."

"This is what I see for you. You should *not* get married to your boyfriend, Stan." I adjust the balloons in my bra. Damn that squeaking.

Yes, yes, love to see that shocked look, sweetheart.

"Think about how Stan makes you feel. Do you feel honored and joyful? Does he simplify your life or make you argue with him in your head? I think we both know the answer to that one."

"You're *amazing*. I know. And you even know his name! But I need to settle down with someone so I can devote myself to building my career. And I do enjoy his company. I have a thing for Italians, too," she whispered, blushing. She probably could tell I have some Italian blood myself.

"If you have a child with this man, like you've been thinking about doing . . . ?"

"Wait, what would the child be like?"

"A monster."

"Oh, I see."

She's crying. I don't blame her one bit. A monster is not good. But crying now, yeah, that's good. I offer her my napkin. I've hardly used it.

"And Stan works in the city somewhere, but I'm not sure what I'm seeing." I look at her with all my sideways intensity. She doesn't say anything. "You're getting together with him very soon. What I have to tell you may shock you. I can see that he won't live long at all after that, if you accept his proposal. Even if you *think* about accepting it. I give you my guarantee. It's a cosmic thing. Sort of like karma. Just don't go blabbing that to the police when he dies that I let you know you're the guilty party, you hear?"

I know she'll think about it. She won't believe me, though that would save them both. "That's all I've been doing. Planning to say yes. How would we have a child if he dies from me thinking about marrying him?"

She got me there. I spilled some coffee to change the subject, and she helped me mop it up with the napkin I'd lent her. I don't know if she could smell the vodka or not. "The world is mysterious, my dear. Nothing is as linear as we think."

She looks confused, but that's OK. That's when they're most vulnerable to suggestion. I've heard people always try to make psychic readings make sense, if there is a compliment. "I can see that you are a special person. Maybe an angel. Do you ever suspect you are one?"

"Well, yes," she says, shyly, looking down. "Someone did kinesiology on me, you know, asking yes and no questions of your subconscious by pushing down on my outstretched arm, like this."

She demonstrated, and hit the waitress with the wonky hair right across the crotch by mistake. "Oh, excuse me!" We both giggled. "And the kinesiology test said I'm one. When your arm stays strong it's a yes. But I don't know. I feel silly talking about it." Her cheeks rosy up. "I do feel my wings, almost can see them sometimes. I use them in my dreams. I know because I write them down in my diary."

Anyone else said that and I'd laugh. "Is he spending the night tonight?"

"No, he's leaving. He always does. Gosh, you know, I hope he doesn't ever read my diary. I don't know what he'd think about the angel thing."

"It's easy for me. You're so beautiful. I can picture it now, no problem. I'd never leave you. He always leaves at ten o'clock. Doesn't he?"

"Yes! He says he can't sleep in the same bed with anyone. And I've never been to his house."

I can identify with that. I never took women to my bridge.

"I never thought about it until today, but I don't even know if maybe he's living with someone or something."

Hell, I don't know. There's not been much point in taking buses all the way to his place in the hills for nada. I don't want to take a chance on getting anything wrong. I need her to tell everyone how good a job I did by predicting what's going to happen to him. I know the rules of business. Generate buzz.

I want her to be happy. She just doesn't know what's good for her. She'll come to me for advice every day, once she sees how real this shit can get. And, so will everyone else in the neighborhood.

I tell her, "You're killing him right now by considering his proposal. But I know you can't help it. It's been in your mind so long. Don't worry. I don't blame you. I'll never hold it against you. I'll be the only one who knows your secret."

She's looking creeped out. I didn't know she could raise one eyebrow that much higher than the other one! Hell, that's almost a talent. I wonder if this was a good idea, making her feel guilty to keep from spilling the beans. Hmm. She's got that, "Get me out of here" expression, and a, "please don't die, Stan," vibe mixed together. Poor girl, it won't be long. She's scared she's going to be living her life alone. No worries, there, little Missy.

I tell her. "I can even help you get back in God's graces."

She looks at me horrified. Funny, I swear it made her hair kinda frizz out. Her mouth's open so wide I can see she had fillings in the back.

She gives me thirty dollars, plus a nice tip in the upturned lid on the table. She leaves the coffee shop. I drink the rest of her latte.

Now, I just have to hire a cab to wait down the street from her apartment at ten, and follow him home. Easy peasy. I've always wanted to take a cab and now I can. I'm so happy I can hardly stand my luck. I don't actually think it's luck. I think it's karma. Haha, yeah, right, karma.

Chapter Fourteen

Warning

Walking home from Random, with her eyes down at the gritty, broken sidewalk raised by tree roots, Becky struggled not to think about marrying Stan. Every thought could be a dagger in his chest. In spite of her attraction to the blond man, she knew life was just that way. Married people would always pass by attractive strangers. What mattered was a secure life together with her husband.

No, no, she had to not worry about it. She had to marry him without thinking about it, because a single thought could bring on his doom.

She noticed a man in flannel watching her from across the street, holding up a cell phone. *So many crazy people around here. And they all are into me lately. What.*

She shook her head, and tried to laugh off what the nutty psychic woman had told her. Anyone dressed in that ridiculous outfit shouldn't make decisions. Becky believed in a few psychics, if they didn't use Tarot cards, Angel cards, numerology, astrology, but just tuned in. Trixie had known a lot of things about her life. But still, Becky couldn't give up everything she and Stan had built together just because of a woman with a huge plastic sapphire ring, and breasts that crinkled like paper wads.

Becky just wished she'd found out if Nancy was OK. Of course, Nancy was a busy woman, teaching piano lessons. She probably hadn't had time to spy yet.

Becky noticed a policeman with a large nose and a big mole on his cheek driving in sync with her across the street, gazing her direction. She sped up and so did he. He looked away. She was shivering. The sun was going down. Her breath wasn't coming as easily. She massaged the muscles of her chest, pressing between her ribs.

She almost forgot to look up to see if the handsome dirty-blond man was still tending the flowers. No special roses there. Just . . . She didn't know much about flowers at all. Just . . . the delicious smell of his sweat got her attention and as she started to look up, she caught him watching her walk, with an appreciative smile.

She put more curve in her stride, exaggerating the left to right sway. She then tried to straighten into a prim bee line instead, hold in those pelvic muscles, take straightforward small steps like a woman about to be married should. Her walk got out of step, as she wasn't watching where she was going. She tripped awkwardly over a break in the concrete.

He laughed, and said, "Feeling a little unsteady, there?" His smile was so lovable. So fresh. The wider his mouth opened, the more the autumn felt like summer.

"No, I'm OK. Those are beautiful flowers." She wondered if liking flowers meant he was gay. She found herself hoping he wasn't. But why? Why should it matter? She had to get used to the idea that that would never matter about any man she ever met again in her life. It felt like being in a straightjacket. She shook out her arms and wriggled her fingers.

"They're local to the area. I never plant invasive species."

"Is this your job?"

"Nope, just volunteer. I like getting my hands in dirt. I spend a lot of time at the community gardens. That's where I get most of my produce, and it's free. Ever work in one?"

"No. Well, I've passed by a couple on walks. They were locked, and there wasn't a number to call. One was completely taken over by weeds but the other one looked like people worked in it."

"I haven't done much with the one that's gone all weedy. I don't like that word, though. Weed. Like some plants are less worthy. But I have the number to get into the other one."

"Like a code? I've never seen anyone working in it when I've walked past it. I've checked it out. It looks magical."

"I work in there, usually around 7:00 in the morning. I made friends with the cactus that's by the gate. Someone had broken off all its big ol' spines. That's got to feel scary."

"Well, that explains it. I'm getting ready for work at 7:00." *And distracted by trying to figure out who broke into my house. Must have been Stan. But what was he doing? Gaslighting me with blobs of gunk on the ironing board? What!*

"I waited by the gate for hours one day. I just set up in front of it and did Tai Chi. Finally someone came by, to work there. I got the number from him that ya call to get accepted into the group and get a day. I can give you the number."

"That would be great, thank you."

"I made friends with the cactus that's by the gate. Someone had broken off all its big ol' spines. That's got to feel pretty vulnerable. The only benefit to the cactus I can think of is getting petted. So I do that before I walk in through the gate."

"I love that."

"The closest active community you can just walk into is five blocks from here. You might have passed it without noticing. There's a wooden fence around it."

"Oh. I see. That sounds handy." Did hip people say, "handy"? She almost wished she'd lied that she knew where it was. She must not seem very much like an earth goddess to him if she didn't even garden. She felt herself blushing. She almost forgot to pay attention to what he was saying.

"Anyone can go in and work, and you can eat the produce."

"I wouldn't want to take advantage of everyone's work up to this point," she said, softly.

"There's plenty to go around. They even donate some of the food. It's great if there's extra when you're taking the plants out that have grown too close together. Only way I'd be able to live here, even though I have plenty of clients as a hypnotherapist. Living here is crazy expensive now, eh?"

That sounded like a very useful bit of information. She could work in the gardens too and if she ate the produce, she might have plenty of money to buy Maiden better cat food. She could be more independent. And not feel guilty about buying Pinot. "I like that."

"There are other community gardens around too, so I work in three of them. I can show you where they are if you want to keep in touch."

She stood there, contemplating a new life plan. Less grocery store. More free. More art. She wanted to paint him, with his shirt off, in a field of flowers. Maybe with a horse drinking from a creek. In abstract.

He showed her the different plants, naming them, and telling her how they also could be cultivated for food, and what the medicinal properties were. "I love them. I talk to them, do you?"

She nodded. Well, she *sort* of did talk to them. "I make tea out of the weeds, so they don't go to waste."

He shook his head. "I seriously don't like the word 'weed.' Like they're inferior because of their relation to humans. I almost got into a fight with someone who insulted my plants friends by calling them weeds." He laughed. "That's when I knew I needed to get out more."

She giggled and agreed with him. He sure looked muscular. A slender waist and sturdy legs, wide shoulders. Weeds must be good. She was all about weeds.

"I can help you get started working in the gardens if you're interested. Show you where the tools are, what kinds of mulch to use where, what the different beds are, how far away the plants should be from each other, all that stuff."

"I'd love that."

He reached into his pocket and handed her his card, which was smudged with black loam. "Name's Buck." He tousled his blond hair, with a quirky expression.

"Becky." She held out her hand, though what felt more natural was a hug. He opened his arms and they lingered, warmly, breathing slowly together. When their hug ended, they disengaged gracefully, and her hands felt like magnets, pulling away from him against the pull.

She hoped Stan wouldn't mind. Sometimes she wondered about his explosive temper. She did kind of like that Stan had lots of testosterone. He stood up for himself. He was "manly." But she didn't want to make him jealous just by working in a garden, or two, or three. What if he didn't understand their friendship, and took it out on Buck? He could seriously fuck him up.

She walked on, and when she glanced across the street, the police car was gone. She took a bigger breath. But when she looked back to watch Buck walk away, she noticed the policeman driving slowly across the street from him, in sync.

When she neared her apartment, there was a man with tousled hair, in flannel, leaning in front of it, looking at his phone, laughing. He moved aside as she put her key in the lock, saying, "Oh, sorry. Funny cat video!" He angled it so she could see it, almost as if to prove to her that's what he was doing, and she glanced only quickly. "Wow, you're so beautiful," he said, aiming the camera at her. Was the camera light on? "Anyway, have a nice day."

When she looked back at Buck, she saw a man in a suit talking to him. He was pointing at her and making a popular rude gesture as if being masturbated, scowling at her with apparent disgust, which Buck then shared. She was shocked and walked back toward them. The man got in his car and drove slowly, talking on his phone, watching her. Buck turned away from her with a sneer and walked away quickly.

She wanted to follow him and ask what was going on, but hesitated. That felt like stalking. Did he hate her? She stopped, standing there. She tried to tell herself the incident she had observed had nothing to do with her. The man must have been pointing to the man in flannel behind her, not at her.

She felt heated. She could hardly stay still. Besides, she decided, Buck was no one to her, just a stranger she met briefly. She could find the gardens and tend the plants without him. She wasn't stupid: she didn't need him to show her anything.

She couldn't stand it. She walked after him. She had to find out what was going on. Ahead two blocks from her, he turned the corner. She jogged to catch up. When she got to the crossing, she saw him climbing steep stairs to a house. She started to call out to him but didn't even hear her own voice over the sound of gunshots.

A black car with black tinted windows squealed away and when she looked back at Buck she saw he was holding his shoulder. He lay at the top of the steps, barely stable, as he was starting to angle precariously toward the edge.

There was blood. He'd been shot!

The steps were very, very, very high.

They were narrow.

There was no railing.

"How bad are you hurt?" she called out as she approached.

"My arm," she thought he said. He was mumbling. "Uh, moving any muscles makes it hurt. Call 911? There was a policeman here a minute ago."

"I broke my phone!"

"Use my cell. Ow! Can you get it out of my pocket?"

She yelled for help from the neighbors. "Call 911! He's hurt!" But she heard no commotion. She ran to the apartment next door and knocked but there was no answer.

"Help!" he reminded her. "Just come on up, Becky."

She gathered all her resolve, girding her loins, feeling as if she were already up high, everything looking too bright and too dark at the same time. It seemed to her as if the ground were far away.

She took a deep breath, started to move, found she couldn't, and took another breath.

She took the first two steps, getting down to crawl by the third.

She held onto the outside on one side, her other hand pulling her up. Her head seemed to be floating in the ethers, growing so large it had no edges. Her heartbeat was hardly even recognizable as human. She used one hand as a blinder, holding it next to her temple.

Each step took her into so much more panic, she realized she was biting her lip so much she'd punctured it. She could taste it: was bleeding too. She licked her lip before the blood could run down. Her muscles were working so hard they were weakening and the cortisol had drained her adrenals almost entirely. She crouched lower to the concrete with each step, so she was eventually slithering.

She scooted to the top of the stairs fast to get it over with, the world screaming silently around her. She achieved her most important mission when she pushed him away from the edge he was about to fall off, pulling him onto the center of the step as he groaned.

Kill me now. She stood off balance, dragging his body. She almost wished the shooter was still around to put her out of her misery.

"It's in my left pocket in my jeans."

She reached in and got the phone, fumbling with the unfamiliar design, her hands shaking violently, and she began to get waves of vertigo as she tried to focus on the tiny numbers with the ground so far below her. She was that high voluntarily, for the first time since she was a child. As soon as she dialed the numbers she hunkered down, holding onto him to steady herself.

"I'd like to repeat a drive-by shooting," she said, "I mean report!" and Buck shouted the address into the phone. "A man is injured."

"Can you describe the injury?"

"Shot in the arm."

"Is there an active shooter there now?"

"No."

"We have no officers nearby so estimated time is half an hour."

116

"There was an officer across the street less than a minute ago. Can't he turn around and . . . "

"Half an hour."

"You'll send an ambulance?"

"As soon as we have time to contact one."

"What!"

She held the phone near his ear. "A gunshot to the arm is not first priority. There are multiple emergencies is this city we respond to."

"You've got to be kidding me," he said. "Do you just not want to respond or something? What the hell?"

And that was the end of the call.

"It's like they don't even care. Don't they want to catch the shooter?"

She saw the blood shooting out in little spurts, and she should be holding him tightly around his shoulder to keep the blood from leaking out too fast to keep him alive. He had hold of his shoulder with one hand and she held tightly with her other hand to match it so together they stopped the flow.

She could barely speak, and when she looked down she froze. Hot and cold waves washed through her and she started tearing up.

"Hey, I'm the one who's hurt here," he joked. "You see me crying?" At first his tone was playful but she watched his eyes refocus and the sneer return she'd seen when he talked to the man earlier. She didn't feel right asking him about a subtle expression in a conversation she spied him in when he was in such a serious situation.

"Look, I can't even believe I made it up here!" she said, with force in her voice. "I haven't been able to go up or down steps as long as I remember."

"Well, then, you've made a breakthrough. I'll bet if you wanted to, you could push forward with progress right now."

She acted as if she were about to push him, trying to make it look like a joke. She had the strong impulse to push him away, feeling as if he was going to make her climb a ten-story building,

117

her equivalent of exploding in hell. "How do you know? It's not so easy!"

"Listen I don't even know why I'm talking to you after what I was told." He lifted his head, but dropped it back down.

"By the guy in the suit?" Becky put her hand under his head.

"Yes, him."

"What did he say?" She wasn't sure she wanted to know.

"Why should I tell you?" Buck's pale lips were squished against her hand. She had to lean down to decipher his mumbles.

"Do you know him?" Her fingers were starting to tingle.

"No. He told me he was one of your victims. When he saw us together he wanted to warn me. Obviously, you know him." He grunted and angled away from her, looked away, shaking.

"No. I don't." She adjusted her seating to avoid getting any more blood on her dress than she had to.

His mouth was going sideways. "He said you entrap men. You entice them, set them up, and then ruin their reputations unless they do you criminal favors. Why? You're sure good at pretending. My ex was a piece of work, too. I should have known better!"

"What the hell? You're delirious. Why would anyone say that about me? I've never done anything like that in my life! That sounds more like the rumors about what the Agents of the Nevermind do."

"They do?" He paused, muscles in his greying face going slack. "Are you sure?" He drooled and tried to mop it off his face with his good shoulder.

She gripped onto the steps with her buttocks as she had never done before.

"That's. Oh, God, this hurts. Squeeze harder. I don't want to pass out."

She pulled him back from the edge again and put his head down on her shoulder. She looked around and saw people looking out of the window across from them. Not too helpful, were they? "Anyone have something to use for a tourniquet? Hello?" She looked in the cars driving by, the kids playing at the mini park half a block away. One of them was pretending to have a gun and the other one running away. He made *bang* noises and the boy fell, clasping his shoulder. They looked back at her and Buck.

Holding on to him as she balanced on the narrow step, she pulled her dress up. She raised up off the chilly concrete. She lifted her arms up and holding on to nothing, feeling as if she were an angel flying in the heavens, she lifted her chiffon dress up like wings to the sky. She was nude. She wished she hadn't removed her slip earlier. That would have helped a lot. She momentarily even wished she had saggy breasts so she needed a bra. She wished she'd worn panties.

She said goodbye to being ever able to wear the dress again and tore it in two. She wrapped half the chiffon around his shoulder as he groaned, and tied it tightly. "Is that good?"

"Tighter. Thanks. You sure don't seem like such a bad gal." He looked steadily in her eyes, his expression becoming more animated and warmer.

She was cold in the slight breeze, making her nipples protrude. She put the half a dress left on her lap, and she realized the neighbors would always recognize her as "the naked woman" when they saw her in the future. It was a nightmare. His eyes were going in and out of focus and his voice was getting quieter as she slumped more. But she was impressed by how he rallied to mumble, "Do you know why you have the phobia?"

"No. I think it's from something that happened when I was a girl. But I don't remember what it was. My mother died in childbirth when I was little. It was just me and my Papa. But later, he left and I was adopted. I don't know what it was all about. We never talked about it."

"The new parents didn't fill you in? That's odd."

"I know. It was this unspoken thing. My memory is really fuzzy. And it seemed like if I thought about what happened, my life would turn into a nightmare. Like I'd fall into hell. And it seems like maybe the phobia might have something to do with that, because I don't remember much before I got it. But what I remember doesn't make any sense at all."

"I can hypnotize you."

She shook her head violently.

"This is the perfect place to do the most effective method. Up high. You'd never go high up again otherwise, would you?"

"Never. I do have to figure out how to get down. Other than being knocked out I have no idea how I'll manage it."

"Unless you move in with me, of course," he joked weakly.

She was glad he was willing to trust her a little, though surely he couldn't take her at her word, considering he was just told she was a liar. She would prove to him she was a true friend.

"Cute," she said. "I should mention I guess that I've got a boyfriend."

"I'm happy to be your friend. What do you think about the hypnosis? It hardly takes any time to induct," he whispered. His lips were curvy and compelling.

That made her like him even better. He didn't just want to get into her britches. "I thought people usually had to take a long time to go under."

"Sure, they do. But I was trained by the very best. Someone who never asked before taking people down. My father." Becky felt as if the air went electric around them. "He knew immediate hypnotic inductions. You know why?" he asked, widening his eyes. When she shook her head he said, "He was an Agent of the Nevermind."

She wanted to reach out to him with her other hand and pet his face. Poor guy. A father in the Agency. Someone who could never talk to his family about top secret missions. Someone you could never trust. She didn't know much about how they operated, but she knew they were in constant danger, and they weren't known for their truthfulness. Having a father like that would make life so complicated, never knowing what was lies. Anyone who could do that job had to have a ruthless side.

Their eyes locked. He was shivering, and she snuggled closer to him to keep him warm.

"You're not an Agent, though."

"I one hundred percent promise, cross my heart," he said.

"You can't do that." She lay beneath his gaze to make it easier for him to speak to her.

He admitted he couldn't cross anything, at the moment, and looked down, making the cross across his chest with his eyes.

She was glad he resisted the obvious jokes about her naked breasts. She refused to look away from him, knowing neighbors had to be looking at her. Probably taking pictures too. Her flat chest would be the talk of the neighborhood. Somehow, she could handle it better than she thought she would, considering how virulently she detested being watched.

He inducted her, touching her body here and there as he said the names of different parts of body that he touched, adding to the confusion, making his grunts of pain part of the experience, asking her to spin around while counting backwards and naming the parts of the body he was touching, overwhelming her senses until the easiest thing for her psyche to do was to surrender to his guidance.

In his hypnotic voice, he talked about the possibility of her getting over the heights phobia, and she started relaxing into an ocean of hope. Her mind went in a different mode altogether, liquid, as if underneath deep water, but able to breathe, forgetting breathing even existed, forgetting she existed. Words swam through her. Something about heights. Something about the memory of how she first got it, and was she up high when something happened? But it was like swimming through the words, as if everything was an ocean, and time no longer existed.

She remembered being young and living in an area with a few trees in the yard. She loved to climb trees. She remembered living two places. One on either side of her favorite tree. Its branches were strong and evenly placed, beginning low to the ground. There was the good side and the bad side of the archetypal tree of life. The side to look at and the side to hide from and run away from and crawl away from in the dark.

She remembered walking through the blue house with her stepfather and stepmother on the way to the Christmas tree, where there were presents. The fire was hot in the fireplace. She'd played in that back yard ever since she could walk. There was a present under the tree from her father. The card said he loved her, and was sorry. That he'd stopped drinking. That he'd gone to therapy. That he'd changed. He wanted her to forgive him if she could. When she opened the card, her stepparents took it away and said not to bother about it. Just to focus on the present. To just forget.

She remembered the beautiful high river flowing powerfully behind the houses. The tall walls and high windows of the house she lived in with her father. She remembered inside the house. The barrel stove. The guns, the deer heads on the wall, the whiskey bottles, the strange smell of her father, the eerie grunting sounds coming from upstairs in a room where she was never allowed to go, and its window was too high to see into. But she wanted to know the truth of what happened up there.

She had been determined not to be lied to, to seek reality at whatever danger, and had snuck into her neighbors' yard. The neighbors she ended up being raised with later. But when she tried to remember climbing it, she couldn't stand it. Being at the top of the stairs was awful enough. Climbing the tree in her imagination was even worse.

"I can't make you do it," Buck said. "It's up to you if you want to persevere. How much do you want to get your independence?"

"I don't," she said. "My life can work even if I never get over this. Stan will take care of me. I don't have to look into my past. I don't have to know." But she hesitated. She felt like a baby saying that in front of a man who was pushing past the pain and weakness to help her. She wanted to be brave too. She would take the risk to go into the chaos in her brain even though it felt like walking into a den of monsters.

"OK. OK. I'm climbing the tree." As she climbed farther, to nearly the top of the branches, until she was able to see over the wall, into the high window, she held on tightly.

She saw the neighbor walking over toward the tree. She turned back to watch and saw her father inside the room, naked. She didn't know what he was doing at the time, but under hypnosis, she recognized it as sex.

He was standing bent over something quivering in a jelly-like way, a bizarre shape of convoluted flesh with what could be called a head with hair sticking up. One eye slid sideways into what might have been a shoulder moving down into an arm that merged with its belly. The rest of the body was like some kind of caterpillar shape, with two holes at the end.

She needed to keep watching to understand what was going on, and wouldn't look at the neighbor. She screamed when she saw him stand up and pull his penis out of the drastically deformed girl. She remembered having heard vague whispered conversations about her mother dying in childbirth. She put it together. That *thing* was her sister.

There was a camera on a tripod. Someone was filming it. And there was someone else there.

Her neighbor shouted at her to look away and come down slowly, carefully. But she wouldn't. She needed to see every detail though he kept telling her to look away.

Her father heard her scream and ran to the window. He grabbed a rifle, aimed it toward her, and shot. The neighbor called for her to come down and her father shot toward him as well, crying, "You two should keep out of things that don't concern you!"

Becky dodged a bullet but in the process lost her balance and fell from the tree. The fall was like slow motion, as she saw each gnarled branch of the tree and the grassy ground coming up to her in some inverted dream of gravity.

The swarthy neighbor ran beneath her and lunged forward to catch her in his thick, short arms, saying, "I told you you should have looked away. You're going to get us both killed!"

Her ankles were twisted badly in the fall and she was crying. He carried her and ran toward his house. Her father shot at them.

The bullets missed.

When the neighbor, the man she would come to call Papa, made it inside, locking the door. He set her on the couch, as she shrieked and grabbed her ankles. He ran, shushing her while he spoke on the phone to the police.

His wife cuddled her, and he said, "Hopefully, that's just a warning shot. I doubt he shot to kill. But that's not OK. Do you understand that? That's not how normal parents treat children. I'll take care of you the rest of your life, if you promise not to do anything like that again. No going off on your own. Listen to me when I tell you to do something, OK, sweetheart?"

She mumbled, with her eyes closed, starting to come out of the trance: "I think I got it. Strange, I don't even feel dizzy any more. Can you bring me out?"

She was already on her way to normal consciousness, but he finished the process. When she came to on the steps with Buck, as revolting as that memory of her father and sister was, liberation was flowing through her, or she was flowing through it.

And when she looked down to the sidewalk below the steps, she felt fine. She squealed. "You did it! I can't believe it!"

"You did it," he said. "That took a lot of courage. You're the one who stuck with it."

She was afraid she'd break her new state by her loudness, and whispered, "I feel like I'm healed. Is this going to go away?"

"I'd say it's here to stay. And your brain hears what I say about that, yes?"

"I was supposed to go into Frame Up this afternoon. But I'm not going back. I can get a job somewhere else now. Bye, bye, el cheapo job!" She used his cell phone to call the owner and quit. Buck tried to cheer her on, but he was fading fast.

When the policeman arrived, driving slowly, then sauntering up to them, Becky recognized him as the one who had been watching them earlier. The one who had cruised along with Buck.

Why couldn't he have been there in a less than a minute? Something was up. She restrained herself from yelling at him. She tightened the chiffon around her.

When the policeman assessed it as probably a random drive-by shooting not really targeting Buck, she started to really wonder why that man with that ugly, ugly mole was so horribly nonchalant and dismissive.

She had the sense *no one* was going to try to track down what it was all about.

"You shouldn't be here, you. Put on some clothes and go away. This is a crime scene. Go home."

He angled his head down, shadowing his eyes. She suspected he was more upset than he should be that she was there. Like he didn't want her going back. But she hoped it was her imagination. *No,* she thought. *Things like that aren't my imagination. I know it will take time. But I'm going to learn to pay attention from now on. Take clues seriously. Not look away.*

Becky stepped forward with a hesitant bounce. Her smile quivered. She both regretted and reveled in impulsively quitting her job, with plans to interview at other galleries that paid twice as much. It was time to celebrate her freedom and upward mobility. She veered off the sidewalk and climbed up and down people's stairs.

A siren in the distance. She wanted to offer to cook for him, after he'd told her where she could get her own food by working in gardens nearby. She could bring him the vegetables he'd helped plant, and help him carry them back once he could start working there some. It felt only fair. But she sure didn't want the policeman to know she was going to do that, just in case.

An ambulance drove up, people getting out quickly who were politely looking away from her.

Naked except for her shoes and blood, when she walked down the stairs easily, holding her head high, looking below her at such an unfamiliar perspective, what she mostly felt was free.

Chapter Fifteen

Psychos

Nancy had always liked Halloween season. All those masks. All those costumes. All that death. The change of season into the revenge of decay. Into the beauty of nothing. Making way, making way.

Her own costume, which she'd put together to try to sneak into the house across from Becky's without being noticed among other costumed revelers, had a certain humor d'ark. She was, in fact, Noah's Ark. Wooden zebras and plastic lions glued onto her in pairs. She'd joked often enough with Becky when they saw people going into the empty house owned by the church, but never coming out. Jokes had stopped seeming very funny.

Anything to do with that church, even tangentially, seemed important to investigate, in spite of the chances of Reverend Red wondering what she was doing there, if he recognized her. This was her first Halloween as a "burn victim" who wore a mask every day she went into the public.

Considering the street address of the church was 666 Daath Street, and it included an obelisk she knew there was some chance the elites who were into numerology might have some interest in it. She'd noticed a few flyers up on poles in the area for missing black cats in the last few days, so she was concerned neighbor's black cats were being stolen to use at the church for a "Satanic" ceremony. She'd watched partyers dribble into the empty house, in costume. But their costumes were so dark for normal churchgoers, she had to wonder why people were going into a house where no one lived, and why they were never coming out.

She'd seen people dressed as Satan, a gory dead black cat, and a grinning cannibal within an hour that night. The humor of the joke was wearing off.

So, a quick trip to the store had given her all the supplies she needed. She'd painted her mask to look like the front of a ship, though she wasn't sure anyone would be able to figure it out. This was her chance to find out, but the people she walked up behind ignored her. They were wearing masks that covered not only their faces but their entire heads: some kind of worm people. Nancy felt icky standing next to them. They unlocked the door, and she locked it behind herself when she followed them in.

The house itself was unremarkable. There were no furnishings other than an umbrella stand, a torn-up pool table, and a mirror. No decorations other than a mannequin dressed as Jesus and a few doilies stuck on the wall in random order. She followed the partyers to a trap door, and down the steps.

She walked behind them, through the simple candlelit tunnel that went underground. Were her jokes about it being the entrance to hell correct after all? She noted a stash of what seemed to be weapons in the corner. She didn't let her eyes linger on them long enough to determine their exact details, because just as she was staring at them, the man in front of her turned towards her briefly. What were they for? She decided it must be one of the caches operatives regularly placed around a city in preparation for whatever might come up.

The tunnel angled upward and opened into the church.

The church was decked out in black and red for the evening. When she was in the entryway, she glimpsed a man making check marks on a piece of paper. He asked, "Are you here for the psychopath training class?"

"Yes." Of course. Wow, she hadn't expected that.

"I don't see you on the list."

"Obviously. I'm teaching it." She gave him the Agency's "secret handshake," just in case.

"Oh, gotcha. Go on in. Is this your first time? The Psych - Training is on the left, second door."

She looked at him with as much disdain as she could, to imply, "Of course it's on the left." She greeted some people casually, coolly, to look like she was at home there and she had no need for anyone's approval.

The couple she'd followed took off their costumes and put them in the cubbies along the wall, next to masks that looked like bubbling lava, Zombie Jesus, and a mushroom. The costumes seemed to be more about getting in without getting recognized than any requirement for a party. This seemed like something else.

There were a few classrooms, nurseries, Sunday School rooms, all closed. Only one classroom was in use that evening. The broadsides along the walls threw her off. The titles were odd. HOW TO SEEM EMPATHETIC. HOW TO FLATTER. People were removing their Halloween costumes they used to get in, and hanging them up in lockers. Many then wandered around reading the broadsides, such as one titled, "HOW TO SHOW YOUR ATTRACTION." She scanned through that one. Seemed to be teaching them how not to seem slimy when they wanted sex from someone. And how to successfully score through pretending to be nice. Oh, grand.

This wasn't a class teaching people about psychopathy. She was familiar with the traits of that developmental disorder. This was a class for psychopaths. And not teaching them now to get better. Well, she'd certainly studied her handlers' psychopathic skills over the years. Observed closely. She'd give it her best shot.

Wearing her medical mask, there was no way she could teach them to read subtle facial expressions, if that's what this was about. They were probably already well-past lessons about mimicking body language. Uh oh. She had to hope beyond hope no one recognized her.

Nancy hesitantly removed her burn mask. She slipped behind a table and assumed a position of authority the best she could in her ridiculous costume full of dangling plastic animals. She wondered what would happen when the legitimate teacher showed up to take the table. What would she do? So, she quickly left her post and searched the church hallways. She found a room with desks and chairs shoved up against a wall. She carried first the desk, then the chair, and squeezed them in next to hers. She couldn't help feeling jubilant. She also figured she had a pretty good chance of being killed.

She adjusted her elephant earrings, while wondering if Noah would have ever seen any elephants. If not, then how did they survive the flood, eh?

A man in a red mesh thong came around bringing water to the tables for the teachers. "And some wine? Red or white?" He stuck his buttocks out toward her and pouted.

"Oh, red, please. *Blood* red."

"Ooooo. That'll get you points." He stuck his arm out, with flair and pointed at her.

Men and women were entering the church. Nancy noticed a certain stiffness in the posture of the people taking their seats to study with the teachers. The teachers' smiles seemed genuine. She stared at them, trying to practice discrimination, as she knew the smiles were most likely fake.

The windows were covered for the occasion, and candelabras along the walls created eerie warm shadows. People were sitting down in the chairs facing the tables and the teachers.

Some teachers had placed laptops facing the students' chairs with slideshows set up. Some of the students connected the cords from the laptops to their ears and listened, nodding their heads, pressing keys.

The oldest of the students, angry because of getting an answer wrong, yelled at the teacher, picked up the laptop, and started to heave it before she was stopped by the brawny guard in a kilt, with plaid underwear on his head, with a dark veil. Apparently, the Halloween spirit was encouraged in Christian churches? She had never realized that. Even for adults? She thought about all the children Trick or Treating, and realized many of them must be

Christians. Maybe they just ignored the pagan sacrifice aspect of the holiday.

Yet, somehow, this seemed wrong. Like the costumes were mocking the church. Nancy had seen the congregation going in and out for services, and had heard them singing. They wore suits and fancy dresses, seemed conservative and sincere. This seemed like a completely different crowd from them. She wondered who had taught Reverend Red to be such a high functioning psychopath to convince his regular congregation he was an upstanding man of God.

The costumes, she realized, all concealed the identities of the people who kept theirs on. There were no fairy princesses or even Robin Hoods. Instead it was a world of ogres, snake gods, and alien femme fatales. The faces of the people who had removed their costumes were scarier than the ghoul costumes. Especially the ones she probably would have eagerly befriended if she'd met them out of the context of psychopathy. The teacher at the table next to hers glanced at Nancy, narrowing her eyes as if she wasn't sure if she'd seen her before, or if she should know her name. Nancy nodded at her in a way that could mean they'd been introduced at a planning party, while imbibing a bit too much, and quickly turned away.

Students coming in looked at her sideways. *What, they don't trust me to teach them how to pretend to be trustworthy?*

She turned her eyes to the far left, then to the far right, to peek at who was teaching. Only one other instructor had no students. The man had hair that looked like the old doormat in front of her porch, sharp bristles going every which way.

A student sat down in front of her. A woman with an angular haircut and lips that went straight across. No cupid's bow. Just little lines around her mouth, emphasized by the crimson lipstick that had crept into them.

Nancy's hands turned clammy immediately.

'What's today's lesson, Teach?" The woman looked pleased with herself for saying a cool phrase. She looked to be around twenty-one years old. Nancy wondered if her role was to congratulate her on being hip. A few decades late, but who was counting?

Um. "How to blend in with people who have a conscience. How to act empathetic. And guess what they're thinking."

"We did that."

"Oh, OK. Of course. So you don't need a refresher course? No? Then: How to gaslight."

"Perfect."

"And how to make a person feel guilty with one look. How to tell if they feel guilty."

"Bring it."

"And how to second guess what a 'friend' will do next from behavioral cues."

"Love it." Being able to say that phrase in a monotone indicated that student had a long way to go. Nancy would work with that on her soon. Then, she would coach her on how to position herself correctly in relationship to a conversational partner. It was important to face away from bright lights, and into the shadows if possible. That would enlarge her pupils enough to seem warm and caring. She summed up all the student's obvious presentational flaws, to quickly prepare a lesson plan.

"You need to develop a bond with a person first if you want to take advantage of them. Do you know how to do that?"

"It's not my strong point."

"OK, sit down, let's go over some ways. Pretend I'm your mark. Use your best observational skills. Do you notice anything about me that I might feel self-conscious about? Something I want people to like but am afraid they won't? It's OK, you can be honest."

The woman said, "I think you're wearing a wig. Are you bald from chemo? Alopecia? Just have hair like ass?"

"Perfect. Yes, someone I want to get into bed with, for example, might think, 'Ew, I hope her wig doesn't fall off while we're fucking. That wouldn't be on fleek at all. I don't want to be her bae. No way.' So that might make me insecure. So your job is to convince me you think wigs are fun. And you even like bald women. But you have to do it in a way that doesn't make any assumptions. You have to feel me out in the conversation. Think nuance. Lead me down the path to get the answers out of me. Once you know what's under this wig, make me think you treasure that quality. Not just pity it, or tolerate it, but admire it."

The woman looked at her as if she were stupid, but would humor her. "OK. Sure. So, I notice you're wearing a beautiful wig. Aren't wig's fantastic? I have some at home. Sometimes, I like to have wig parties with my friends."

"That's pretty good. That makes wigs seem like fun accessories. But what if the reason I have it is not for fun? What if I'm fighting cancer. Find a way to coax that information out."

"You're tough, Teach. Um . . . Your hair is gorgeous! I love the color. Of course, I guess I'm unusual, but I like a variety of styles. I even like the totally bald look, you know? It's hot."

"Well, that's what I have. I never thought of it as hot. It's not by choice. I had chemo. Have a couple more sessions to go, actually. It did me in. OK, now act concerned. If someone tells you an intimate secret about a health problem, angle your head sideways a little bit. Use this tone of voice. See how that sounds? Say you're sorry."

"But it's not my fault."

"I know. It's just a language thing."

She sighed. "I'm so sorry about that. I'm glad the chemo is working? But the bald look, mmm, yeah. I love to do photography, and I seek out beautiful bald women as models. Have you ever modeled? You could, you know."

"Excellent! Great job. Doing that, your mark will open up to you, feel you have special understanding of them and everything else. You must be smart, to see how appealing I am, right? I want to go home and think, 'this brilliant woman said I was hot. I don't want to think, 'this stupid-headed bitch said I was hot.'

Completely different effect on my self-esteem, right? I'll believe what you say if I can."

"That's all it takes?"

"It's a start. Use all the tactics at once. Like — laughing together at a common enemy. Who might I feel frustrated by, but I'm a nice person so I keep my feelings to myself? I'm polite to them, but underneath, I'd love to be able to joke about them to someone?"

"I don't know!"

"Look at me. Work your mind. What do you notice about me?"

"You're muscular. Flat-chested. You're tall. You look smart. You've got an unusually pale face. You don't care how you look, or you'd be wearing make-up. And you've got dents in your face. Bonding like this is always strange. But I've made progress, from coming to these."

"That's a good one. So, if I'm smart, I might resent people I think are too dumb to make good choices, so they influence politics in a negative way. And it wouldn't be an emotional knee-jerk resentment because of some meme I saw. I'd be angry at them for not researching specific vital facts. For letting themselves be taken in."

"Yes, I get it. So, I just need to figure out your politics. Today it's not easy because you're in costume. Normally, I'd go by grooming to see if you were Conservative, or Christian, or whatever. You know how there are certain make-up and hair styles that identify people?"

"You're right. Now, assume I'm wearing heavy foundation. I obviously use a curling iron, and a little one on my lashes. Let's go totally into imagination, here. So if that were true, you might guess I'm Conservative, and I'm fed up with Liberals, yet I live here, surrounded by them. I have to just go along with them, to get along. But underneath . . ."

The woman looked off to the side as if glimpsing a Liberal, and poked Nancy with her elbow, grinning. "Tee hee, check out that stupid bubble butt, with her T-shirt slogan. She's the kind of person who thinks the U.S. should police the world to make it better. She'd obviously make a great policewoman, wouldn't she?" She played, imitated the woman's walk while mimicking carrying a gun, and trying to look tough, but looking more like an offended, pouting child. She then got back into character, pretended to watch the Liberal walk past into the distance, then stepped closer to Nancy. Meta.

The student whispered, and again imitated the imaginary Liberal, crying while dropping her gun: 'Halt! How can you support that candidate? How can you be such a patriarchal raschcist? What have you got against women and people of color? Bam, bam!"

Nancy laughed at the imitation and continued in the voice of the Liberal. "'You should support *my* candidate. He only wants to murder third-world leaders of color and install brutal puppets that kill women and children, to stop all the murders. *He'd* never make fun of anyone. Ever. Got it! And he's not an aggressive lover, either. You white-supremathcist.' So, you'd keep the joke going. Every time you saw me, you'd make it more insulting, in worse and worse taste. You should probably get me drunk at least once. We'd start making jokes in our emails. Then, you'd have the record of them. Imagine that hanging over my head. You'd have some power, eh?"

"Why, exactly?"

Nancy remembered psychopaths didn't care what others thought about them. Being disliked, or being caught talking behind someone's back, didn't make them feel shame. "Because I'd be horribly embarrassed for my Liberal friends to think I made fun of them. Embarrassment causes pain. It's just different from a broken arm or something. But not *that* much different. But in the meantime, joking about a common enemy creates a bond, especially if it's a secret joke, and you let each other off the hook about whether you're actually being a nice person. I'd want to trust you, because I'd feel like we were conspiratorially on the same side. We share a world-view and we're being secretly naughty together."

The woman kept up the acting game. "So, you say you have four older brothers and sisters? Well, you're lucky you weren't conceived in a Democrat family. You would have been aborted to save space on Gaia for all the cute weetle animals."

"Haha, yes, perfect. Now, what if I'm a Liberal instead and I want to bond over problems with Conservatives? What would you do, then?"

The woman paused and then jumped into character. "I met a smart Republican today. No, really! Amazing, eh? He convinced me same-sex marriage was actually an abomination."

"Really? Why, what was his logic?"

"Logic? What do you mean? Like I said, he's a Republican."

Nancy pretended to laugh at the weak joke. "OK, needs some work."

The woman furrowed her brow. "How about this? So, look, there goes Mr. Sensitive. Just the kind of guy you'd want to share all your dark womanly secrets with at night, right? You know he cares." She waggled her head and opened her eyes comically wide, pushing her face into Nancy's when she said, "He really *cares*."

Nancy genuinely laughed and she congratulated her work. They toasted her progress in being manipulative with some Halloween punch. Then, she came up with the next instructions. "Here's another technique. Do you think you could convince me you're spiritually advanced?"

"I don't even know what 'spiritual' means. I've never felt whatever it is."

"No problem. Let's go for it. Close your eyes and tilt your head back. Open your arms out wide, and smile really big, like you're relaxed and you know everything will always be fine for me. I'm just getting caught up in faithlessness. But really, God, or the aliens, or angels, or whatever."

The woman did so, and said, "You were a special birth. I can see it. Images are coming to me from the great Egyptian Osiris-flamingo god, Bennu. He says you were meant to be born to bring light to this world. You have an important mission. I see Archangel Michael standing behind you, with his hands on your shoulders. He's so beautiful. It's like you two are Twin Flames. Working together to enlighten the world and help people see their true nature."

"Fantastic ploy! Just acting like you're superior isn't enough. You have to have an inside scoop on me being special too. Wow, you're good. Now, reach out and touch me while you talk. No, not like that. Just a slight touch. Do you know how to crinkle around your eyes to make a warm look?"

"Yes, the last Teach taught me that. Where is he, by the way?"

"I don't know. Looks like he doesn't care, eh? It's just you and me, baby." She sidled up to her and put her arm around her waist.

"I see what you did there."

"Good. Do the crinkle-eye thing and barely touch me while you talk, casually, fast. Being touched makes a person feel trust. Unless your hands are cold. Don't do it, in that case."

The woman poked Nancy as she blathered on. With practice, her touch got more feathery and compelling. Nancy almost started to like her until she caught herself. *What am I doing?*

"OK, you're taking care of my old father. Act self-sacrificing. Go."

The woman pasted on a smarmy smile, petted Nancy on the shoulder, and said, "You go to bed, honey. I'll wait up with him. You know I can't sleep until he's resting peacefully anyway. I'll be sleeping right here in case he needs me. I learned how to sleep sitting up with my last patient. It's not as hard as it looks. You just have to let love take you away."

Nancy, in character, said, "I give you an A."

The psychopath said, "'That's not enough for me. From you, the best teacher in the world, I'm going to work and work until I earn an A plus!' How was that?"

"Very convincing."

They sipped some more blood colored punch, Nancy beginning to wonder about the strangely believable blood flavoring, until Nancy was ready to give away the primo tip to her psychopath. "Now, here's the best secret weapon of them all. Stay in the con artist caregiver persona. Repeat after me: 'I love you so much. We're almost the same person.'"

"Weird." She dutifully repeated the phrases, then smiled. "But I see where you're coming from with that. Actually, yeah, that's excellent. I'll definitely remember that one.'

And, thus went the first of quite a few lessons that evening.

Nancy improvised quizzes and scored the students' work. The men and women did well enough under her tutelage over the hours of teaching that she felt sorry for whomever they were going to trick more successfully next. *I'm an anti-heroine. I create destruction wherever I go.*

***

The payoff came when Nancy "went to the restroom" and took a scenic route, past the empty daycare and Sunday school rooms.

As she walked down the hall, she brought attention to how she crinkled her eyes. Or, on a meta-level, she tried to look like a seasoned psychopath trying to look genuine. So many layers. She stood, leaning against the doorframe, pretending to yawn, looking around unconcernedly. She opened the heavy, decorated door and walked into the largest room in the church, with red velvet curtains around the periphery. This was certainly not another classroom. The red velvet curtains around the very tall room added to the luxurious gorgeousness. She caressed the cloth she was standing next to, and rubbed it against her face.

She couldn't help it. Her pale cheek was usually languishing inside the mask, and no one ever touched her face — not since her young lover, whom she'd had to move away from suddenly, after she and the older journalist, Brandon, had teamed up to bring information to light. The mask had become her new identity. A formally stunning woman. Hidden behind a fake burn accident.

Never touched. Never revealing anything about her life to anyone. A piano teacher that filled her students with pity.

She pressed her face against the velvet in an intense, slow, sensual, subtle dance, which pulled her behind the curtains. She followed around the edges of the room, and realized one wall was almost entirely a beautiful stained glass ceiling. *They must pull the curtains back for the regular service.* Bronze candle holders, with milky unlit candles, curved up out of the wall like young breasts, in elegant intervals.

It seemed a poor use of space. To make the room purposefully smaller by creating a passageway around the edges that went nowhere. Making it dark, so no one could see even movement on the other side of the windows. It felt like a womb. The seemingly continuous curtains were a surprising number of narrow ones hung next to each other. She walked into the inner room through one of those slits.

She passed near some men talking as they walked around the building moving things around, banging and adjusting. "At their peak, when they're terrorized, there's a surge of electricity in the heart. The adrenalin in their blood charges it up." The bangs made it hard for Nancy to hear everything they were saying, only bits. "The piezoelectric effect in the. . ." Bang. "When a person is traumatized badly enough, she dissociates. Part of her astrally projects. That part is easy to suck in with the specially provided straw-claws, as we call them."

One of the men asked her, "Are you one of the designers?"

One of the men answered. "She's one of the teachers from the workshop. Can I help you?"

She nodded whimsically up at the images with ancient images of Mother Mary being handed dead babies and legs to hang on the strings behind her. She remembered seeing those before in old books and wondering what they were about. "Getting ready for Halloween?" she asked. She controlled her tone to mean either she just had a slightly dark sense of humor, or she was into some sort of non-Christian ritual herself. But also, that she barely cared, was just bored and stretching her legs. Maybe she was a jaded insider, of high standing and power. Maybe she had no clue and was not a threat.

She read his subtle expression as a "yes." A carefully played yes that could mean something different depending on if she were naive or if she were high-ranking in whatever those people were doing in that room. She had to act both ignorant of, and approving of, the impending ritual sacrifice of the gold-diggers. She had no idea how she could stop the ritual. Obviously, the elite and everyone in the legal system was involved, and the media protected them. All she wanted was to discover something solid she could use against them to stop it, something that could prove it was going to happen, something that wouldn't rely on her revealing her sources or how she obtained the information. So far, nothing. Maybe this was just impossible for one underground woman without recourses to prevent. Sexual favors and bribery were the main currency making international societies go around. There was no stopping it. But she'd damn well find some way to keep Becky from going to it, some way that didn't just end up getting both of them killed.

Nancy saw a couple men walking toward her with purpose, their necks stiff, no bounce in their steps. Something about them seemed subtly menacing. She walked quickly toward the tunnel she'd come in through, but found it was meant only for one-way passage. The men were gaining on her. She jumped behind the red curtains along the edge, and ran behind them along the walls to the other side, feeling the wall, trying to find the proper exit. She peeked through one of the slits in the fabric and saw the men angling across to cut her off. She ran back the way she came, and around the other side of the building, hearing the men's footsteps continue as they were, then angle toward the curtains on the other side, where she had been earlier. One of the men must have gone in through the slit in the fabric and looked up and down, as she heard him cursing about how she had disappeared.

Her foot slid over a rough spot on the floor, and when she looked down, she saw an indention in the surface. She grabbed it, and lifted it up, finding a trap door that led her into a tunnel that exited through one of the other empty houses owned by the church, releasing her on the other side of the block than the house she originally had entered through.

Chapter Sixteen

Preparations Underway

Friday

Been a long day of giving readings, making good money, I have to say. Well, long day for me. My days are short. I need to sleep so much. They say sleeping all the time is a sign of depression. Go fuck yourself. I do feel like ass, though, gotta admit, even with coffee. No wonder no one else is asking for a reading. They can see misery on my face. Well, I'll just turn my sign over and call it a day. I've got to think hard about Becky for a while. That's what gives me a reason to live. I just want her to be OK.

After I finish off all the Random coffee, I feel kind of heavy in my legs when I stand up. Got to make myself stand straight. Why does everyone else in the cafe get to just hang out and read, and talk to friends, and I have to be here *working*? I can even hear someone watching a movie on his laptop. It's not fair.

OK, I'm heading straight for the bridge, just a few streets away, to get my characters' clothes. I'm going to pin this thing on Connors. *He* has all the luck. Haha, Connors.

I love being back home now at the bridge. So, first thing, I put on Connors' outfit, carefully folding my wig and putting it in the box. I remember to wipe them all off my body.

I take a shit next to the box. I leave the toilet paper and Handywipes scattered around. I definitely don't want anyone taking this stuff, now do I? This is a treasure trove of people to be, places to go. Best way to keep it safe. Guard turds.

I drink the rest of the final bottle of wine in my stash. Pinot Noir, in Becky's honor. One with the label peeled off so it breaks just right. I love breaking bottles.

I feel a lot better now. I'll make a big step up in my career if I can pull this off. People will be paying me even bigger bucks. I'd rather be sleeping. Got to get pumped. Got to do this thang.

I wonder how you retrieve the data from this silent recording in my brain – or whatever it is — so you can hear it, Mr. Interrogator. Sometimes I feel like cameras are watching me and listening to every word I say or think. Sometimes I don't. Maybe only aliens or angels can hear this recording of my thoughts.

I wonder if Becky really is an angel. She could be. No, because then, she could hear this, and my plan wouldn't be working so well, now would it? I won't hold it against her if she's not one: we all make mistakes. No one's perfect.

I'm trying so hard, girl. I just hope you appreciate it. Can I turn you into an angel? Being together with you. That would be Heaven. Almost like souls exist. Today, I almost feel like they could. Like there could be a God.

All right. I'm putting all self-doubt behind me now. I'm doing it — my workout routine. Lifting rocks. If I don't do it every day, I look like the wimpiest guy in the world. But if I do it, I can do anything. I can do anything. Anything. Anything! And I will.

Chapter Seventeen

Hitch

Nancy stood near the last bus stop on the way to her porch, turning her face up to the sunshine for warmth. She almost didn't see a car pulling over to the side, or the arm through the window, gesturing her over. She picked up her bag and ran, peering through the dirty glass to try to make the usual quick determination about whether the driver looked trustworthy. So far, they all had. She'd never had anything go wrong yet.

This one, well, he offered her rice cookies. Couldn't be all bad. At least it wasn't rice cakes.

The man didn't introduce himself when she did. He just nodded like he already knew everything. His white fur collar created a fuzzy contrast with his tan skin and intense blue eyes. He leaned back as if he were satisfied after a fancy meal, ready for a cigar. He smiled at her like she was the after-dinner sherry. She decided to be flattered. She decided life probably *should* be more about gratification. Comfort. Pleasure. She settled in to talking with him about the recent rise in the stock market. He commiserated with her about not having bought into it when the time was right.

When she started to tell him where he could drop her off when the time came, a place with no obvious landmarks, he said, "No, no, don't bother. I know. Of course I know." His blue eyes fixated on her. The car seemed to drive itself.

"I'm sorry. Do I know you?"

"We know you. We know who you are."

Agents! She grabbed the door handle. He locked it from his side. Cool. Casual. Steely. Gloating as if he and the car were one, and he could take credit for its trapping mechanism.

She lunged against him, knocking him out of the way and pinning him down as she reached for the unlocking lever on his side. She jammed the gas pedal, and spun the steering wheel, as she bit his hand. He yelled and shook his hand in the air while trying to remedy the situation coming at him from all sides. She grabbed the back of his head, his hair in her hands, and pulled him back so he couldn't see the road. She stomped on his foot, leapt out of the car, and ran.

A gunshot zinged past her.

A car drove by, then backed up, and stopped near her attacker's car. The driver got out, asking if he was OK. Nancy kept going, as she heard the man trying to convince the do-gooder he was fine. She ran toward a nearby tiny church she thought might be open. She heard footsteps approaching in the distance, and more shots. She zigzagged without looking back.

She pulled hard on the church door, but it was closed. She ran into the small cemetery in back and quickly formulated a plan when she saw a partially-dug grave, probably abandoned for the digger to get lunch. She lunged into it, and pulled clods of dirt over herself. She moved like a rabid dog, digging the sides of the hole, glad the dirt was soft. She reached up and grabbed fallen leaves and lay down, scrambling to get underneath the rough earthen covering. An earthworm crawled over her face.

She breathed as softly as she could, not moving a muscle. Her arm was showing. How could she make it look like dirt? How, how, how, before the driver caught up with her? She heard him running past, hesitating only for a second. The worm crawled into her nostril. She needed to sneeze.

She pinched herself so hard the pain overcame the sneeze mechanism. She squeezed the muscles along the sides of her nose to make the entryway less welcoming.

145

The driver ran on. She risked pulling out the worm. She ran toward the road, and found a better hiding place, from which she could watch him get in his car and drive on.

How could he have known where she was going on that obscure road? No one even knew she lived there other than the owner of the house, whom she paid cash to each month. She was definitely innocent. Nancy got no mail, paid no bills. How could anyone have figured it out unless she was being stalked? She couldn't go home. She couldn't tell her landlady. She couldn't keep teaching piano. She had to go deeper under cover. Even less traceable than before.

She was dirty enough she surely scared off all the drivers. She didn't get a ride back into the city any time soon. When she did, she got him to drop her off not too far from Becky's place, but not so close she'd be noticed, at a bridge she'd once thought would be the best place to take shelter in if she ever needed to. She put her things down on ground that looked like dogs had lived there recently, and she wondered if fleas lived in mashed bits of shit and hair.

***

Nancy laid her belongings out on the steeply sloping concrete under the bridge not far from Becky's house, then chasing them as they rolled downhill. She had a lot of things in her bag, like her change of clothes, and she felt a little silly to be carrying around the rock the ice cream person had thrown at her window. It had become a talisman. It felt smooth and strangely comforting in her hand. She'd have to gather more practical things to make life more comfortable, such as a sleeping bag. She wasn't used to envying homeless men for their bags. She stared longingly at the set-up on the other side of the bridge on the mirroring sloping concrete. She couldn't tell if anyone was in the plump bag or not.

She wondered what the man, or woman, living there, was like. It looked to be a man's stash, but it was so neatly arranged, she wasn't sure. Especially because sticking out of a box was what looked like long blond hair. She hoped it wasn't someone's head that had been chopped off. Someone who had been living there.

Or, maybe, someone the person living there had murdered. Oh, God, no. She pulled her jacket over her head and went into hibernation mode.

She peeked out around her jacket. She had to know.

She climbed down, crossed the ditch stream under the bridge, and climbed up the other side, quietly, so as not to wake the person up. She peered into the box at the hair. She poked it a few times before grabbing it. She knew it surely wasn't a head in there. No one had been decapitated. Or scalped. Surely.

The Bible next to the box comforted her.

She reached down and poked the hair again, bending closer so she could see it more clearly. She lifted it up, squeamish. A wig. Nothing but a wig. One of many wigs, both male and female. There were dresses and a folded business suit, turquoise sandals and lipstick, a mustache, and a razor. She heard something rustling nearby and leapt back, pretending to be casually walking by on the slope. She needed water. Her neck was starting to get stiff. When she jerked it suddenly to hide her curiosity, it hurt. She needed hydration. Toilet paper. A flashlight.

The rustling seemed like it must have been birds hopping in the dried leaves. Maybe a squirrel. But she wasn't sure. She kept looking, while trying to act like she wasn't.

Best case scenario, she had stumbled across props for a theater group for the homeless. Maybe lots of people took shifts using that sleeping bag. Or maybe the person just didn't care what kind of clothes he wore, as long as they were clothes.

Sharp teeth hurled toward her, sharp and ragged, and eyes fiercely focused. A raccoon! She swung it around, its teeth in her jacket, until it let go and hit the side of the bridge, running away. She checked for punctures. She couldn't possibly get vaccinated. She couldn't officially exist. What if it came back while she slept? She'd always liked them but had never seen one behave like that before.

Someone had taken a shit next to the other giant box. No, no, no. She wasn't going to look inside. Too close for comfort. But, then she did. She held her nose and stepped gingerly up to it, lifting the flap. Papers, mostly. Some sort of scrapbook, bits of photos from magazines that looked like they were escaped from a collage. She felt ridiculous being so invasive. It was like sneakily reading a daughter's diary. She told herself she just wanted to know if she was going to be safe living across from that setup. She *was* a good person, even if she was a bit of a snoop.

That was the most important thing to her at this time in her life: to be recognized as a good person, the closest she'd have to being in community. Even if it meant lying to her friend and landlady, by leaving out everything about her entire life. To squelch dangerous impulses she'd been trained to have. Her propensity to take things in her own hands, like a tough-man vigilante. She planned to hunker down and keep her dark secrets forever. And thus, to find love. Community. That magic word. To connect with others who thought like she pretended to think. She'd given up on finding others who thought like she thought. She knew too much about how society worked behind the curtain. She could only dream.

She explored the trash around the bridge, most of it shitty tissues and condoms, porn magazines and a cast-off love seat that was probably swarming with some awful kind of vermin. There were a couple of old broken wooden chairs, though. She set them up in her space, propping them up with sticks, and draped a muddy sheet over them. She pulled a frazzled browned ball of twine out of the mud, making a memorable sound. She tied the chairs down so they didn't slide. Twine was attached to everything, each piece of the chairs sticking up and down and sideways.

It was a fort. Just like when she was a little girl. She would make it a pleasure-fort. Life would be good. She had her skin. She didn't have much else. But she could entertain herself with that.

She searched around, with nothing else to do, and found a fluffy flower, a chunk of moss, and a pine twig. She wanted more. She went back down the slope, slopped across the ditch, and over to the other side of the bridge, and up the slope on that side, to the box. It reminded her of playtime dress-up.

She picked up a very soft skirt she'd been hankering for since she'd first seen it lying on top of the box. Who knew if anyone was even staying there? She was going to take the skirt back, anyway. She wasn't the sort to steal from the homeless.

Was she?

She could always give it back.

She carried everything into the sideways web/nest/fort. She took off her mask, closed her eyes, and swept her skin with the pine needles. It felt wonderful. As if she was cleaning her aura of everything stuck there. Cleansing her lymph, making it flow beneath the surface, saying goodbye to stagnant emotions. She caressed her inner forearm with the flower. She nuzzled the moss. And she moved the silky skirt over her eyelids.

Chapter Eighteen

Saturday Evening with Stan

Saturday

When Stan knocked on the door at 7:30 in the evening, Becky was already dressed in her most elegant gown from the thrift store: long, red, and velveteen. She'd lit candles all over the house, and had warmed up the meal she'd prepared for them the night before. She'd put out the pewter goblets, not sure if they were appropriate, but they were different.

She didn't have a table, so once he came inside, she spread everything on a cloth on the hardwood floor, as usual, with pillows on each side. This time she'd even lit incense, again not sure if that was done with a meal, but she wanted to do something different to mark the big day, in case it did happen. For appetizers, she set out little plates of apples and cheese, celery and peanut butter, and dates. She brought in more food as he ate heartily. She hoped she'd have something left for the next day.

She didn't bring up the earlier phone call over dinner, not wanting to ruin the mood. She was so happy, she assumed it had been nothing, anyway. Nancy probably would have told her if it had been bad.

She gave Maiden a scrap from the meal, and Stan kicked the fluff ball away before she could eat it, saying, "It needs to learn manners. What does it think it is, a dog? At least dogs kill intruders. What does a cat do?"

"She lets me pet her! Just like you do." Becky reached out to him, and ran her hand along his leg.

He leaned over and kissed her.

Becky wanted to gather Maiden up, rock her, and tell her it would be OK, that Stan wasn't mean, really. But she tried to be reasonable instead. Men were supposed to be disciplinarians. Otherwise their kids didn't obey them and could get into trouble. He'd make a good father. Their child would never misbehave. He or she would be scared to. Becky couldn't hold back a tear.

But what if their child was a monster? What if Miss Trixie was right? She'd heard people whispering about there being a monster in her neighborhood when she was young. So, it was the *thing* that was her sister.

What if Stan treated their child as badly as her father had her? Everything buzzed, and her own saliva tasted like metal.

Maiden gave them a miffed look, then walked to the kitchen and noisily ate dry food pellets, pushing her bowl around with her nose. Becky wanted to protect her from Stan's moods. But she wanted to be able to feed the cat better with the money marrying him would give her.

That made her envision instead just living off produce she grew in the gardens. "I met a new friend today. A hypnotherapist. He got me over my fear of heights, for free! It was terrible timing. He'd been shot, and I was helping him. But he did it anyway."

Stan got quiet. "A male friend, eh? Hmm. Well, all that matters is that he didn't keep you from being here with me tonight. Let's say it's karma that got him. You know he has to want to take you away from me. Doesn't he?" His voice was low and controlled, with energy steaming behind it. It reminded her of a pressure cooker.

"Well, he might like me. But, so do lots of guys. I'm likable, if you haven't noticed," she teased. She sashayed, letting the wind lift her dress as she spun around, smiling to distract him from her tears.

"What was his name?"

"I forget." She didn't want him to ask where he lived. He was too jealous. He wanted her all to himself. In a way, that made her feel like a vivid, wild, dancing Italian woman in a traditional town.

A woman so beautiful, the men fought over her. She wanted to protect Buck, though, so she lifted her skirt.

He wasn't smiling. "You just be sure to not let *anything* keep you from getting together with me tomorrow night, honey. Not anything or anyone. And bring your wedding dress with you. This will be your most spectacular performance. The church will never be the same. You'll be amazing."

She felt proud. But she wished he'd be gentler about it. He was ruining the beauty of the proposal by being like that. Why couldn't he just get more competitive and be nicer to her when he got jealous like most men did. She was used to raising her value around them by showing off a little. But she'd learned not to use that tactic with Stan.

Becky wished they'd done the sexy video and made love *before* eating. She didn't like how eating made her tummy bloat a little bit, not as good as she'd like to be remembered when they watched the videos lovingly in future years. Stan hadn't liked it when she'd eaten a full meal before and gotten a little rounded belly, even though she was exquisitely slender and shapely. She wanted him to love her no matter how much was in her tummy, but she wasn't sure it was that way.

Until the last couple weeks, they'd never done anything like the videos before during their reasonably short relationship. They'd gone to a playground and hung out on the swings. They'd watched some movies she had enjoyed, and had gone to hear some classical concerts in the park. He could even dance well. That's when she liked him best: when he was having a good, light-hearted time.

Recently, they hadn't done much but the sexy videos. That evening's movie would be the thirteenth. Just one more video to go, on Halloween night. Just too perfect to waste that special date, so he told her he'd rented the church for just them. She was glad the videos were going to be over after that. He'd promised. It hurt to get in those crazy positions. She didn't like being tied up, though she smiled and looked around at him in as sexy a way as she could manage. And she knew it was pretty good. She just tried to get into the pain, telling herself masochism was a tool to have in her box.

The third and fourth video had been with her in the same pose, but different naughty clothes on consecutive days. If they could even be called clothes. The tenth and eleventh had been a different pose than what she'd done before, but were identical to each other.

He handed her the outfit to wear that day. The leather smelled like some other woman. She tried to be delicate when she sniffed it. Maybe he'd gotten it at a thrift store, she reasoned. She didn't want to act as if she thought he was cheap. Maybe he was having money troubles.

She wished he'd let her keep them. She thought some of them made her look spectacular. He said he returned them to save money. But he had a Cadillac. She suspected instead he was going to give all the clothes to her when he asked her to marry him.

She disliked the black tarp he made her pose on for video shoots. She liked floral sheets better. But one time he'd had her pose with a white rose and that looked beautiful against the black. She'd gotten giddy when he showed it to her. She wished she could show it to people, because she looked so good.

The pose he moved her into was similar to day eight's, but not quite as dramatic and pointed, slightly more rounded. She was to get in that position that reminded her of a camel's two humps, while he video-taped her for a minute. He tied her up into the almost unbearably painful pose, attaching the leather ropes to the hooks he'd installed above her bed. He squeezed her neck hard. She moaned, moving her head back and forth, trying to make a sound.

He pulled his hand away. "I'm sorry. I'm just trying to get you into a good position for the light to make you look your prettiest. You're so lovely."

"I am, aren't I?" She giggled. The Pinot Noir made everything better.

Then, she could move around a little bit against her restraints, invitingly, before he turned it off. She sometimes liked that part, not having to feel so restricted. Like an object. But sometimes it made her feel cheap, the way he told her to act like a whore.

Why would he want to remember her that way? She was so long-limbed and lithe. Why couldn't that be enough for him? She knew once they had a family, he'd get over it and start to respect her more. *Think positive*, she told herself. *Anything you can believe you can achieve.*

He said, "Tell me you want me. Beg me."

She did as she was told. She thought maybe she should be an actress as well as an artist. Maybe he'd help her be great at two things.

"Tell me you want to be with me forever. Tell me you'll do anything for me if I stay with you."

She did. She meant it. She could hardly wait for him to ask her while he was recording, to marry him. She would scream for joy.

He pressed against her windpipe as he kissed her. She struggled, trying to speak but couldn't. He'd been reading about breath play. She could get into it, she decided. It's what the cool girls were doing.

He let up, saying, "Good. We're done. One more, and we'll have something *sweet* to remember the rest of our lives. My BDSM Baby, you're so good at this. You're a natural. You're so beautiful I can't stand it."

She stretched out of the uncomfortable contortion, rubbing her neck. She was glad to be out of the pose as fast as possible. It was almost like being in a shape of a giant M, she thought, laughing. Mmmmm, she said, and purred at Maidy, who butted her with her head.

She wanted to ask Stan for a massage, but she knew that wasn't very much like foreplay. So instead, she reached out to him and ran her hand along his back, the way she knew he liked it.

He blew out the candles and snuffed out the incense. He'd apparently forgotten the roses. That was OK. Halloween was wedding gown day. He'd bring them then. He'd rented the church for the occasion. And they'd be getting together for dinner before that. Maybe he'd be nicer then.

She had her eyes on another special outfit at the thrift store to replace her chiffon dress, as long as no one bought it before she got there. She'd need to get a new phone too. But she was finding it hard to be quite as excited about it as she wanted to be.

Chapter Nineteen

The Fort

Nancy pushed the grocery cart full of recycling, and left it at the base of the bridge, angled in against the ditch. She had to trust the person living across from her wouldn't take it from her. What else could she do? She wondered how she was supposed to mark her territory. Was she supposed to shit by her things? She wasn't sure she could do that. What if someone walked past? She'd hold onto it until the middle of the night, and try it then.

She scrambled up the slope, to rest her back, take off her gloves, and wash her hands by opening the jug of water, pressing it against the shirt she'd set aside for spit baths.

She'd wait until the next day to go back to the recycling station and cash out. She was too tired, and was going to take a serious nap, late as it already was. She couldn't make it until proper bedtime. And, why should she? Besides, night time was the best to go prowl unseen around Stan's.

She realized she'd somehow had a sense Stan was dangerous to Becky long before her friend had asked her to spy. She felt as if she'd already disliked him before she had any reason to suspect him at all. Yet everything Becky had told her had been glowing. Was it raw instinct or was she tuned in spiritually to — everything?

She reached for her comb, out of habit, and found something thin in her pants pocket she hadn't noticed. She realized she'd been feeling it there all day, without thinking about it. Money!

Some kind benefactor had given her something. She wondered if it was another recycler, taking pity on a newcomer to the trade.

Maybe someone who had passed by in the night and taken it upon himself to climb the slope and make her life better.

She'd been wondering if she could live by waiting for fruit to fall from the stands in the Chinese market. Now, she could not only live, she could pursue her mission with all the technological needs addressed. She wished she could thank the generous donor. Someone brave enough to approach a sleeping homeless person and lift her blanket. She was touched by the kindness.

But the concrete was still ugly muddy beige and trash floated by and the water in the ditch stank. She wanted clean water to drink. Would she buy a filter and see if she could get anything from that murk?

She tried the pleasures of her skin again, but she had lost the playfulness she'd been able to muster the night before. The flower was pathetic. Browning, with a dark crease, and a hole where a bug had had a snack. She missed having shelter.

She didn't know if her bridge companion had made it home to the bridge. She'd slept so deeply, she would never have heard him. Nothing looked different, but since he'd folded up his bag, she wouldn't have been able to tell. Maybe he always folded it like that when he left.

She crept to the other side of the bridge again for the only entertaining thing left in her life. Snooping. She took out some papers from the box. Receipts, recipes, doodles, nothing very interesting, all in the same handwriting. It looked feminine enough she decided maybe her companion was a woman. And it did have some things in a costume-bag, like a hairbrush and make-up.

She felt sorry for her, less afraid. Nancy usually gave money to homeless women, more often than she did to men. They had it rough.

She wondered about some of the homeless women she'd seen in the area lately, and wondered if it belonged to them. As she sifted through it, she felt a strange calm. Like the calm inside a tornado.

She was glad it was probably a woman. They often were scarier than the men, though, she had to admit. Yet, there were men's work boots and a plastic bag with a clean, quality suit in it. She came to think of it as a genderless being, but her fear level, never knowing when the person would show up, maybe even discover she'd been rummaging through the stuff, made her think of her bridge companion as male. A rough male. Unpredictable, powerful, crazy, or maybe a kindly artist run out on the skids by the housing market. She cleared her jacket's large pockets of small apples she'd picked, onto the sleeping bag, as a gift.

She was about to go back to her side and stop being so nosey when she noticed a word on one of the papers. "Stan." How ironic. How many Stans were there?

Was her companion into someone named Stan? The synchronicity made her feel like dancing. She liked it when life curled up into little paper wads like that. Distant edges touching, things connecting that had no reason to be.

She found a little diary. She opened it. Ah, again, with the Stan thing. The handwriting looked strangely familiar, though, of course it would, after having seen it in the box here and there. "I think he's going to ask me to marry me. My body says no. The ligaments along my groin tighten at the thought of sex with him, even when he's not there. Even when we're not having sex. Even in my dreams. I wake up and have to rub my pussy to get all the little knots out. All along the tendons on my thighs. Can I do it? Yes, I can. I can overcome. I can be his, forever. His, and Maidy's."

What! That was Becky's diary! How the hell had Nancy gone to the bridge, admittedly, the livable one near Becky's apartment, and found Becky's diary? Did that mean Becky was camping there? Had she fled the apartment because she got scared? Did Stan or her stalker do something to her?

Or, did that mean *Stan* was camping there? Who else but him could have been going into her place and stealing her stuff?

Nancy was so flabbergasted she stood up and dropped the diary into the box. She heard something delicate break beneath it. She didn't stop to look at what it was.

She ran back to her tilted fort, and cuddled down against the blanket she'd scored. She had no idea what to think. Her thoughts didn't take her anywhere. It was like blankness, itself, eyes open wide, stared into the vast, nameless weirdness of the world.

Only later did she get up the gumption to search again, using the little flashlight as she sifted through everything. A simple collage of photos of Becky, Maidy, a wedding dress cut out from a magazine, another magazine image, of sparkling empty jars along a window ledge cut.

Her head hurt.

But it was worth it when she found a torn, dirty piece of paper with Becky's handwriting. Must have been in recycling. It said, "Stan told me he loved Maiden Reverse so much, he uses her name for passwords. How sweet is that?"

Chapter Twenty

Bottled Up

After I sleep the Pinot Noir off, I'm ready for my big night. It's my last drink. Ever. Why would I need to kill the pain? After what I'm about to do, there won't be any. Of course, if Becky wants to drink with me, I'll make an exception for her anytime, anything, anywhere. I'd drink Draino for that lady.

Calling a cab. Pretty soon, if my plan goes well, I'll be able to buy a car. Be good for work and all that. And taking Becky out to movies and dinners and plays and art museums, goes without saying.

I meet the cab down the street from her apartment, and tell the driver: "In a little while that Cadillac ahead will pull out. Just follow it." *This way I can catch him when he's for sure home and awake and alone and not in some inward space or whatever.*

No one would ever guess that Connors is me. My accent, and my make-up, my comb-over, and my sideways smile. I'm getting good at pretending to have Bell's Palsy. Took me a long time to perfect that plus make it elegant. And now I'll never get to use that skill again. Who would ever put Connors together with my usual self, or with Trixie? I'm so good. Best actor in these parts.

I chatter to the cab driver, as Connors, about growing up in Hawaii, haha, someplace I researched in all the *National Geographics* people put in their recycling, my words coming out all slurred from the way I keep one side of my face from moving. But he doesn't respond. Oh well, not much of a conversationalist, I guess.

We drive up the hills around the edges that would make Becky cringe but I love seeing the city down below. I can see my old home, the bridge I'll never have to go back to now. I wonder if anyone who moved in under there kept that smelly Bible I left as a gift. I let the cabbie drive on for a few blocks past Stan's house before I get out.

Along with the cabbie's tip, I give him some advice. "The stock market insiders have said Reber's going down fast this week. Believe me, I have solid sources. Bet on it. Have a good night!"

I'm sad to see the cabbie drive off. I hope I see him again, but he won't recognize me. Especially with the lifts in my shoes that make Connors so tall, the bronze make-up, dark shades, a curly blond wig scratching me under the hat, the clip-on ear ring, clip on tie, and all that. If he puts together anything, he'll tell the police he drove a stock market dude to the neighborhood, is all.

I won't get to dress up like Connors ever again. Connors must die. Poor guy. It's been good knowing him. Being him. But I'll have to set him on fire before the night is done. He can fly up to Heaven. I'll bet the angels sing.

Everyone I like goes away. Connors is just the newest about to leave my life. But not Becky. She'll be mine. She's all I need.

I walk down the street to Stan's house.

One of those nice weeknight neighborhoods with bushes to hide in, and no one out and about. I hang out behind a bush with red leaves for a while and take out Pete Zelite's clothes from my bag, so they'll be ready to change into fast when the time is right.

I put on my gloves.

I take out my broken wine bottle, the last one I drank from and will ever drink from alone.

I wipe it down for prints.

It's been long enough.

I knock on his door, calling out, "Stan! It's me! It's Connors! That stock market deal we talked about is peaking right *now*. Don't miss your chance."

He'll recognize my voice. I made a good impression when I was dressed as Connors last week and said I'd give him a stock tip sometime. Well, this is that time.

I kind of hope he told someone about the inside trading possibility and I kind of hope the neighbors hear me framing poor ol' Connors; he can't win for losing, eh?

Stan opens the door, the spikes in his hair leaning sideways, his shirt buttoned wrong. Becky must have tired him out, that feisty vixen.

I head up the steps. There are so many of them!

When I lunge for him at the top of the stairs, he steps back, shaking, his eyes open wide. His olive skin gets crazy pale.

I grab him.

He calls out to the neighbors, though people are so used to drama on the streets these days, I'm not worried. Kids yell "help" all the time, guys yell how they're going to kill someone on their cell phones walking up and down the sidewalks, women scream when they have sex, people fight, there are gunshots, and nothing happens. No sweat.

I do see someone running toward me a few blocks away, though, a thick man with a flopping belly. He's getting out his phone while he runs. Must be calling the police. Of course, since he doesn't say anything about me having a gun, they aren't likely to care about that call at all, are they? If they come out, after a couple hours or so, they'll be looking for Connors, and plenty of people have seen him around the city, when I dressed up like him so many times over the last year, making my profile come alive.

A witness like this is perfect. Good luck with that call, buddy. I have a slab of meat in the bag in my pocket I got out of the trash yesterday, in case of an attacking dog, and this guy looks like that trick would almost work on him.

Stan presses against my arms with his, squeezing me, making it hard to breathe, and I feel one of my ribs move where it shouldn't.

But I know the moves.

I waste no time.

I shove the glass right into the center of Stan's neck so he can't make a sound other than a disgusting, long, wet gurgle. Yuck.

He grabs me, looking at me like a child pleading with his mother, and slides down my body, slow, thudding down the concrete steps.

He bounces down, the blood dripping, and I have to step back to keep from getting it on my clothes.

Of course, I'll be changing them anyway. I'll be rolling them in the mud and sticking them in the recycling bin where all the homeless guys will pick them up and get their fingerprints on them before they take them and wear them, and that's that. They're out in droves tonight since pickup is in the morning in the hood. I cover all the bases. They'll pick them up before the police even think to start searching.

I throw the glass shard over his fence into the recycling bin, where it shatters. Nothing unusual about that. People hear that sound all the time. Even down the street right now people are crashing around in the glass recyclables.

I drag him into the house, grab one of his video cameras in a dope bag, why not? I close the door, well, at least part way, and get the hell out of there.

I run toward the stash of Pete Zelite, a hell of a lot faster than the sloppy neighbor can. It's way too dark for his phone camera to pick up. I tear up my gloves into tiny pieces with my teeth and throw them inside a diaper in the neighbor's trash. Time to wash off the tan make-up with the Handywipes. With my acting skills and set of characters, I'm my own witness protection agency. I be whoever I need to be to stay out of trouble, and that's just how it's going to be!

The neighborhood will be amazed by my powers of prediction when Becky tells them Stan got killed; my prediction. Trixie will get *so much business*!

Ha Ha! I'm so clever it hurts.

Chapter twenty-one

Perfect Timing

Nancy was not the kind of person to be easily shocked. She'd seen everything. But as she walked up the hill, past the bus stop, toward Stan's house, her tote bag full of any possible sleuthing necessities slung over her shoulder, ready to see what else she could learn, she saw blood on his stoop.

She couldn't believe it. Had Stan already killed Becky?

Nancy'd thought she had until Halloween to find some way to save her! She thought he was keeping her safe as he could to make sure the final video was valuable to customers.

She crouched down. The blood could be from any of the gold-diggers he'd recorded. Did he propose to all of them or record the videos when other men did propose? Did he do it secretly, or did they even pay him for his work? How many of them did he kill at home, roll up in a rug, and let the police cart away? How many did he wait to kill in a ritual — or whatever the video flavors of the month were?

She knew if the police got there before she could see what happened, they'd cover up Stan's crimes. She wanted them outed. Yet, she couldn't be caught there, or anywhere, considering someone was apparently onto her troublemaking with the Agency.

She watched carefully for any witnesses. She slunk up to the door and peered in. She gasped. Stan's body lay just inside, twisted on his back, eyes open wide. Blood pooled around his neck, the bottom of his shoe preventing the door from closing.

She stepped over him, put on her gloves, and dragged him a little way inside, before closing the door. This was crazy. The police would probably show up any minute and find her there, interfering with the scene of a crime.

But this was her only chance to find out what he'd been up to, and maybe find some way to do something about it. Becky was finally safe. Sure, prison would have been better, but that would have never happened. Stan had been planning to kill Becky, had killed others, would have killed again. The Nevermind would have protected him and all the powerful people in the network.

She wondered if it was Congressman Rawlings who'd killed him. She wouldn't put it past him.

Or maybe it was one of the gold-diggers who'd escaped. Vengeance would make sense.

She even wondered if Becky could have overcome her fear of heights and made it to his house, and done it herself when finding out what was going on. She wouldn't blame her.

It seemed like a fresh wound. What if the killer was *in the house*?

What if he was watching her? What if she was next? She picked up a paper weight as she walked through the house, pulling back the shower curtain, opening closet doors. She could finally breathe normally. Until she saw the room: black background, video camera, still camera, tripods, lights, everything.

His laptop was open on his desk. She sat down and tried the password, Maiden Reverse, to access it. Voila! The images drew her in. She delved in, ready to run out the back door if the police showed up. There was the video series of Becky in back-breaking poses, each in the shape of a letter. WILL YOU MARRY ME? The last one was not yet entered. Nancy's heart fluttered, and while she was in the room with death, she couldn't help sitting up straight and tapping her foot quickly. There were others in the Gold-Diggers series, all without the final installation. The empty slots for the last video were named, referencing the ritual in the church. She downloaded those to Stan's empty flash drives.

Nancy grew impatient, wanting proof of the murder the Congressman had told her Stan was capable of. Had the Congressman just made that up? Was he trying to frame him?

She took a chance. She didn't want to just take the laptop yet. It was hooked into the internet and she could send Brandon all the files using Stan's email, before erasing the emails from the sent file — if she had time before the police or neighbors got there.

The screen went gray. Oh no! Failure. She fidgeted, growing shaky with hurry. Then, she remembered what she'd read in Becky's diary. Maidy in reverse. She typed ydiaM. It worked!

She scammed the project names. One was called, "Incest Kidney." Another called, "Incest Stem Cells." "Incest Blood." Hmm. What the hell was that about? Did people have children so they could use their blood if they needed to? No, that was too weird. Paranoia's a bitch.

Only the three projects already open could she access and download onto the drives without a code. They would shut down as soon as she wasn't able to keep engaging with them on the laptop. She had to work fast to copy them. She had no internet cafe or library to access them from, and if she used anyone's device it could be traced to them, creating havoc in their lives.

Maybe she could find a way. She typed in the codes she'd been given: GD:0724pohb and FS 080poih87 and RES: 8y908oiu.

One of the projects was about the gold-diggers, and the other focused on people with deformities. Then, she found scenes that made her feel faint. A series in the Freaks Show project titled Blob. Stan had not shot those. He would have been too young. Nancy herself was only a teenager at the time.

She knew because — she'd been there.

There was the little girl, if that was even the right word for such a creature, who'd been called only The Blob. The girl had been born with an incredible deformity, leaving her shape barely recognizable as being even remotely human. The man having sex with the twisted girl in the video was The Blob's father. Nancy knew, because she'd convinced him to sell the Blob to the Nevermind. As he was probably already having sex with her regularly anyway, she'd persuaded him to film one last sex scene with the girl with an extremely challenging disability, for added monetary reward.

In the light of those movies, the scenes looked lurid and disgusting. If The Blob had been shot in black and white photographs by the famous photographic artist, Joel Peter Witken she would have been painfully beautiful.

The father had told her he'd gone into debt when his wife died, and he had to take care of both his daughters, and pay for their house. He'd seen no clear way out and it was driving him mad. He hadn't seemed evil. He seemed very sick. Confused and twisted. She hoped he'd gotten counseling, was put on medication, or if he never reformed, was locked up in prison for life.

Nancy's face grew prickly and hot. She almost felt the reddening of her skin reflected on the screen. She'd done terrible things under mind control. Terrible things.

Only in the last year had she recovered from the splitting of the self she had endured from childhood through deliberate trauma too intense for anyone to bear without disassociating. She'd remembered. She'd put the puzzle pieces together several months before she moved there to be near Becky.

The Agency had made her into an assassin. A honeypot. A means to take down countries for the sake of U.S. Interests, supposedly, but was it globalist, instead? Or was the network behind the scenes guiding the balance of power doing it for whatever strange desires they had that only extreme profit and control could allow them to slake?

She had been a spy. Supposedly admirable, therefore. Even more specialized than a soldier. Elite, sophisticated, doing highly specialized, dangerous secret agent work for the government in a vital position for maintaining the desired balance of power.

She could not be held responsible for actions the Nevermind had forced her to take. But she felt like throwing herself at the police and saying, "Take me! I deserve to be killed. I'm ready to pay my debt."

She cried, and had to remove her mask for comfort. She wiped her tears. She looked through other videos of the Blob. Some were simple sex scenes — as simple as they could be with a body contorted in that way. In other videos, The Freaks mated with her. Nancy turned away, nauseated, seeing the Blob nearly torn by sex with a man with gigantism, a condition which had become popular for a while with adolescents discovering the effects of human growth hormone, started at the right age, in large doses.

Nancy had even had to participate in a couple of the videos, herself. She'd forgotten any details about who she'd worked with. They'd blended in. And then, there it was. *She* was in one of the videos with The Blob. She'd had to hold the poor girl's "head." It was slimey.

Besides just the difference in decades, she'd looked different from how she currently did, after having had cheap cosmetic surgery to hide her identity from facial recognition. She'd been beautiful, feminine, with clear skin and a button nose instead of the lengthened one, with fuller lips back then. Her body had been curvier, before she'd starved herself to hide her past. She looked lovely in the videos, but what she was doing was hideous.

And there she was, with The Blob and a young man. She remembered him, vaguely. He was so young, hard to make out distinct features yet. Then, a light went on. She realized he'd grown up to become a newscaster on a popular news station. Holy fuck. Tom Tellen was doing The Blob.

She worked double time. She looked through the videos in both projects to see if she could find any other people who worked at the news station. But how would she know? She downloaded the list of names of everyone involved.

She began a check on the names of everyone listed as working with that station. Then, she did a cross-check analysis to see if there were any matches with the list of experiencers. Yes. There certainly were. Some of the names were not relevant. The names didn't seem to belong to the same people. But, bingo, there were the producer and news director, who worked with Tom Tellen.

And a clip of the director and Angela Ageless together with The Blob.

In that moment, Nancy went from the need to hide her identity to find a community — to the willingness to, if necessary, put her visage on national TV.

No. She couldn't. Children could be watching. That would never fly.

But the internet. All sorts of things made it onto the internet. Brandon had his own website independent of any host's specifications. Brandon would show that video if he needed to. She knew it. She just had to overnight it to him.

Her stomach turned into an acid knot of pain, and she curled over. Maybe it didn't have to be that one. With her in it. No. It did. A vile action by Tellen. People would never trust his stupid propaganda again.

Or would they? Basically, it would out him as a pervert doing something that would shame him forever. Him caught having sex with a beautiful woman would blow over. Even win him points. But being with a deformed person would sear into the eyes of all the viewers. It would go viral. But what would it ultimately accomplish?

The Nevermind would never own up to it. It would get away with that legally because of national security issues. That video had been made either to blackmail him, to bribe him with the experience, to sell to fund the Nevermind's covert activities, or to be used to traumatize young people into dissociation for the sake of being programmed by the Nevermind. In all cases, it had been sanctioned, done for the good old United States. The Blob's feelings were collateral damage.

Nancy barely remembered a little girl downstairs the day she'd convinced the father to sell The Blob.

The Blob had to be taken to a different location, a little place that later burned down, called the Freak House. The father had left the area with the money he'd been given. Nancy wondered if

The Blob had died once her usefulness was up. The thought made Nancy bury her head.

Sweet dreams, Blob-girl. May they be better than your life has been.

She looked at the raw footage of The Blob, outtakes that had been stored in the archive, to see if she could get a sense of what had happened to her. She wished she could wave a wand to liberate all the Freaks she'd recruited for the videos and other sexual experiences. But the Nevermind would simply recruit more of them to take their places.

There was the kitchen, downstairs from The Blob's attic. Not a bad house. Ordinary. Could have had a little better upkeep. Looked like a nice yard outside the window, just a little wild and weedy. And there was The Blob's younger sister, walking through, oblivious. A sweet little one. Nancy hoped her father hadn't mistreated her too. She hoped at least he'd used the money he'd been paid to send her to the best schools, buy her special presents, and healthy food.

Nancy locked the front door, so if the police came, she'd maybe have a little time to dash out the back. She unlocked the back door and planned the quickest route past the hedges and through the neighbors' yards.

She went back to the laptop and decided to take it with her, if she could. She downloaded short videos, pictures, detailed records. Suddenly, files started spontaneously deleting. Some of the most damning ones were gone. It had to be a dead man switch. Stan must have had some way to communicate with the machine regularly, and if he didn't, evidence went away.

She then saw some of the files preparing to send. Auto-posting couldn't be good. That was not happening to blow the cover on the operation. Agencies had been collecting dirt on politicians and decision-makers, not to arrest them, but to control them. They'd been encouraging the dirt, setting them up with sexual perversions, encouraging their darkness. She watched the files going away, and wondered how much better it would be for them to disappear. They could not be blackmailed into things like

171

supporting terrible laws, voting against impeachment, and hiring insidious people. But they could also not be brought to trial if it was ever allowed. If the powers that be ever became integral.

File after file disappeared, one at a time, at a fast rate as she watched, and she didn't know what they were yet. She wanted to be able to delete whichever ones she felt would be a good idea to protect the victims. But mostly, she decided, it was better they existed, just not in the hands of the Nevermind. *She* would do the blackmailing, here, and the Nevermind would not like it.

But how? What could possibly be the signal that went to it if he was alive? Was it something he did regularly to check in, manually? If so, it had to be from a distance. She ran to his corpse and felt around, thankful for gloves.

She felt his pockets, emptied them out, scrambling through all the contents. She discovered something that looked like a dog whistle. She blew it, heard nothing, but the files stopped deleting. She was impressed. The Nevermind had some advanced technology she'd always been in awe of. She'd seen the prototypes to those in a meeting, but had not followed their further production.

She continued to study what was left. There were more archives of embarrassing sexual encounters. Some of them in occult rituals. Goat heads, horns, pentagrams, incense, gold.

Did this mean she could finally go to see Becky, and no one would be surveilling? She didn't dare take a chance. Anyone who could help Becky figure out Stan's plan could be suspect. She didn't know if Becky had gotten the message from Frame Up, or the messages she'd finally taken the chance to leave on her phone, from a random stranger's phone she'd asked on the bus.

She fumbled with Stan's professional, top notch cameras, trying to teach herself their unique workings fast enough to take photos of the incriminating photoshoot scenes, being careful not to disturb anything, keeping her gloves on.

Then she came across something bigger. She pored over the material, her hands moving faster with excitement. Perverted covert sexual alliances between the elite decision-makers and the intelligence community was nothing new. The existence of snuff porn was no longer shocking to people, who had other things to think about more relevant to their lives. It was considered the realm of extremists to care about such undignified things. People would just say its existence was a conspiracy theory if anyone in their favored political party was accused of doing it. But this. On Stan's largest laptop, there was an entirely different set of editing projects. The subject was the Rescuers.

The video Brandon had pointed out with the Rescuers killing children was real. They had killed them. Here it was, again. But this wasn't a clip as it was shown on the news, with the men (who happened to *actually* be Rescuers, in fact completely missed by most viewers) touted as terrorists the U.S .had to take down.

This wasn't the clip used, as Brandon had, to analyze how the media was lying about who the Rescuers were, first portraying them as kind people bringing aid and toys to a country war-torn by terrorists, when in fact, they *were* the terrorists. This was obviously snuff pedophilia. This showed the whole clip, in close-ups. The Rescuers violently raping the children for a long time before killing them. And Stan had edited it, framing in a way to make it appealing to trusted customers, paying a lot of money to get off on it. Nancy found the list of subscribers, and next to their names — letter and number codes.

She searched further and found the specific blackmail programs the codes referred to. Each subscriber could be trusted to keep the snuff porn to himself because otherwise, he could be blackmailed with something he had done even worse than subscribing. Many times, the blackmail projects involved the person being invited to The Experience Room and engaging in something awful, such as snuff porn, himself. Apparently, the most embarrassing ones, with the most stars, weren't pedophilia, but Freak Show sex. It seemed sex with beautiful women and children was more accepted by the populace than sex with someone deemed ugly.

She couldn't believe her luck, coming across Stan's house with the door open, him dead, his computer running, and the police not showing up yet to hide the evidence. Maybe they didn't have a clue about his death. She wondered if any of the neighbors had heard anything and called them. She had to work fast. She breathed double speed, as if that would make time be more fruitful.

There was satellite footage from far above, showing the entire city, then zooming down, covering the cityscape where the Rescuers were supposed to be giving toys to children, strengthening the buildings, bringing food to the restaurants, giving medicine to throngs of people lining up. The scenery from the satellite was barren. Other than the men in Rescuer costumes, and a few stragglers they seemed to be keeping in pens, grabbing onto them as human shields when strafed, there was nothing. Animals. Birds, wild animals that had wandered in, a few domestic creatures who had escaped the destruction.

No buildings any more. Some Rescuers were feasting around an outside table. The terrorist mercenaries the U.S. had covertly funded, armed, and trained had been extremely effective, and moved on. They were nowhere to be seen.

Meanwhile, across the U.S., newscasters furrowed their brows and chattered earnestly on how the U.S. had to protect that city's huge population from the U.S.-sponsored terrorists — without mentioning of course that they wouldn't have existed without U.S. support. Newscasters spoke of the need for heightened military spending, new Defense contracts galore to fund the other U.S.-sponsored terrorists, which they called "moderate rebels." The good guys. Like their buddies, the Rescuers.

Their big message was — time to declare war the first week in November. The newscasters just had to convince the population to get behind it a little bit more. Just a little more. Never mind that it would lead to WWIII. Nevermind, indeed.

Nancy had to stop them. There was evidence at her fingertips. Sure, Brandon and others posted forensic breakdowns of the obvious flaws in some of the videos purported to be coming from the city, and other videos actually coming from there which twisted the truth. But most people dismissed anything but the mainstream news. They might share something about something sensationalized but a mind-boggling, convoluted political situation far away? It wouldn't get enough traction. Those people would just be marginalized and called conspiracy theorists by their friends.

No, it needed to be on the mainstream news. She had to make it happen. It would be her mission. She jutted out her jaw, and breathed in testosterone vibes. Her muscles tightened, and she narrowed her eyes as she bent to the desk, searching, copying, and sending the material to Brandon in the meantime, using Stan's email account.

She needed horrendous blackmail material so she could force people to confess to the Rescuer scam. A political scam could soon be forgotten. A picture on the internet of a man having sex with a deformed person? People would eat that up. She didn't want to put it out there, though. She wanted to respect the privacy rights of the disabled people, even if the pictures might lead to their liberation, and the freeing of many others held as sexual slaves for sanctioned psychopaths.

"Hello?" called a large, sloppy man, hesitantly by the front door. "Police? Anyone there?" He had food around his mouth.

No! What she was emailing to Brandon had to go through. The future of the world depended on it. If she could convince people about the scam with the city empty of everything but ravaged chickens and two-legged dogs, they wouldn't support the war. The major powers wouldn't have to defend their territories. Everything could calm the hell down.

The best email of all was in the process of sending. Just another minute and Brandon would be stunned. But she couldn't be caught. She closed the laptop, put it in her tote bag with the video camera, took off her shoes so she could run quietly into the back of the house, with her medical mask. She hid them under a bed and stood by a closet, wondering what to do.

She heard him coming inside, and gasping loudly. "Is anyone there?" he called, and started through the house.

Hiding was too dangerous. If he caught her in the closet, she'd be a suspect. She rubbed her face, messed up her hair, splashed water under her eyes from the bathroom jutting off the bedroom, and went back into the living room.

"Hello?" she said, with a shaky voice, looking as devastated as she could.

"What's going on?"

"My boyfriend just got killed."

"Oh, I'm so sorry to hear that. That must be horrible." He hugged her shoulders, and backed away, his eyes darting around.

"I didn't see it happen. I don't know who it was. It's so awful. Just so awful."

"I live two doors down. I was out walking. I saw a well-dressed white man just come up the stairs and jab him with a bottle or something. He ran away down the road. I called the police. I don't know why they're not here yet. Maybe since he's already dead, they're focusing on more urgent cases? Weird, though."

"Maybe they have time to get a whole team together. I don't know, a medical examiner. Ambulance. Do they even use those for dead people? I don't know. I can't think straight. I'm sorry, I'm not in a very sociable mood right now." She bent over, and rocked in a position of maniacal grief. She yelled into her arm, biting the fabric of her sleeve.

"Do you need anything?"

"No, no, I'll be fine. I just need to process. It happened so fast. I need to compose myself for when the police get here."

"OK, I'll let you have your peace. I'm sorry for your loss."

She just wanted him out of there before the police got there. How could she run away if he was there? She nudged him toward the door, where he stepped over Stan. Then, he hesitated, and stepped back over him again toward her. "Listen, if you need anything, you'll let me know? I didn't know him very well, hardly talked to him, but maybe . . ."

She couldn't listen to what he was saying. Her heart was beating too loudly. She thought the sirens in the distance, not an uncommon sound, might be coming up that road. She had to get away fast. Had to, had to.

She pushed him toward the door, pleading, "Please, please let me just have a minute to deal with this before I have to face the police. I can't handle this. It's too much. OK?"

"But."

"Hey, you know, you've disturbed a crime scene. You're better off not telling the police you came in. You could get in a ton of trouble. Just forget about me, and let them do their job."

"Oh!" He scurried out the door, and she took off running, put on her shoes, grabbed her bag, and dashed out the back door, locking it behind her. She watched for the neighbor as he walked home, and she hid behind trees and shrubs in case he glanced in her direction. She leaped over a hedge, the laptop falling out of her tote bag. She pushed her way back through, grabbed it, and pushed through the hard wood and scratchy leaves, bleeding a little, and found herself in a neighbor's yard with a dog tied up with a rope with plenty of room to spare. It was jumping at her throat.

She screamed into her bitten arm, pressing it against her mouth to dilute the sound, and held the laptop up as a shield for her neck. The dog growled and snarled, its eyes fiercely glinting in the moonlight. It tore into it, and she hit its soft nose, much as she hated to. She'd vowed never to commit violence again. She loved animals. She loved people. She didn't want to hurt anyone. She'd been forced to do it so often in the past. She cried as she pelted the dog with the slender metal, running away backwards, watching the lights come on in the house, looking for the neighbor, who could figure her out and send the police any second.

She delved into the shadows and ran through yards and side roads, finding a hollow bush to crouch inside, and stayed there all night, shivering. Wondering if there was any life any more in the laptop at all. Drops of rain. She crouched over the camera and laptop, holding them under her shirt against her stomach, off the wet ground, for hours.

Chapter Twenty-Two

Glinting Forever

Sunday

Becky's stomach growled. She could hardly eat, feeling so much appreciation for Buck while preparing to marry Stan. She couldn't stand it. She almost wanted Nancy to show up before Halloween and tell her Stan was a dumb-ass. She'd have a valid reason to turn him down. She'd do it at the moment he proposed. That would show him. But what if he was true to her? In that case, she didn't want to be the jerk.

To Becky, the sun seemed to shine more brightly on Buck's blond hair than it did other people's. Something about the yellowness against his tanned skin, the brilliant whiteness of his teeth, and his easy broad smile seemed to live in the daytime. She'd only seen him when it was light, though the days were short. She felt closer to the sun when they were together, gardening, making each other laugh, stealing subtle glances and looking away. She couldn't imagine him at night.

Stan was the opposite. He was scruffy, with dark hair and dark skin. He slouched in his black leather jacket, which he wore even when it was warm, while clicking the flash that made his dark stubble glint with silver light.

Sunday morning after her successful job interview at a far better paying gallery in the hilly part of the city, up a substantial part of the stairs, she walked fast, trying to make time go faster so she could burst out her good news.

Buck stood in front of her apartment, emanating rays of joy when he saw her face. Before she said anything, he burst out: "I knew it!"

"All thanks to your hypnosis. Good thing you got shot."

"Any time, Miss."

"This gallery pays twice as much as Frame Job and is five days a week. I walked up and down all the stairs and it was no problem at all."

"We should celebrate. Can I take you to lunch?"

"What?" She broke the flow to look around every now and then.

"What?"

"It's OK. Stan and I don't have plans for today, but . . ."

"Oh. Should I . . .?" His eyes searched hers. They had light grey branches and a dark rim, with blue depths that looked like caves she wanted to explore.

"It's not . . . It's just. He didn't show up for our date last night. So, he could come by and tell me what happened. Set another time for our next date. I don't know." She felt the foundation of her life, the support she was planning on, fall out from under her. She remembered her dream from the night before. Walking along and then suddenly falling into an infinite abyss the sidewalk had become, waking up with a jolt.

"Oh, that's right, you're still saving for a new phone."

In golden daylight, she almost couldn't believe Stan would show up. The leaves were wet muted collages on the sidewalk. She moved her left shoulder back in a circle, then the right one, leaving her posture more open, like Buck's.

"Let's just go. Let's just get to work, like we planned." She was ready for him to show her another community garden. This was the fifth day in a row she'd learned from him about how to become more self-sufficient with food. He'd already helped her put the things that could be planted in the autumn in the garden they'd made on her roof. He'd helped her ferment sauerkraut and pickles, and put the dates on her calendar for planting cucumbers and cabbages.

She was surprised Nancy hadn't come by yet with news of either Stan's infidelity or fidelity. Waiting was wearing her out with images of him with another woman. The sound of the woman's voice on the phone with Stan still haunted her, though not so much as it used to. She was starting to get immune to the constant barrage of worrisome possibilities. Was it someone he worked with, maybe, at Wedding Company? Getting the brides ready for their photoshoots, taking shots they'd remember forever. What a romantic job. They were surrounded by flowers and lace, gauze and looks of love. Women looking their most beautiful. Maybe getting it on was women's version of stag parties.

She wasn't sure what she would say when he proposed at the church. She knew it was going to be all set up for their bridal video series. Some kind of abstract art. She had great respect for conceptual theater and was glad Stan was into that kind of thing too, personal work. Not just tied down to the regular wedding documentation. He needed a creative outlet.

They biked to a community garden, and Buck introduced her around to the regulars. She and Buck built a wooden planter on stilts, easy to stand and plant in rather than having to bend over. The oldest woman at the garden clucked over it while they worked. When they were through, Buck, Becky, and the woman held hands and danced in a circle, wiggling and bending this way and that. Buck threw his head back and laughed. His teeth glinted, and in that glint of pure white light was Heaven.

Chapter Twenty-Three

Through the Bathroom Window

Monday

OK, so I'm sitting at my table at Random, giving crazy expensive readings as usual, as you well know, my Interrogator, my love, my shadow, my surveillance king, my invisible listener, my angel-headed madness. And thank you for the gifts. For taking me somewhere in my dreams so I can bring back things I stashed in the bushes. Some things are hazy. Some things are clear. My life makes no sense until I think about Becky, and then it doesn't matter. Then the holes are filled with her.

They love me here. Becky's friends started the trend after she told them how good I was and how I even predicted a death. They told everyone else, and now I'm famous in this neighborhood. I'm glad she only knows people around here. If I started doing readings for lots of people who weren't local, I'd be in a hell of a lot of trouble. As it is, a few outsiders, well that's fine. Everyone expects psychics to be wrong sometimes. The times they're right make everyone forget about the failures.

I do miss going into Becky's house. Before long, I'll have enough money that she'll be inviting me in anyway. She'd better. She'd better serve me some nice meals, too. Should I ever let her know I'm her savior from Heaven? One day after we've been married for years, I might spring it on her. Heheh, she'd be so grateful who knows what she'd do.

I still have to go through people's recycling of course, to get up-to-date information on them. I can remember the people by name and address. See, all I ask of them is their address when they sit down, in case I've forgotten their faces. It's kinda scary when the ones come in from the apartment complex, the giant one six streets away, because it's hard to tell whose trash is whose, sometimes.

The repeat customers haven't noticed me, when I dress regular, going through their stuff each week. The other recycling guys like me too, because I don't bother pushing the carts full bottles and cardboard and cans to the recycling station anymore. Hell, I make 300 dollars a pop now and I can do fourteen readings a day. That's 4,200 a day.

So now I have a new magnifying glass to read people's tiniest scribbles in their recycling. A business expense. I can't wait for my shift to be over so I can go back to the motel. I'm so lucky the motel dude rented his room to me for cash while he's gone, and the owner has no idea I'm there at all!

I've got to take some papers by my incinerator under the bridge, now that I've got the magnifying glass to start a fire.

I love getting rich. I can stop lying to people about being psychic, soon, get healthy, get my papers in order, have an address and phone, make fancy friends who can be references for me. I can be a real career actor.

Man, the only break I get is going to the bathroom. And it's that time . . . I call sitting on the can at Random, like I am now, a vacation. People pay this much to famous readers all the time, but it still amazes me. I keep doing the math because I just don't see how it can add up but it does.

I've been taking fish oils and detox formulas to help me think better. I feel like Mr. Normal now. Here's the weird part: I don't even think you're listening to me anymore. It's just habit, I guess, talkin,' now. What else am I going to do?

I look a lot better. Been using creams on my face. Teeth whitener. Pretty soon, Trixie won't exist. People will be so sad. But a psychic who predicts someone's death is bound to cause a stir eventually. What's that commotion outside in the shop? Oh, damn.

I don't like that guy's voice, the way he's talking to the barista. FBI! Well, hell! I've *got* to get out of here. I can't go into the cafe or they'll nab me for sure.

Won't I look extra suspicious if I just stop doing readings the very moment they come in? It's not quite closing time. Damn.

This could be my last day as a free man. All I did was kill a guy before he killed a bunch of other women. But they'll give me the chair for that, goddamn it. What am I going to do?

OK, that's it, I'm done. No more readings for me. Out the window it is. Tee hee!

I just hope the sink doesn't break when I stand on it. Oh, no, they don't make sinks like they used to. I didn't mean to turn on the water full stream with my foot. But, I ain't going back down to turn it off now. Got to sprint into the back alley and get to my Pete Zelite outfit fast like nobody's business. Bye, bye, Trixie-pie!

Chapter Twenty-Four

Growing Things

Tuesday

Becky and Buck worked together putting the new vegetable garden on her roof. She was glad the landlord had said yes, and the micro-area was zoned for that. His arm was in a sling, making her feel needed and capable, helping him while he helped her. Through the roof-gardening, and working in community gardens with him, she learned how to save food money. She could focus on promoting her art shows. Her new floral-inspired paintings were vibrant and colorful, more contagiously joyful than anything she'd done. She incorporated airy rooftop landscapes into lit-up abstracts.

There were also deeper layers and tones of browns. Stan's murder made her want to just put her head on Buck's chest and cry. But she'd already done that. She couldn't expect a helpful neighbor she'd so recently met, to be her handkerchief. Still, her head drooped toward him.

"You seem to be holding up well after Stan's death," he said. "I know it's got to be terrible. Let me know if there's anything I can do?"

"Look what you're doing now, helping me plant my own garden. I mean, of course, you're welcome to eat from it, too." Becky blushed. She hoped that didn't seem like an afterthought of a selfish woman. Of course, he could, without her permission. Her arm muscles pressed in against her bones. She couldn't tell how he felt about her, and she felt hypocritical for caring so soon.

"I know Stan would have taken care of you so you could make it as an artist."

"These plants and the sun and rain can support me, now." She touched his shoulder softly. "Besides, I have a job that pays well. Finally."

"I just hope whoever killed Stan isn't going to going to go after your suitors." His face was inscrutable. His eyes narrowed in the sun. His mouth up on one side and down on the other.

Becky couldn't stand it if he was hurt because of her. She put her hand on his arm. "You think Stan's killer's the same person who shot at you? The police told me it was probably just a robber, who got scared off or something. I wish they'd talk about it on the news so I could learn more about it. It's hard to believe doing that would really cause copycat murders."

Was Buck saying he loved her? Had he called himself a suitor? She searched his face. He'd been polite about her having a boyfriend, and then going through the death. He hadn't made a move on her. The magnetic draw she felt toward him tingled. Burned. Pulsed.

He handed her an edible flower, which she promptly shoved in her mouth, pretending to be feral. He growled and ate the leaves off the flower fast, vying to finish before she ate the whole thing herself.

Becky picked up a small pile of weeds and turned them into a wreath. She put it on Buck's blond hair shining in the sun. He held onto her hands, with his good hand, and spun her body like a child's, in a circle, her laughter tinkling in the wind.

Maiden Reverse — sniffing the scent of flowers, covered in catnip, already a little slenderer — wove back and forth, pressing herself against Becky's shins. That action wrapped the green, life-filled tendrils around Becky's legs, which were getting tanner, and stronger, as she worked, surveying the cityscape that looked so much more picturesque from above.

Chapter Twenty-Five

Soul Mates

I ain't been to Becky's apartment for a good while now.

I hope I still know her habits well enough. *The liquor store, please, Becky, go to the liquor store today, get your wine. It's your day. Please, don't go with a friend. Just look at what I did for you. Well, if only you knew. You owe me. Look, I lied, so I can support you. Who else has seen your debts, and your trashy reading, your mess, the old clothes you keep around in case you gain weight again? I've seen the bad selfies you don't let anyone see and I don't care.*

There you are! My Becky. Becky, my love. "Hello, how are you?" God, I hope I did that right. I think I've finally got my voice sounding nice and low, after practicing all week to make it resonant.

"Oh, my! You startled me." She's being so polite. She can see I'm a well-dressed gentleman worthy of courting her.

"I must say, you're a beautiful woman. What's inside shows through, you know? You have a profound face. If I was still an artist, I'd ask you to pose for a portrait."

"Oh. Well. Thank you. I do care more about my mind than my appearance. I'm an artist, myself, you see. My name is Becky."

How cute. Now she's blushing, like she knows that was a sort of silly thing to say. She's looking down and back at me, standing a little closer.

I want to talk about her art for hours. She has no idea I've seen every painting in her stack.

"I'm Dave. I like oils best. The new kind that's quick drying." Only kind she buys. That will win me points.

"Me too. I can't believe how long the old kind took to dry. Insane."

"What kind of a crazy world is this, right?"

She has such a lovely laugh. I think it's my first time getting her to do that. I want to make her laugh all her life. I want to help her with her art. Make sure she never has to worry about nothin'.

I like how she lets her arms swing so free. And how she doesn't try to get away. She's acting like she has all the time in the world for me. My attempt at being charming: "This neighborhood is awfully quiet right now, isn't it? It's like it's holding its breath, hushed, listening, to this special moment. Me, talking to you. Not all noisy like the neighborhood gets on Tuesday nights when the recycling bins are out and all the guys are coming around diving into them, right?"

"Yeah, that makes it hard to concentrate. Or sleep."

She's been nodding, and didn't stop nodding when I said that about it being a special moment. She even smiled more brightly then, and softened her eyes. So, I say, "That black market keeps the recycling stations from making as much money as they should. And makes you have to pay more for garbage pick-up." I'm not sure if that came out as romantic as I had hoped.

"I know it's illegal, but I can't blame them. Everyone's got to make money somehow."

She's perfect for me. We share the same values.

She's staring at me. Not sure I like that after all. "You look really familiar."

"Feels like I've known you all my life, too." Yeah, could be that she sees me going through her papers, cans, and bottles every week. Could be that I gave her a fabulous reading. Could be that she's my soul mate and we met before we were born while the angels sang. Nah.

"I've seen you around the neighborhood when I was passing by. I've always been intrigued by the way you walk. How you carry yourself. I've wanted to know what's going on in your head. What your passions are. Your hopes and dreams. I wanted to know what you were like as a baby. Maybe you've seen me, too, and had some thought like that, yourself, for a moment, before moving on to the rest of your life?"

"How wonderful. Yes, maybe I have. I would have that those thoughts, if I'd seen you, I'm sure."

Sure, as long as I wasn't homeless. Then, none of those things matter, do they?

"Would you like to go with me to the new French cuisine restaurant on Franklin?" Did I need to say, "cuisine"? Is that redundant? "They have some organic items on the menu. If you're feeling hungry, that is. If not, I'd be honored to take you another day. Because I'd like to do the three-course meal with you."

"Lovely. I'm famished. You're so right about me. I do like organic – it's just kind of expensive."

"Of course, I'd pay your way, my dear." She's not reacting to that statement like she would have not so far in the past. I thought she'd be getting all breathless about a man who has money.

I walk her to the restaurant I'd seen a flyer for in her bin. She'd marked an organic entree, but thrown into recycling. No doubt this place is out of her range. And if you don't mind, I'm not going to tell you everything right now. I want to concentrate on enjoying my food, for these prices, and getting to know this talented young lady in front of me.

***

I can tell she's taken with me. Her body language shows *definite* attraction. I hate to be indelicate, but so does that scent she's exuding. Listen, my homey, she even reaches out to me and touches my hand when I say, "I hope I'm not keeping you." I hope you're not jealous of Becky.

"Oh, no," she says. "It's *really* nice getting to know you. I'm flattered." Her eyes shine, and when we stand up to go, she gets close to me. Closer than any woman would stand before I got cleaned up.

My breath doesn't smell like alcohol now. Using the shard from the bottle to kill that meanie left me satisfied. I haven't felt like drinking since.

I ask her, "Can I take you out for a nice dinner here again? Just let me know when and I'll make reservations. They have the best Pinot." I stand so straight, almost like Connors used to. But without being such a stiff-ass.

"I was just thinking about Pinot."

Heh heh, I'm sure you were, little missy. "How could anyone like anything else?"

"I don't usually go out with strangers. Your face — I guess you just inspire trust?" Her pupils are huge. She does like me. Maybe she already loves me!

"Do you like the grove? We could share a bottle of Pinot there under the moonlight."

I'm so happy when she says, "That does sound kind of exciting." She looks up at me. I like being taller than her. She looks so cute when she does that.

"I have a fantasy that I find just the right woman, an artist who needs a push to be discovered by the world. Someone I can take care of."

"I thought that was going to be my future. A patron helping out like that. Someone I could love." She looks down. I look down to see if there's something wrong with her shoe or something.

"And?"

"Disaster. I don't want someone's money to sway me anymore. Anyway, I'm self-sufficient, now." Somehow she doesn't seem as much shorter than me as she did. Not as much as I'd like.

"You have something against people with money?"

She nods as she says, "My ex made lots of money. I think he did it in a bad way."

"But. You see bad when you look at me?" I can't wait to hear. Finally, I'm being myself, my true self. No costume needed.

"You're *very* handsome. You have a delightful voice." Funny, her voice imitated the way I talk, when she said that.

"Thank you, darling." Success! All that vocal practice paid off. Her sweet dimples turn into a comma when she smiles.

Her mouth is on funny. I'm not surprised when she looks down, purses her lips and says, "But I should probably go back home now." When she looks up, her eyes are shining, though her eyebrows are raised in a subtle question. "I'm treating the guy I've been spending time with to a movie downtown. It's a kind of a thank you. He helped me get over my fear of heights."

"I *see*."

Well, *that's* rich.

Becky hugs me when we get to her apartment, standing outside her door where she seen me going through her bins. I'm glad I live inside now. I can smell her better. Oooh, I can feel her ribs. So delicate. She's like a ballet dancer. We're breathing in sync.

I kiss her cheek. I'm so glad I'm not a hairy guy. I like feeling my smooth skin against hers. So I can nuzzle better without scratching her. I kiss her on the lips, I use my tongue, I grab her around the waist. I nibble her ear, I pull down her hair at the nape of her neck, and she gasps and grabs me harder, and we kiss so hard our faces almost turn into the same face.

She's breathing so hard I can hardly tell what she says. I notice my cheek is getting wet. When I pull back, I can see a tear. And another one. "Just . . . I'm dealing with my fiancé being murdered. And there's the guy friend I care about. . ."

Well fuck a damn duck.

No doubt she'll paint *him*. In that weird way of hers, with all those transparent layers. And no one will even be able to tell it's him. I will, though. Ah hell, now everything she ever paints I'll probably see him in it. I wanted to see me in her art for the rest of our lives. I could paint her from memory, if I could paint.

I gotta stand back. Got to change the way my smile goes up on the end. Gotta think like I'm her brother. Got to practice. She's like a sister to me. A sister. Not my everything. Not my doll baby. Not my sweetheart of eternity, my soul mate, my all.

She pushes out her lips almost to the edge of hope when she says, "Maybe I'll see you around here? Are you a neighbor?"

"Sure. I know this neighborhood like I know the back of my hand. Even when I wear gloves."

Chapter Twenty-Six

Betrayed

I love Riad Tamir. He's the most bad-ass Rescuer hero of them all. His character in the movie didn't do him justice. They should have picked me to play him. I'd have done a fine job. I have the noble silhouette for the role of unselfishly giving humanitarian aid. Sure, I'm small. But I'm big enough to hold the little victims, comforting them, acting out stories for them. After those goddamn government army guys blast their city, I'd be going in and saving them, and giving them toys, toys, toys! And more toys! And not plastic ones, either. Nope, nope, nope!

All the good people support droning the hell out of that stinking country's government army, and if stupid Russia doesn't like it, WWIII be damned. Who cares what Russia thinks? That bully. I can't stand them. If that's what it takes, that's what it takes to bring those kids freedom from a dictator who uses chemical weapons on his own people. What a monster. A monster made out of dangly bits.

I read newspaper headlines at all the stands lately. Sometimes I even buy the papers. They come in double handy as TP, but damn, we might be going to war any day now. I wonder if they'll call me up. Even if they don't, I'd go. I'd fucking go.

Well, well, what a pretty young lady. Not as cute as Becky. No one is. But oh, she's coming toward me. Got to stand up straight and tall, flash my teeth, they're so white now. She'll like that.

"Well, hello, there." I've got to stress my good points. I'm a little older than her, so I'll go for the look of the wisdom that comes with age. Plus, a dangerous hedonist edge. I think standing askew gives the best impression of that, looking at her with one eyebrow raised. A cigar would help the image. A fedora would be perfect about now.

"Oh, thank you, darling. What's this?" She looks like a wholesome person. The kind I like.

"A flyer about the sarin gas hoax, and the ratline that happens in countries the U.S. overthrows." Wait, what? I wasn't expecting that. Got to get up to speed, here, and put on my thinking cap.

"Thank you, dear."

"I'm sure you're familiar about the whole nonsense about the president using sarin gas on his own people."

"Yeah, I hate that guy for that."

"It was a total lie. It was a false flag the anchors talked up on the news to get people behind ousting a legitimately elected popular leader. Remember Tom Tellen going on about that every day for a month?"

"Well, I don't know. I don't have a TV where I live."

"That was just what the Nevermind told him to say. Their president never used the gas at all, didn't attack the citizens."

"What makes you say that?"

"Check out the proof in the flyer. And the false accusations of mass public hangings?"

"What a bastard, right?"

"But, that didn't happen. Their president's the victim, not the bad guy. He's being slandered. The Nevermind is just really good at covering it up and putting out the faked videos to make people think he did bad things to his people, and then they show Nevermind pictures of the poor kids he's supposedly bombing. Give me a break."

"What! Why would you say such a ridiculous thing? That's absurd." She's not as attractive, actually, as I thought she was. She's got a pretty heavy mustache, to tell you the truth.

"The president was set up. Take it and read it. The flyer shows the details." She does have nice arms, though. Her muscle is flexing nicely as she hands it to me.

"If it's true, why haven't I heard about it on the news?" HaHA!

"Do you follow indie journalists dissecting mass media cover-ups on the internet?"

I didn't even know that was a thing. I've never used the damn thing. But nodding like — of course I do — is the best option. Makes me look smarter than her. Heheh, I should sell my dating secrets. I get the girls every time. I just haven't given it a go with anyone for a long time, other than Becky-wecky.

"A guy told me you'd be a good person to give the flyer to. I mean, I've been giving them out for hours, but he specifically said I should talk to you you about it."

"That's weird as fuck. Where is it? Point him out?"

"Sorry. He wants to be anonymous."

"Freaky." I wonder if it was that guy over there that the other flyer-girl is talking to. Looks like a university professor. Maybe he could tell I'm smart enough to understand. Nice, he's smiling back at me. Or is he smiling at my flyer-girl? I can't tell.

"Some of the people reporting about the sarin false flag got killed for you to be able to read this. Feel free to pass the flyer along. Take some extras and put them around your neighborhood?"

"You're saying — what, exactly?" I feel like I'm made of one giant tear and I need to cry myself out, to get rid of all the toxins inside me, until I'm not there anymore. Goddamn, why aren't men allowed to cry? Why are we supposed to just not care about *shit*? "So, the whole thing about the rebel uprising that we're supporting. Since it all started because he supposedly used sarin gas . . . Then, there's actually no actual humanitarian biggie-big reason for the people there to be rising up against the president? There's got to be lots of other horrible crimes he's committed worse than any other country's leaders, right? Worse than Saudi Arabia, Qatar, all those places?"

"He's not an angel, and there's naturally going to be religious conflict. But people in his country really like him. It's irrelevant to why we're droning civilians, though, in any case. The U.S. isn't getting involved because they feel sorry for his people. Haha, no, not so much. Stealing their resources, more like it, including human resources. Destabilizing the region so the U.S. and Israel and Saudi Arabia can have more power. And killing them all off so the pipeline can go through. And, you know, keep the weapons manufacturers rich with good salaries. And the international banks are always playing around behind the scenes, with the boys who owe them the big bucks. And of course, Wall Street has a hand in it. The elites have their hands in everything."

"What?" I don't know about this chick. I want some of what she's smoking.

"Investors that take down countries to manipulate the market for the sake of investments?" Is that what she meant about Wall Street? My head is spinning. She's saying this stuff like she is a smarter person that me. It sounds like it kind of makes sense. Sheeut.

"France and the UK transfer money into an organization."

Transfer. Organization. What does that even mean? And I always forget, what countries are in the UK? And is it the same as Britain? Is Britain the same as England? Why don't they just call it what it is? Damn, is it Northern Ireland or Southern Ireland that's part of it? So hard to keep straight. Wait, what's she saying?

"The organization isn't actually using the money for humanitarian aid. The money's used instead used to finance the mercenaries, the so-called 'moderate rebels,' that keep the war going on and on. They pretend it's a civil war, but it's run by the intelligence agencies. The 'moderate rebels' are supervised by a British military contractor in Turkey, and funded by the U.S. and the UK."

There she goes again with the UK biz. I don't know which one sounds cooler to say. UK . . . Britain. I do love the sound of those words. London. Hard to say it without an accent. If I was from a foreign country, I'd definitely play up my accent. They sound so sexy. Maybe I should bring in a little English to my voice for this girl. That thing where they leave out the t's is pretty cool.

"The war is given a good spin by the Nevermind branch." I like the Nevermind. They have a great amusement park. I remember when they first got started, and my parents took me to the park. That's where I learned the word "surreal."

Oh, wait, she's still talking. I think I heard her just say something about black budget projects. Does that mean some dollar bills are black? Or one of those budgeting books in black leather. I don't get it. She says, "They've got total control of mainstream news. It's funny, though, how they keep getting their story wrong. Did you see the one yesterday where they were showing a picture of a hacker's computer? Some guy who was supposedly taking down the grid? And the picture was from a video game about the Rescuers."

"Woah. Do they think people just won't notice? Or what."

"I think they want people to see the clues that things aren't what they seem."

"Why? That don't make no sense at all." It's all too much, at the same time, to even try to think of a word that I can leave the t out of. Too much, too much!

"It doesn't seem like it would, does it? It's Alice in Wonderland. They show us what Magickians or Satanists or whatever call predictive programming. Some of them actually think the occult stuff is nonsense. But they still get a kick out of when all the numbers add up into some OCD arrangement. What else are they going to get excited about when having a career means getting a lot of people killed. And, then when 'conspiracy theorists' do forensics on the videos and see the Nevermind made the whole thing up, they can sound ridiculous, and they can also be tracked. Like the ones that watch the big video channel dues, you know those people are in the database big time."

"OK."

"The elites even let their hoaxes fall apart in front of us, and make it obvious to people who take the time to look beneath the surface. They tell contradictory stories on the news that couldn't possibly have happened. I guess they can say it's our fault if they put it out in the open and we don't do something about it. We can't blame them, or something. I'm not sure, really."

This really is Wonderland. It all makes sense though, more than anything ever has in my life before. Not that I remember much of my life. And that's an understatement. But now, I feel like I almost remember more than I did before. Things I can't make out. I must have been off my gourd.

Get outta my head! "You're so pretty. You wouldn't be *lying* to me, would you, smiling at me like that? Are you messing with my head? Hey, I'll bet you are. You leave me alone! Pretty ladies talk to me all the time. Obviously, right? I'm irresistible. I don't have to listen to you." Bullshit bitch.

"I'm sorry. I know it's hard to wrap your head around this." I do like her more when she reaches out and puts her hand on my arm. Ah, that feels so relaxing, the warmth of her hand. I'm breathing slower already. She's not so bad, really. Kind of sweet.

Her mouth is such a nice shape when she talks. "It's the Nevermind, and their dumb Rescuer movie. They're the ones fucking with everyone's mind. It's the news stations making shit up."

"*Dumb!* What are you talking about, dumb? That's my favorite movie. Ever! I love kids. Don't you think the kids deserve toys?" Fucking moron. Why did I even listen to her crap?

"Yeah, kids deserve toys. But that's not the point. Your donations to the Rescuers go to kids being *killed.*"

"*Oh. come on! For Pete Zelite's sake! Killed by who?*"

"By some of the Rescuers."

"I don't believe you."

"It's not all of them. But some of the sneaky ones who work night shifts, man, ya gotta watch out for. They'll send your corpse off in a DieCorp body bag."

Wait, is she threatening me?

"And their buddies, too, the 'moderate rebel' factions, that is, the mercenaries sent in by the CIA, who are all branches of the worst terrorists — you know, in that so-called "civil war" the U.S.

and its allies like Saudi Arabia and Israel and others are supporting? When it comes to the people pulling the strings, it's not about some religion-phobia or racism."

"What's it about?"

"Resources. Putting pipelines through to be more competitive in the market. Profit for Defense contractors and their investors."

"You're saying they're psychopaths?"

"You know, they send the mercenaries and agents over to whatever country they want to overthrow. They sic a gang on them, to destroy the country from the inside. The use organizations to start revolutions here and there. They get the U.S. citizens to get behind the terrorists by tugging on heartstrings through TVs and radios back home, by acting like supporting terrorists is great because they want freedom from a mean ol' dictator. Here's the weirdest thing to me. That a year ago, the terrorists were still supposed to be the ultimate evil. Then, the story switched, and no one comments on it. Surreal."

"Yeah, that *was* weird."

"They use the exported terrorists, and all the other millions of people involved in the operation, to brutalize the person they want to take down and take from. The CIA intimidates the main guys in the construction industry, and they make a union out of it."

"I thought unions were good. You can't tell me you're anti-union."

"But the CIA runs it, not the construction workers. It's good for bidding from 'blah blah blah' that way, and that's how they make their billions." Listen, Interrogator, she's throwing out bunches of letters I never heard of and probably never will again. I wish she'd talk English! Anyway, bidding? Like an auction? Is she just crazy or what?

"How do they get away with it. I don't believe this is happening or Tom Tellen would be talking about it."

"All they need is the Nevermind to put a positive spin on it, piece of cake. All those great scripts for the news anchors with pictures of war scenes — believe me, they're explained it as being just the opposite of what is actually going on."

"Total *Alice in Wonderland*, man." I wonder if she liked that movie. Maybe I could invite her to some kind of surreal movie sometime. They have them at the art museum, from what I understand. I'd buy her popcorn.

"Then, DieCorp shows up."

"You're kidding me. *DieCorp?*"

"Haha, I know. It's a CIA cutout for covert operations. They have contracts, like training the police to set up the system to nab the country's resources with slavery and trafficking, mining, and stuff, and they blackmail everyone who might try to put a stop to it. Not all of the guys in the organization are bad, I think. Just some of them. The Rescuers, land in the war zone, and you get ratlines set up to take out the country's resources."

"A ratline? Like the Nazis? Like smuggling?"

"Moving everything, including taking kids for sex. The kids in the commercials the Nevermind makes bring in big bucks. It's all one trafficking project in the countries the U.S. overthrows. The Brownstone thing that happened, you know? The U.S. presidential blackmail sex scandal with the orphans, the one that was related to the Nevermind branch splitting off? The journalists only found part of what was really going on, back then, and they didn't even publish that for a long time. The thing is, it's even more sinister than they knew. It's just that when witnesses, whistleblowers, journalists, judges, police chiefs, mayors, ministers, and, whatever, who try to expose it, they get suicided. It's bigger than you can imagine."

"But I *want* to imagine it. If it's true. Why?" Oh yeah, the diagrams on the flyer. I forgot about the flyer. Lots of typing there. Words make me a little dizzy. But I like how she's pointing the flyer. I like that she doesn't use fingernail polish. She doesn't bite her nails, either.

"Well, for one thing, look at the path of the pipeline. See, each country along it that resists it gets taken down in order. See there, on the map? The news is all total theater. They make up false flags to pretend the country they want to overthrow has done something terrible, and it's our duty to go make it right, or to defend ourselves against them. Those false flags either didn't happen at all, or they were the reverse of what they told you. The war is nothing like they tell you it is."

Can't. Take. It.

"The pipeline is competing with Russia's. It's balance of power. I mean, don't get me wrong. I love the U.S. But I don't like to see so many people killed in my name, you know?"

"I guess."

"Stopping 'evil dictators' is about going in and taking their stuff, including their people. Like for sex. Including kids."

"What?" God, that gets me in my heart. I thought those guys who did the trafficking got busted a long time ago.

"France and the U.K. were transferring money into the accounts of the Rescuers, but none of it was being used for humanitarian aid."

"That's some wild shit, lady." I hate crying. I'm *not* going to do it. Not. "Have you no patriotism, woman?"

"Look. The flyer shows the URL that explains where all this stuff can be found today. Who knows where it will be tomorrow, if that website gets blasted. If you see anyone with an arm band like mine, you can ask for the flyer of the day. Volunteers keep the URLs updated."

"Is this real?"

"The Rescuers are a media campaign, got it? They're there for the regime change, because that's what the U.S. and its allies like Saudi Arabia want."

"You say that like it's a bad thing. I *love* the Rescuers with all my heart, do you get that, lady? We want to do what the U.S. doesn't want? We don't want to be powerful? That what you're saying?" Is she dim or something? I mean, not that it matters, with tits like that.

"No, I'm not a globalist, who wants to tear down the nation. I'm not betting for the U.S. economy to crash like some of the guys working riots to change the value of stuff on Wall Street. And the bankers and the banks and securities."

"Wait, banks? I'm not following you."

I like feeling her breath on my face when she sighs. "I just want people in our country to be decent to other countries. Doing things in U.S. interests is bad when it's so destructive of so many billions of people, for selfish gain of a few people, who are really international."

"Isn't it important if we see bad being done in another country to stop the dictator doing it? If someone is going to have more oil or natural gas or whatever the fuck it is in a pipeline, wouldn't it be better to be us than some other superpower? Is it bad just 'cause the U.S. wants it?"

"Have you ever yet seen a country that the U.S. intervened in, destroying and installing a puppet dictator, that came out ahead? I mean, look at Vietnam, the U.S. taking the poppy fields, getting the G.I.'s addicted, sending drugs back home in their corpses. And that was just the start. Look at Libya. Don't you see how it leads to extremism instead, and the weapons that are left behind are then used by terrorists to destroy countries?"

"So, you're Islamophobic?"

"No, you're not listening to me, sir. Please pay attention instead of letting emotion screw with your head. So, OK. A security contractor founded the Rescuers. A marketing company run out of New York helped him come up with their brand name. A British PR firm manages them, in conjunction with the Nevermind. They're using other children they 'rescue' for sex trafficking. Normally, they execute the masses who have no use for them, and imprison the rest. The prisoners they take are forced to donate blood. People who have rare blood types are kept alive as long as possible, so they can take as much blood from them as they can. In fact, soldiers, or whoever, rape the women, then kidnap their child to harvest the blood and tissues. Best policy for organ transplants, because the women raise the kids, and when they're needed, the organs won't be rejected, that way, and there's no wait. It's like farming animals, or vegetables for that matter, until it's time for harvest."

"What the fuck, sister? Now, that's just absurd."

But wait a minute. There were those handmade cards Stan gave Becky that were obviously some kind of sick joke. I didn't get it at the time, and obviously Becky couldn't have either. What kind of sick jerk gives his girl cards where there's real blood stains on medical drawings of hearts. Disgusting. Could Stan have known about that kind of shit? I mean, the way people were sneaking around, laughing, stealing people's hearts in those drawings was a pretty weird way to say *I love you*. God, even if he didn't, the thought just makes me want to blow some shit up.

Insane flyer-chick's lucky she's not a dude. I'd deck her right about now. This is just too much. Organ harvesting, that's just the grossest thing I've ever fucking heard. I had no idea anyone did it at all, and she's telling me it's big business? Come off it. She must be on her period.

"It's just how it's done. Don't shoot the messenger. I know it's awful. The wealthy (or bribed) rapists can then go to the ships floating nearby, which have diplomatic cover. They do transplants in the hospitals on board the ships, using their kid's bodily materials. It's hard for decent people to imagine it could be true."

"You got that right. I'd never hurt anyone. It's bizarre to me."

"Human trafficking after a country is taken down is facilitated by some of the UN peacekeepers in the buffer zone. The nasty ones in the bunch use slave labor to dig the gold and lithium and stuff. They loot left and right." She looks pretty upset. But, *really*?

"Come on, tell the truth. Are you some right-wing-nut or something? Do you like men more than women? Or wait, maybe I mean, do you like women more than men? Are you all about guns, guns, guns?" I'll bet you've got a shotgun at home. I'll bet you look tough shooting it. Kinda gives me a hardon.

"I'm not a member of any political party. I just go issue by issue. This isn't about parties or blind loyalty to a candidate, or Identity Politics. It's about people dying. If you don't like guns, why would you want to support the U.S. arms deals with all these countries like Saudi Arabia that kill innocent people with them in their countries? Look at the before and after pictures of the proxy wars, right?"

I'm so confused. "I support arms deals? I don't get it. What's the big deal about the pipeline they want to put through their country? Why does the U.S. want to stop it?"

"Sometimes it's about stopping a pipeline, sometimes it's about forcing a pipeline on them, depends. The pipeline would mean they'd be able to bypass the petrodollar. Gas from Iran could be traded as an alternative currency. It's also one of the only countries left with a state-owned central bank, so the IMF wants to change that."

I have no idea what she's talking about. Now she's showing me more pictures from the countries the U.S. is bombing. God, their faces. I can't handle this. It sounds real. It's logical. Facts, goddamn it. Too many facts!

"My mind hurts." Someone looks at me weird when I say that. I want her to hug me. I want her to show me more pictures. I want her to show me how what she says is true.

"Take a closer look at the flyer. It shows the proof. You can see the photos showing where the canisters were made. The sales receipts. The CIA officer whistleblower's sworn statement. The itinerary for the training camp."

"Does this happen here, too?"

"You bet it does. DieCorp trains some police officers at Green Beret Special Ops training sites in the U.S., especially sheriffs. Like Fort Bragg and Fort Benning. From what I understand, some of them set up sting operations targeting mayors, judges, everybody. Eventually, they're sent off to Kosovo, Bosnia, wherever the UN peacekeepers are stationed."

"A sting? Stinging them? Like a bee? Is this a special pointy weapon, or what?"

Oh, Interrogator. I know you remember all this stuff for me so I don't have to. Thanks for being my backup memory. Because this is too much for one person to take in. Now, she's talking about some company that manages ratlines and my head is spinning. And she's going on about some council that sprays people with viruses from helicopters. What an odd idea. Kind of sounds like a graphic novel. I like those. They're really cool.

And now she's saying something about some kind of railroad that goes underground. It's like the world is shaped different than I thought it was. More folds and tunnels and shit, I guess, because that's a new one on me. I didn't even know that was possible to do, wow, seems like the ground could fall in on you. I ain't riding one of those.

I can't keep up with flyer-girl. I think she knows even more than *I* do! How can she be so smart as to find out the news station was lying? I mean, who would ever think of that? That makes no sense. Wouldn't everyone make them stop once they found out? But she's saying there's a whole internet subculture that knows about lies like this? Keep track of whatever it is she's saying; maybe you can explain it to me later, gator! Haha, they's how I'm going to say bye to you after this. Dig it. But, seriously, people aren't calling the news stations out if they're fibbing?"

What the hell? Oh my God. I can't believe this flyer! She finally shut up and let me actually read the damn thing. So, it actually shows proof here, that the U.S. really faked the whole thing about the dictator using sarin gas? Rescuers and the rebels and the terrorist groups were given sarin and trained by the CIA, Pentagon contractors, and U.S. Special Forces in how to use it. And to pretend it was the dictator who did it."

And here it says there's this company was caught getting people to donate organs when they shouldn't. And trafficking in the ladies of the nighty-night, if you know what I mean. So, this citizen journalist has put together the evidence with the help of lots of folks sending information to him online. Wow, what a cool thing to do: figure out the truth and share it for folks to spread around. Says: *Some members of DieCorp train some of the policemen to steal from the countries where they support the terrorist "rebels."*

Oh, God. My stomach hurts. I wonder if they harvest stomachs from dying people. Ugh. Mine feels like it just shrunk enough they wouldn't find it. I remember something about a police chief killing people for organs in Moldova a long time ago. I think it was called DieCorp. I thought it was just those few guys. I didn't know it was going on in droves like this. Shit! "Yes, give me more flyers. I can't talk to people about it good as you can, but."

Goddamn! So, I'm sure most of the guys working at those organizations are trying to just do regular jobs, and they have idea the weirdos trafficking. I don't think I ever used that word until today. Trafficking. I just thought it mostly when I was walking across a street. Or how loud it was over my bridge.

So if this is really what's going on, it looks like it's not just a few criminals doing it on their own. It's like the web that holds the world together. All this shit done by DieCorp and all those other organizations working together is spun by the Nevermind. They made going to war seem like it's all necessary to do if we're good people. They make us believe lies. That way, everybody's all calling for saving the poor people by droning them.

Oh, she's waiting for me to say something smart. "I know about Iran-Contra and Mena Airport and heroin from Afghanistan and shit. So, hm. So, tell me if I've got this. They want people to be all, *We support all this so we can feel self-righteous and good about ourselves about all this humanitarian aid and policing the mean dictators.*"

"Pretty much."

"The world is worse than I knew." Stay out of my eyes, sweat! God damn it. How did I not know this shit all this time? I can't believe all the big guys know this is going on and they don't blow the whistle. Or maybe they have been and I just haven't been going to the internet or whatever she was talking about.

The little boy coming up behind flyer-girl has the audacity to yell at me. "Hey, man, don't kick over all the trash cans, eh? Someone got to pick that shit up."

"Oh, go jump off a bridge."

"Hey!"

"What, you're scared to? I'd do it. Look, I'm going to jump down from this here tree." I've never climbed a tree so fast in my life. It's like I'm tearing into it like I'm killing a dinosaur. Or some shit. I don't know. "I don't know!"

Ugh, landing on the sidewalk knocked the wind out of me for a minute, there. But ol' Dave's not done in, yet. Not done in.

I can't stand it. I've never smeared mud all over myself until now. But now I look like a warrior.

Yes, I'm dancing, *yes*, I'm climbing up on recycling bin, *yes*, I'm shouting, "The humanity! It's tearing me apart!"

I'm sorry, Mr. Interrogator, wherever you are, if you're even listening anymore. If you ever were. If you even exist. I don't know what to believe about *anything* any more.

I don't know why you listen to me. How you listen to me. Why you do, if you do. People tell me I just think you listen, because I'm cray cray. But if you are listening, please. I can't take this mind-fuck. Stop listening if you're not going to tell me what to do. Tell me what to do

Chapter Twenty-Seven

Freak Lord

Having gotten the address of the Experience Room from Stan's laptop, Nancy wasted little time. Or did she? She ground her teeth and bit her fingernails while she rode the bus. Why was she always napping, unable to handle her life, getting overwhelmed and getting too drunk to remember what took her down? Well, of course, there was an easy answer to that. She'd been purposely traumatized since youth and trained to dissociate in response.

She closed her eyes and leaned her head against the bus window. She wanted to eat, to drink, to dance, to have sex with a random stranger, to go to a movie and stay in the theater all day, re-watching it until she fell asleep. But sleep seemed to be a joke in her life. She sleepwalked. She slept so fitfully, she kicked off everything in her whole life, her whole being, her whole past, present and future. Linearity was irrelevant. She wanted life to be simple. She wanted to be good. She wanted love. Honor. A legacy of sweetness beginning with her move to the porch.

Maybe having a baby would work. A little darling she could tell fake stories of her life to, so she would love her always. That, or swallow a bottle of dopamine supplements and die in the process of becoming her own Heaven, her own sudden belief in a god, in angels, in classical music wafting from the skies. No, music changing into music more to her taste quickly, before she got bored. Music with cellos, a bit of nihilism. No, not nihilism. This was about her fantasy of feeling ecstatic. Nihilism was just how she felt every day. Sure, it made grunge, metal, punk, and heroine cool sound good. Gave it that distortion edge. But no, if she was feeling heavenly, she'd probably be able to handle classical music like she used to when she still believed she was a good person.

She missed teaching piano. She thought about how the students must feel betrayed when she stopped showing up for regularly scheduled classes. At least there was the darling anonymous donor who left the money in her pocket she woke up to under the bridge.

She looked around. Some people on the bus were wacked. But most of them looked normal. Living regular lives. Why did she hang onto the habit she'd gotten used to her whole life, since childhood, of ignoring details that didn't make sense? Trying to ignore any cognitive dissonance? Even though somehow it felt useful. Necessary. She liked to tell herself it was even productive in some way she didn't understand. Yeah, and she was the woman who told herself wine was good for anti-oxidants and chocolate was good for magnesium. Behaving that way was still wrong. She'd been trained that way, to ignore cognitive dissonance. But now she was free of the Nevermind and she should be able to think logically. She resolved to become more present. To not sleep away her life. To get with the program. To make a difference. Now.

She had to start being honest with herself. She'd always told herself wearing a burn mask was only to protect herself from surveillance, but was it also to cover her intense shame? How horrible a person she'd been molded into? She told herself moving across states to make friends with a woman she'd never heard of, for no discernible reason other than being told to by a stranger, was rational. She pretended to believe Becky loved the real her, even though she'd given her no chance to know who she was, and that they were best friends. And if Becky did know what Nancy had done, whom she'd killed for the Nevermind, she'd hate her as much as Nancy hated herself.

Nancy had no one. She just couldn't admit it. If Becky, and her landlady, knew the truth, Nancy would be utterly alone, which felt like acid scalding her skin. She had no community. No one she could talk to about what she knew about the world because of her past, but everyone else around her was too brainwashed by the news to see. And community was what she wanted more than anything else in the world.

Looking away from weird things about her life was not healthy. Dissociating into alcohol and sleep. Walking away from anything that made no sense to her. Sliding sideways into the arms of nothingness and illogic, covering up her own clues and failing to put pieces together. Instead, blocking out the pieces. Just looking straight ahead at what other people were doing wrong. Ignoring the strangeness of her own psyche. Sure, she'd been trained that way. But, now, she was free.

She got off the bus and wandered around, putting printed packets about the Experience Room in as many places as she thought she could get away with. She didn't have time to wait for the mail to deliver them. She walked to the Child Protection office. She told them what time to meet her at the huge Experience Room building, so many people could go in together. She figured once she went in, if anyone was there to catch her, or if she showed up on surveillance tapes, the codes would be changed by the Agents and there wouldn't be another chance for anyone to observe.

#

In the parking lot was an entry to drive down into. But it was only accessible after putting in a code. She tried all the codes she'd been given, including the one marked: "Entry." What if none of the codes worked and all the people she'd just given packets to couldn't get in, and had no reason to believe her? She parked down the street and walked back to the building. She couldn't tell if anyone was there. She'd chosen 5:00 in the morning in hopes it would be in sleep mode rather than entertaining experiencers. There were no windows. It was so large, it not only had a front and back site, it had an inside too. It could be empty, or thronging.

The building was nondescript: grey industrial walls behind a spiked black fence. The kind that would puncture anyone trying to go in or out, after tearing them up with razor wire. She sure hoped the codes worked. If all those people showed up and she couldn't get in, that would be embarrassing.

She figured not too many people she'd given the packets to would show up, considering they'd be citizens expected to mess with government business, getting involved in something nasty that had nothing to do with them, taking the risk of being shot at, being called traitors, being blackmailed, themselves. Still, wouldn't *someone* want to help if they knew there was sexual slavery going on in the neighborhood?

She tested it first. Figured she'd try all the codes to the door if need be. The code marked Entry worked to get into the building. But she closed the door again. She didn't want to go in alone. She was relieved to know that whoever had given the codes to her knew the procedure correctly.

She climbed a tree to wait until the crowd showed up at the allotted time. She thought about what might happen to someone who turned up. Nancy could be responsible for his murder. She wanted to go back to the places she'd taken the packets. She wondered if someone on the list had some kind of business with the Agency on the side. They could snitch and an Agent could walk up and take her in. Torture her to learn everything she knew.

She waited forty minutes. No one came. She'd hoped they could free someone from the Experience Room together. No one official would do it. No one was coming to help her. Was it up to her? What could she do alone?

She opened and closed the door softly, took off her shoes, and silently walked through the hallways. She peered around corners before turning them. She barely breathed. She walked through the halls, wearing theatrical make-up instead of her mask, and a wig she hadn't worn in a long time. In fact, she'd grabbed it from the other side of the bridge, since her neighbor seemed to have abandoned the boxes.

She peered around corners, heading away from the sounds of distant footsteps, and vague voices. She had her story ready if discovered: she was there to have oral sex with a giant. Having someone with gigantism there was inevitable, as giants had become such fetishes after the HGH trend at the time the Nevermind were legislated into existence in the 80's. Back when life took a turn no one saw coming.

Her cover story was that she'd been given the FS code by Stan a couple weeks before, and had been told to go on in if he was late, since he wasn't sure of how his timing would work out that day. In reality, she didn't have a plan. She had the codes. That was enough.

Room after room. Each one had a label. Girls. Boys. Death. The FS code worked for none of them. Until she came to the one called Freak Show. That's what she had suspected. The same code to the Freak Show project folder on Stan's computer worked for the pod the Freaks were being held in. Of course.

Specialty sex to satisfy powerful people. She'd been forced to recruit people to sell their wards, from hospitals to caregivers, parents to adoption agencies, to the Nevermind, to use as blackmail and bribery to keep the horrible secrets about how coups worked, something all PR for the elite required. The people with deformities didn't have good lives, she'd told their families. Parents could make money by selling their disabled children. The Freaks would even have love lives, which they'd have no chance of otherwise. Perhaps the parents could even be persuaded to break them in, for extra money.

The Freak Show would be used for the sake of intelligence, for the sake of the country, to curry favors, to blackmail and bribe, to reward, to fund, everything that made America great. Policing the world. Taking down dictators who "gassed their own people," who "hated American's freedom," who needed to be "stopped from being evil." America had a "duty to save countries from their dictators." And sometimes there had to be casualties. Wasn't it better to save a country and sacrifice a Freak who probably had no idea what was even happening at all? That's what she'd been aggressively trained to think (or pretend to think) since childhood.

But what was it about, really? The dirt on people who enjoyed the Freaks and gold-diggers, children and adult slaves, living, dying, and already dead bodies, in the designated special pornographic worlds inside the Experience Rooms could be used against them if they ever tried to speak the truth or vote their conscience. For instance, to keep them from talking about how the Rescuers were just the opposite of who they were said to be, how they were really mercenaries playing a role for the news stations to disseminate. How they in fact killed the children after filming the toy scenes, and raping them with knives. How those scenes were sold to trusted subscribers, through people like Stan, to fund the Nevermind. How those subscribers, and those Experiencers, were then beholden to keep their silence about the reality of the Rescuers and how DieCorp and so many other organizations working together internationally regularly trafficked in humans. Because the public must never know. And the public was gullible enough to never grasp it, because they were good people, and couldn't fathom how psychopaths thought.

The halls echoed silence. Would there be caretakers of the victims in the building, assuming anyone slept there? Was everyone on a different wing of the building, at the moment? Her skin felt like one big goose bump.

She tried the next code on the short list with various doors, but none of them worked along that hall. She heard people walking around in another part of the wing. She tried to look like a sexual predator herself. The right way of bending forward. No, maybe it was bending back. She got tickled at herself for bending back and forth, trying to find the right stance. Breathe. It helped her breathe.

She looked in the corners. No visible cameras. Cameras would surely mean death if anyone in charge figured out who she was.

She went back and put her ear to the thick door labeled Freak Show. Perhaps it was this very room some of the deformed people she'd recruited when she was young had been taken to. Some of the people had been amorphous, similar to The Blob, something she'd never heard of happening to people until that time. She wondered what sort of chemical had been in use that had done that to the poor babies. She knew The Freaks didn't just stay in the state they were recruited in. They were sent around on a circuit to a limited number of locations for the most sought-after people with dramatic deformities concentrated the possibilities. This kind of secrecy was not possible just anywhere.

She had recruited three Freaks during her life. They surely couldn't recognize her if they were there. What if they did, though? Would she turn away? Would she begin to forget? Split into pieces and hide in the dark spaces in between?

She slowly opened the amazingly thick, sound-proofed door. She missed the old days of carrying a gun. That would have come in handy. But she did have a knife. And not a small one.

When she peeked in the door, she wished it was a sword.

A wild-haired woman with dwarfism and some something that looked like translucent sacs sticking off of her body, showing external organs through the skin, ran screaming at her, so fast Nancy could barely catch her breath. Shining teeth bared below her. Long, colorless, matted hair flew, whites of the eyes showing all the way around the pupils, leaping up to her face, and biting her on the cheek.

Nancy jumped back in pain and held the Little Person by the shoulders on the ground, pressing her into stability, dodging her punches. The Little Person suddenly flew through the air backward. The dog collar around the woman's thick neck led the way, and she was jerked back into place by a man sitting in a chair. He didn't look up. He applied a shock. She jumped into the air, screeching, and was shoved into a bean bag chair by a naked, warty man, who looked very much like a giant toad.

The man's face was covered by his large-brimmed red straw hat with silk flowers. A long-haired 600-pound woman with four eyes waddled sensually to him and lifted up the man's hat a bit, and stroked his hair, putting her little fingers directly into his ears, while licking her lips, then slathered his face with her tongue, turning her eyes toward Nancy. Nancy suddenly recognized the man in the hat: Congressman Rawlings.

Within moments, he had graciously bowed off the overweight woman and was embracing two people with gigantism, surely from the HGH craze that happened around the time the Nevermind was created. Nancy couldn't tell at first if they were male or female, old, or young. Just the overhanging brows, the outsized hands and feet. The Congressman told everyone to take his seat, and be quiet while he talked to Nancy. Two moaned, reaching their hands toward him as if being pulled away from their mothers. The Freaks retreated to sit on the pillows along the walls. Some rocked, some chatted, others laughed, and one curled up in a ball.

A door opened on the opposite wall, and a pinhead entered the large Room. Nancy spied inside that room a bed, the walls painted gold, and a pyramid design along the side. All along the walls of the Room were doors, with names listed, including Giant Nate, and Little'un. Another simply said Restroom. Some had stickers on them, but Nancy had no time to examine.

"Can I help you? This room is mine for the night," he said, nodding and jiving, slowly, very slowly, lifting his head to look at her. He looked like a king.

Nancy took the risk. He could have paid for the room. But her sense, from what he'd said before, was that he'd broken the rules, had gotten the code and the location from surveilling Stan and was taking advantage of it without anyone but her, and the policemen liaisons, realizing it. And they probably didn't care. They'd probably hit him up for the code, themselves. In fact, that could be their footsteps, as they enjoyed the goodies for free as well.

Some of the undesirables nodded and squealed.

One of the women was chanting something in the corner, with a desperately peaceful look on her face. Nancy went over to her and put her hand on her head. Nancy, crying, bent down and kissed the center of her skull, and patted her softly as she walked away, the woman's forehead furrowing as she remained focused on the mantra.

A young boy with a hair tale scooted across the floor, grinning at her, wild eyed. She laughed and bent down to him, grabbing his hand as he slid sideways, both of them giggling. She wiped away tears as she looked back up at the Congressman. What beautiful people were in the room.

The Congressman was not beautiful.

He bashed her across the forehead with a thick book.

She saw red of the book's cover coming toward her. She mostly remembered red, and then it was all over, and she had him pinned under her, on the floor, her knife at his throat. She narrowed her voice at him. "What are you doing here? The Nevermind is not happy. Not happy at all."

He laughed beneath the blade. She pushed the edge of the knife against his forehead. He raised his eyebrows, lifting the blade. His eyes, in partial shade, held her attention, but her hand had no mercy. He grunted, rolled her over, grabbing the knife, overpowering her forearm, and pushed it toward her sternum.

Red heat inflamed her cheeks. Thing was, she had to pick her revelation. Only one revelation to the press could be the big blast. The world could handle only one at a time. A moment on the news was enough for an underground woman to pull off. She was only one person. She pressed against him, and he didn't budge. Pure muscle, in spite of his gray hair. He leered as he looked around the room. "My pretties," he said. "All of you are pretty. I love you all. Come snuggle with us."

He lifted the knife from her throat, as if he were dancing, perhaps in a Spanish style, with great flair, and clicked his heels together, standing straight, arched back a bit, one hand up in the air, and twirled. He sang something she didn't understand. A line or two. He never put away the knife. It glinted as he turned, pointing at one freak and then suddenly moving to point to another, then another. The Freaks seemed to not notice the danger, just watched the dancing movement. He was angling the knife just right for her to see, as he peered over his shoulder at her, his mouth sharp in the corners, his lower lip straight across but curving up drastically, showing his lower teeth and the pink gums scalloping them.

She played along with the dance so as not to disturb the people in the room. She moved in sync with him, watching his eyes to see if he was about to lunge and kill her. She watched out of the corners of her eyes the other people. There were half a dozen, from the person with dwarfism to the person with gigantism.

She was glad none were ones she'd recruited, like The Blob, who wasn't there among them. She was probably in Washington D.C., she was such an intense phenomenon, she would be in highest demand. If she was even alive after all this time. Nancy hoped not. A life like that, whether she'd interfered with her or not, must be hell.

The Blob had looked at her with the most profound eyes, her pupils large and gaze soft. It had been horrible.

Was she willing to tell Brandon to release the images of The Blob and the newscaster? To destroy the poor woman's life even more? If she had that kind of awareness. Nancy hadn't been able to tell how cognizant she was, and if she had anything resembling speech. If she was aware of her reputation, was Nancy ready to grind her down into the ground of embarrassment, her images famous at their most debased? Would the woman rather remain hidden from the shame forever? If she was alive, unless someone had sprung her, she was no doubt still being used, and kept in a pod like this, away from awareness of anything in the outside world.

Nancy had laughed hysterically once when her handler had said, "How dare you insult her. Her actual name is Sum Wat Blobbee."

Nancy decided she was willing to sacrifice The Blob once again . . . assuming her targets at the news station didn't go for the blackmail. If they disregarded her deal, video clips of them with The Blob would be released by Brandon onto YouTube. They'd have to deal with the personal embarrassment. The shame of being seen having enthusiastic sex with someone most people would consider astonishingly ugly. Inhuman. Even demonic.

But it wasn't what she wanted. Yes, she wished she could free the Freak Show. She didn't *want* to walk away from them. Not by any stretch of the imagination. She felt ashamed of the thought this was like being at a dog pound. But she had to make a hard choice. She'd been trained well in how effective blackmail could be. Would it matter whether she exposed the Freak Show if she didn't free the world from the impending WWIII instead? If the Rescuers hoax won over everyone's minds, and they supported imposing a no-fly zone, and declaring official war, Russia would retaliate. There were only a few days left to change people's perceptions, to overcome the propaganda. It was her, and Brandon and the other indie journalists, against the entire war machine, against people who had jobs and assets in the Defense Industry companies who wanted to make money through endless war.

A boy with a humongous head and rubbery lips came up to her and tugged on her shirt. She reached down and touched his round cheek. She knelt to him and hugged him gently. He laughed melodically and pulled away, throwing his arms up in the air and spinning around, yelling. His tongue was red. Looked like a lollipop.

When she looked back at the Congressman, he was shirtless. He was holding his arms out and curved forwards, holding the knife in one hand, and dancing elegantly back and forth over the Freaks, his muscles shining as if he'd only recently been oiled. He looked impeccably proud.

"You have no fear of the Nevermind?" she asked him. He'd overridden their rules. He'd gone around them to get to The Freaks for free.

Her exotic make-up, black dress and black wig that he'd seen her in last were no longer there. She narrowed her eyes, trying to ascertain if he had put the pieces together and guessed who she was. Maybe he had learned that she had no authority over him at all any more. And in fact, should be reported to the Agency immediately. This was just about right for spooks during Halloween season.

He sighed, shaking his head as if talking to a cute little girl who didn't understand anything. "I'm no longer bribable. What more could they offer me? I've found Heaven. With my Freaks. I even have the code to change the code if I want to. I've become king."

She filled her voice with grit. "You're saying you've ruled out blackmail? Do tell, Lord Ruler."

"We all know sex trade is the warp and woof of society. People involved in it protect each other. Anyone going down takes more down, right?"

True. The Nevermind had nothing to gain by exposing him anyway. They'd be disabling themselves. They'd have to kill him instead. But who would be that upset about the monetary loss other than Stan?

"Look at what's come out about all sorts of people already. People just get on with their lives unless the issues are what the cool kids are raving about, at the moment. It's not trending. It's far too similar to the 'scandals' that turned out to be nothing lately. Just a bunch of nutters reaching too far to try and see a pattern. Now, anyone who exposes anything resembling their overwrought accusations will be laughed down."

She knew he was right. That was the worst of it. Reason trumped anger. The stupid scandal he was referring to was in fact real, but had been picked by the Nevermind as the most absurd-sounding one to publicize to make conspiracy buffs go wild. That would make people interested in truth look insane. The scandals had been investigated by the perpetrators and found to be innocent. Then, of course, the PR company had hired an actor to blow up the building where the trafficking was going on, and make it look like he'd been driven mad by the conspiracy buffs and their "unsubstantiated" claims.

On the other hand, Nancy had the recording of the entire conversation happening with Rawlings in her pocket.

He turned to her, still hazy, his jowls relaxed and flopping. He held his arm out in a magnanimous gesture with the knife. Then, he gracefully danced his other hand into a pack next to him. He withdrew a gun. He pointed it at her.

She started to run to the door. But how could she put in the long code to get out in time?

"Move and I shoot." He twirled the gun. He put the knife in his mouth. The crimson blade clashed with the red straw hat. But it went well with the pink flowers.

A lion-headed woman sat alert. Her muzzle chewed. She made a grinding, growling noise.

If he killed Nancy, would the country's citizens have a chance to find out about the Rescuers? If they didn't learn about the real role of the Rescuers, how would everyone in the world fare when the U.S. went to war with Russia?

The Freaks gathered toward him, standing in front of him, glaring at her, growling, sticking out tongues, turning and licking him. He stood on top of the chair and raised his hand with the knife high, breathing deeply, holding his chin high. The gun was still on her.

"I've been taking a different Freak home with me each night during beddie-bye time. Showing her around. The lights. The city. Fancy drinks. Fancy drugs. Fancy clothes and mirrors, music, dancing, fucking with style, with colored lights in a canapé bed."

The Freaks cheered.

One snarled. Was he about to bite Nancy? She knew if the Congressman said the word, they'd attack her. She'd have no chance to even begin pressing the code to get out or to lock the door back again. They'd rush out the door with her, pushing her out of the way, before she could lock them in. She'd be devoured, bones and all with those giants' teeth. No one would have to know.

"Listen to me. Just for a minute. I promise I'm telling you the most important thing you'll hear in your lives. You're being held slaves. Being treated like this isn't normal. He's not being nice to you. You're not supposed to be OK with this. It's not like other people live and it's not how you have to live. You're being used. People pay to do what they want with you," Nancy said. "He's just getting you for free. He doesn't love you more than the other people who rent you out. He just has figured out the code to get in. That's all. Most people are not slaves. I want to help you be free like them, if I can. I don't how. I don't know when. I want you to all be able to leave. But."

"Like The Blob did?"

"Free like Little'un was last night?"

"Snacks? Dwinks?"

"Tell us the code to get out!"

"Let us out!"

"Take us with you!"

The giant that Nancy decided was male grunted and turned to the side, shyly retying his animal skin loin cloth.

A little girl who looked to be around nine covered her face. When she removed her hands, Nancy saw how she was smoking a joint. Children were often made into drug addicts to confuse them and make them less credible if they revealed how they had been raped. Nancy thought about how Oedipus Complex theory had been developed by Freud to cover up child abuse

"I can't promise I can rescue you later. But what if you didn't have to have sex unless you wanted to? That's how most people's lives are."

"Oh, are you playing Rescuer now?" the Congressman taunted.

Lion sprung, roaring, and grabbed the Congressman around the neck. She bit his jugular and held on.

The Congressman knifed the lion-woman. She continued to hold on with her locked jaws as he stabbed.

Both fell into each other's laps, dead at the same moment. The Freaks screamed.

"I love you," yelled one of them to Nancy. Another held out her arms towards her as if to a rescuing mother. She wanted to be a true rescuer to them.

But she ran to the door and put in the code. One of them, wailing, pulled her hair. "Take us with you!" Another threw himself to the floor and grabbed her ankles, sliding across the floor with her.

Nancy slid through, kicking them off, kicking one in the face, pressed the door against their arms until they squealed and had to pull them in. She slammed the door, and heard them wailing. Calling, "Miss! Miss! But we love you! You can't leave us here! We're *slaves*!"

Chapter Twenty-Eight

Have You Heard the News?

Wednesday

Nancy organized the video material she had gotten from Stan, adding in with what she had shot herself. There was so much to work with, and she had to make a succinct, persuasive, clear, shocking, horrific, yet doable segment for the news. Turned out the sneaky bastards had gone through France to do the operation to avoid the finder — having to go through the Senate intelligence officers. By early the next morning, Halloween, Nancy had worked diligently, drinking coffee to stay awake, and had deftly edited the most important scenes of two projects. The news director's involvement in the Freak Show was ready for the internet, and the PR firms' fake stories about the Rescuers was ready for network TV. The choice of which would go public was up to the TV station. One thing she'd learned well during the course of her life was the tactic of blackmail.

She didn't know how long the TV segment would be allowed to run before someone shut it down. Blackmailing the key players might work, and it might not, considering there were so many people at the station who could overpower them and stop it from airing once it began. So, the first images had to be potent. They would be going viral, even on the social media accounts of people who had refused to believe the stories when they were on the internet only, and people all over the world would wake up. She would give the news director the gruesome choice of which one to enthusiastically report during breaking prime-time news. TV viewers could only take in so much at a time. Their minds were going to be boggled either way the news director's choice took the future of the world.

Becky would have been murdered that very night. Someone had the heart to attack Stan more violently than she would ever do — other than when she had been ordered by the Nevermind when she was out of her mind. Stan's murder broke the case. Ha, the *case*, as if she, an escaped agent gone rogue, was working an official case and being paid by anyone to complete it. Everyone was working to *stop* her solving the case.

Much as she wanted to get Becky fighting for truth, she knew that could darken her life. No, Nancy would do it alone. She wanted to let Becky live simply, basking in the sunshine, like a child painting. She wished she could continue to be her friend. She'd have to flee and go even further underground, and never contact her again, once the day was done, assuming she survived and remained free.

In her favor were her lack of traceable identity, her skills at evading capture, and her contacts that could help her leave the country immediately after, where she would pursue more surgery to make her look so different no one could possibly guess who she was. She would probably have to do the surgery herself this time, for monetary reasons. This surgery would mean basically beating herself around the face so violently with a tire iron she'd change its structure forever.

The bus delivered her to the door of the news office that afternoon. It was going to be a momentous day.

***

The VIP tour was only sixteen dollars. She watched the status update for whether the day's breaking news would be incendiary enough to cancel the weekly tour of the station, as that happened relatively often. Back-up plans roiled through her mind in that contingency. But this was too perfect. The news director was the one who gave the tours, and they did the tour on the cusp of the evening news going live.

The station wasn't far from Becky's apartment and the church. Her plan was in full fruit.

The food court, international flags, wax figures of newscasters, and the new station's logo hanging from the skyscraper's ceiling didn't impress her. She did like learning on the tour about how the curved walls amplified the sound. That was interesting.

The tour guide pointed out the social media producers' desks, the floor manager, the teleprompter operated with a pedal, the reporters' earpieces, news editors working at their desktop computers, listening to police scanners for breaking news, the backup control room for special effects, the technical director, the newsroom control room. Tom Tellen was there, looking smug, drinking coffee from a Rescuer mug.

She recognized the technical director as she passed him by, but her theatrical make-up meant he'd never know her. When the tour ended, the crowd wandered out. Some stayed to thank the news director, who had been their guide. She waited until she was the last straggler before she went up to him.

Everything she'd learned about being a law-abiding citizen, a nice person, polite and sweet — it all railed at her with every step into the room where the news director stood. She stood against him, holding a pen in her fist and pressing the tip against his back.

Balanced on her toes, she leaned in, to whisper, "Turn around and pretend to recognize me as an old friend. In fact, you do know me. You just don't know it."

He did so, hugging her, whispering, "Do you realize how many people work here who can take you down in seconds? How good the security is?"

"You're going to want to hear what I have to say."

He sighed, and nodded.

"Brandon is watching the evening news. If the anchorman doesn't read the script I have prepared here, and show the video about the Rescuers, Brandon's going to release an old video of you and Agent Angela Ageless, when she was underage, holding The

Blob while you were having sexual relations. Obviously, it will go viral. It's up to you. Your choice. Which will it be?"

He whispered, "Goddamn it! Not The Blob. Jesus Christ. Everything is already pre-set for the news. Just like I said in the tour. It's all robots these days. I can't do that. There's no way."

"You have to make it work or Brandon will release the videos and will keep doing so. You know how well protected he is. It can't be impossible. The cameras can keep the same setting. The time slots for reports can remain the same. The video that's shown behind the anchorman is all that needs to be changed. Put this on the teleprompter. Change out the backup script on his desk. Or, your face will be synonymous with Blob-lover."

"Oh my God. No."

"The story to be released on the news, if you choose that option instead, has nothing to do with you. Purely world events. You'd be remembered as the station bold enough to tell the truth. I have material just as humiliating on producer, floor manager, and the technical director. Gold-digger snuff. And Freak Show stuff. If they don't believe you, show them these photos." She opened up the folded printed pictures, showed him one after another, then folded them back and put them in his pocket.

"Fuck! Put those away before someone sees them."

"Get the producer to call the anchor on the red phone. The show is starting. Just show however much of the video fills in the space already allotted to the video segments behind the anchor. It won't matter if some of what I've prepared is cut off when the camera is programmed to switch back to the anchor. Arrange it now."

"How do I know you won't release that shit anyway?"

"I promise I won't. It's true, something might possibly come out eventually about the Freak Show. Of course we know the FBI and the NSA collect information on people to blackmail them, before they're allowed to have jobs like yours. And the Nevermind has plenty of evidence stored on Brandon's secure server, sent to him from a non-registered machine." She liked to keep him off-guard, wondering if she was an Agent acting on orders, or gone rogue, or not an Agent at all.

"It's not possible to make the changes you ask for."

"Never fear. Your connection, and the technical director's, and the producer's also will be destroyed. If the news segment goes well. You have my word. What else could I possibly give you?"

"You really think you can get away with this?"

"I'm going to walk out of here a free woman and no one but you will know I spoke to you. If you get me arrested, think of your legacy. Is Blob Lover what you want your friends, family, fans, and haters remembering you for? Brandon is watching. You sucking an elbow shaped like an umbrella and being humped by a neck that's part shoulder — that's about to go on his website in an hour unless you make it work. People archive those shows. They upload them. The images will become who you are. More than anything you ever have said on the news."

Nancy curtseyed and left.

***

Entering a carefully chosen restaurant nearby, Nancy went into the bathroom and changed her face. When she emerged, a little boy pointed at her, exclaiming to his family, "Face! Face!" and shook his head. But no one paid attention.

Nancy winked at him and made funny faces through the theatrical make-up, but it only made him cry.

She watched the evening news on the TV blaring in the corner. Then, she realized it was showing a different station's news. She walked up to it and flipped to the station she'd just toured. She was ready to defend her right to watch it with a fist fight if needed. She had to see history go down.

"Hey!" said the only other woman dining alone.

"Hey," said Nancy. She squeezed the muscles in her face at her, reddening, bringing out veins in her forehead.

The woman looked down at her salad.

The waiter came up to her, and Nancy said in a quick monotone she'd have a salad, and that's it, and put her hand up over one eye like a blinder, and he got the hint to leave her alone.

Everything seemed normal. The anchors talked as usual about crime and weather, sports and a celebrity scandal. *The Rescuers* movie had made more money than any had ever made before, and the franchise, with video games, comic books, costumes and toys, was an equal opportunity employer, leading to more jobs in the U.S.

The anchors discussed the escalating problem of "fake news sites," which major search engines and social media sites were now refusing to monetize or let be posted online. The main focus, however, was the impending decision to go to war in the next week. The newscasters were adamantly for it. Something had to be done to police the world so little children the Rescuers were taking care of could be safe.

They featured a segment of video showing Rescuer heroes, Dayan and Riad, giving children toys with money people were donating, interviews with people about their austerities they went through to give the children vaccines, food and warm clothing. And Rescuer action figures and dolls. The heroes giving out their own dolls elicited shrieks of excitement.

"The hero found this girl, huddling in a pig sty, afraid of the terrorists. Her name is Nao. He took her to his Rescuer camp and got her all cleaned up. All cleaned up. Just look."

A girl in a shiny purple dress stood outside a billowing domed tent, her hair blowing, obscuring her features, teasing the viewer, as she came in the frame, zooming in on her face. She flipped her hair out of her eyes, which were huge, ringed with long black lashes. The effect was startling. Being confronted with such sudden innocent beauty, looking straight into the camera couldn't help shaking people to the core. It was the best trick the news had. And they were tricky.

The regular programming was interrupted gracefully with the breaking news segment. Her thoughts raced as she processed what was happening. Was this it? She waited for the words of her script to come forth. All the little bits and pieces floated through her head, such as, "While previous reports have claimed that the Rescuers were there for humanitarian aid to clean up after the destruction by terrorists, new video and photographic evidence proves they are in fact, NATO-sponsored terrorists themselves. They have participated in genocide, wiping out an entire city and much of the country. There are few people there for them to save at this point. There are only a few citizens left there, and they are only there because the Rescuers won't let them leave, using them for human shields, for organ harvesting, and for sex. Especially the children they have been recorded giving gifts to. You have been shown faked videos to give the impression there are many people there, and to put the Rescuers in a good light. Seeing this evidence should change your minds about the need to go to war. Please look at the evidence with an open mind."

An anchor in the station introduced, Tellen. He said Tellen was on location at the Rescuer camp where Nao had been taken.

The camera panned on the scenery, looking like it had been, all along, on the news when they showed scenes from there. Nancy felt crazy. She imagined how much crazier everyone else was about to feel if this was how they were going to deliver her script. Fucking mind-boggled.

Nancy knew the reporter wasn't really far away, in the country the Rescuers were destroying. The country had been Balkanized, and most people in the world didn't even try to remember its name or location. But she certainly knew an airplane flight couldn't happen that fast. All the people on the tour, and other people who worked at the station would also know that was impossible. That would start an internet discussion somewhere, and lead to excited comments on social media.

Normally, nothing but frustration would come of such a discussion. But this time, since its topic *was* the fakery of mainstream media, it would be meta enough that *something* would happen. And by something, that meant mentioned on the mainstream news. Nothing else officially mattered.

And by mention, that meant denial, false accusation, demonization, polarization, turning all the viewers against the people who paid attention to the comments from the people who had been on tour.

Or would any of the people on tour even notice? Cognitive dissonance was built in already by the gaslighting media, always contradicting themselves and saying illogical things, giving images from the wrong location and time. If the people saw that he couldn't possibly be where he said it was, would they all just be silent, and go about their lives, trusting everything the newscasters said?

Normally, yes. This was no doubt far from the first time that had happened. They had to change up the timing and the tourists had to forget about what linear time even meant. But they'd do it, if it meant believing what they saw on the news. They adored the station. They'd just brought home mugs, tee shirts, and bears wearing jumpers with the logo. But this time, the topic she'd written about in the script took the meta sword and plunged it into the viewer's eyeballs. They had to care.

The reporter said, "This is probably the biggest story in the history of television news. Tune in and alert everyone you know to listen." His voice was loud and pointed. People eating their meals in the restaurant got quiet and turned to the screen, though some people continued talking loudly about their intimate lives.

That surely couldn't be introducing her story. She'd expected a shaken, scared, bewildered anchor choking out her script about how there was a secret movie production location where some of the scenes with the Rescuers were shot before being interspersed with some scenes on actual location.

"The heroic Rescuers, the frightened children. The sand and moonlight over the tents. It's all here around me. And it's a set. A very well-made set, with props, backdrops, and green screen."

Nancy gasped along with the others. The restaurant got mixed up together in a cacophony of conversations and shock. Why would the station proudly draw attention to humiliating *themselves* as being knowingly involved in the fake Rescuer scenes? That was taking it a step further than she'd expected. Not just a foot. The entire concept of a foot. It would blow everything to bits. Shatter the glass.

It was fantastic. It was the best day of her life.

She ordered another cocktail from the stunned and mumbling waiter.

She checked herself. She'd been getting plenty of sleep, but over the last months had been feeling increasingly sleep-deprived. Was she going into mania or something? Her heart was pounding fast. No, this was real. The fourth wall was being broken.

"These are simulations of exactly what actually occurred. We take pride in the acting and set design. We wanted to be the first station in the world to break this technique to you. We want to come clean and show you our state of the art work."

He was lying of course. Naturally he'd try to put a good face on it. But it was a start. The video recording was what she had provided, running along silently on the left on the split screen.

"These reproduction scenes are regularly interspersed with scenes from the actual location. We pride ourselves on making the pastiche seamless. This is the scene we are bringing you tonight. We were provided this satellite image this evening. Now here we zoom in." Yes, yes, yes, it was happening! The video she had edited was being shown to millions of people. The city where the news on location was from in fact was not about to be brought back to a thriving throng. In fact, there was no one there, other than two camps.

Zooming into the familiar tents, the Rescuer logos branded on them became clear. There were news cameras, a news copter on a pad, and the crew. There were other people there. Children wearing glamorous clothing with a desert theme, cooks, locals tied up, gagged or screaming. Zoom out, to the vast nothingness inhabited by only animals.

There was no one left to rescue. No one to go to war over. No reason to donate to them any more to save people because there were no more people there to save.

Tellen was not reading the script. This was even better. Brandon would be beyond placated. He would not humiliate the three men from the station with the dirty videos. The humiliating recordings would be deleted instead.

In fact, instead of the sudden tank she'd expected to ruin the station, it would surely be getting record numbers of viewers, calls for archived material, analysis, controversy. Viewership would continue to rise, at least for a while. Other stations would no doubt immediately join in the "transparency" competition.

Still, it was strange Tellen was taking all the credit for fooling the public. Nancy wondered how much he had improvised, himself. Someone had made a radical change in her story.

She swerved a bit as she walked out of the restaurant to the bridge and collapsed into her sleeping bag. She didn't want to celebrate alone. But who could she tell?

Nancy wanted to tell Becky. To display before her eyes what she'd found out about Stan and complete the investigation. Was the surveillance of Becky over, since there was no more video for her to do? Nancy wasn't sure. She would risk visiting her as soon as she could. It was a bit hard to fit everything in.

She wished she could have saved everyone in trouble in the world, everyone hurting, sex freaks and doomed gold-diggers, children and homeless people. Staying moral was limiting. But she was determined. It was her newfound freedom to do so. She couldn't go killing people and blowing shit up. Was blackmail moral? She couldn't remember.

She was exhausted, her muscles twitching. Stopping a world war would have to be enough for one day. She closed her eyes and took the strangest nap of her entire life.

Chapter Twenty-Nine

A Crowd is Born

Well, thank God. Thank you, Mr. Interrogator, for finally giving me information. I'd started to wonder if you were even real. I thought I was maybe just nutso.

Why did you wait so long? That's a massive chunk of revelation, to hold onto, don't you think? So, let me guess. You listened to my thoughts all this time. Debriefing, I guess you'd call it. You helped me do what I needed to do during my blackouts. Like get up and walk up someplace I needed to be when I needed to be there. You made me believe crazy stories you made up, didn't you? And you did it to fill in what I did when I was off my gourd. 'Cause that way, I could pretend life was normal for me, like other people's lives.

You couldn't have filled me in a little *sooner* about the sacrifice ritual the church across from Becky's house is hosting tonight? Maybe even the *day before*? Jesus Fucking Christ!

But it was your plan, wasn't it? To drive me wild. To pump me up. To keep me in the dark about what was really going on with the Rescuers and all that shit and then let me find out. Well, you waited till the last minute, didn't you? I mean, that was a random event, that flyer thing. Were you counting on catching me at my most off-the-wall moment, when I'm maddest to tell me about what's going down in the church?

Clever you, waiting to tell me about it until just when the ritual is starting, a crazy thing that will kill who knows how many women? Or was that just luck? Everything just happened to come together for you, didn't it? You've been waiting all this time, snapping your invisible fingers to wake me up out of my . . . What did that woman call it? My stupor. I don't like that word. Makes me sound stupid. I'm not stupid!

Becky's probably home, in a matching outfit with her fancy-dancey man, waiting for Trick or Treaters. I can see it now. I guarantee they both are snuggling up with a bag of organic candy corn in their hands. Yeah, they're both holding the same bag. Creepers. Meanwhile down the block from her: the gold-digger sacrifice to the vampires.

No, I *can't* stop crying. Fuck you. You fucking well know I'm not going to take this sitting down. That's why you told me. You're a smart one.

I wish I'd known what kind of team we were. A good one, I can tell you that. If it wasn't for you and me working together, Becky'd be headed for the church, to be killed at the moment Stan proposed to her. She'd be deaders, just like all the other girls the men are going to propose to tonight. I knew he was bad news. I knew it. Fucking *knew* he was a dipshit months ago. I don't even remember any time in my life when I didn't know it. He's always been my demon. She's always been my princess bride.

. . . My princess, anyway.

I guess, really, it was my fault. I was so stubborn. I could have listened when the kid in the Halloween store told me about the Rescuers. There were other times. I just didn't get it until the last minute.

Maybe it's past the last minute. I gotta act fast to pull off my new scheme! Now!

Already feel psyched up enough so I can skip my workout. I've got my muscles on for the day already. Putting the Halloween outfit in my duffle bag. Always have your Halloween get-up with you, I say. It's a way of life for smart folk.

Time a'dime for Walmart.

***

I've never felt so tall as I do now, on my way toward Becky's apartment once again, just like old times. Except I'm sly, on roller skates. With a bullhorn dangling over my arm next to a Walmart special: a portable video projector sticking out of my bag. And my other bag o'costumes in tow as well. It's heavy, but I can walk straight without leaning over. That's important to make a solid impression.

When I bought the projector, they didn't even repress a laugh like people do when they hear me talk for the first time. I've been working on it. Nice and gruff. People are starting to look at me with respect. Finally. Pretty soon, I'll be an international hero. I'd be the star on the news if the news was honest. I always thought it was honest, before. It's sick they're calling that revelation of the method, "The Honesty Report."

It's a smart bag I'm carrying, wish you could see it. Black leather. Stole it from Stan. Beat up my legs while I was running along carrying it. Along with his video camera that went inside it. That was a good find. I was finally going to use the video camera today to interview people on the street. You know, ask them questions about the big news about the news. Show them the flyer about the news stations giving false information about the war. I need to talk about it with people. We can't keep quiet now! This is the craziest thing I've ever heard. This is big!

But it makes total sense. I don't know, something just told me this was a good time to use the camera. Oh, wait, was that you? Because of what happened on the news earlier? When I opened the camera, there was that horrible video inside. Stan's video. An hour's worth of out-takes. That flipped my world upside fucking down.

What was on it but scenes of the Rescuers? Fake shit, totally completely fake-ass shit. My big Rescuer hero is a goddamned mass murdering actor. He fucked the kids and killed them, for the camera. And sent it to the States for to Stan to edit it.

After that, he splices it in with scenes from some film set location around here made to look like that set overseas. He sends some for the news guys to show on TV. Makes great advertisements for *selling the snuff of those darling foreign kids*. All the creeps want to see their favorite kid raped and killed. Those kids are worth millions.

That's how I found out tonight. You didn't even have to tell me. That's *how* you told me, isn't it? Why do you have to make it so complicated?

I never know if you might actually be able to see me, Mr. Interrogator. Mr. *Overly Silent*. What is it with you? I almost feel you hovering around me. You could be right there beside me, just drooling, waiting to fucking *dress* me. Put some new persona on for me. Pete Zelite, or whoever. I can't keep track of all the wigs and dresses and things in all those boxes. They get away from me. They go places on their own.

Why do I have to tell you everything, describe my life to you all the time? Why do you even care? And now, I know what you want me to do. I know you do. I know it. Well, I've already got my rock collection going. Starting with the painted one, with Becky and me on it, and the mouth behind it. That one has power. I can feel it. Someone put the power there. I think from lots of years of magic. Magic equals longing made of pain. This rock fits right over my heart.

And explosives in my pocket, from that gang banger on 52nd Street. That should do it.

And, yep, there's the one store in the neighborhood with a pay phone. Time to call my man. The news stringer with the helicopter. "Dude, it's me. Dave. You interviewed me about the homeless problem and recycling. Yeah, you gave me your card and said to call you any time I had a scoop. This one's totally different.

But it's big. Snuff films, man. Fly over the corner of Grant and Gaft in half an hour. That big church, you know? And I promise there's more. This is about the fake news breaking news. You think that's something. There's going to be a private showing of the rest of the footage you're going to want to capture from the air. Seriously."

"Got it. Thanks."

I swear he's going to go. I could tell by how he breathed. I think. I mean, yeah, I'm shittin' ya. I have no idea.

The thing is, can I project and video record and yell and start a march all at the same time? I wish I had more hands.

Stashing my costume bag in the bushes for a quick getaway. OK, up and at'em. Here we go! The skates are keeping the projections of Stan's movies nice and steady on the walls of the buildings all along Becky's street. Brilliant move. Is this how it's done in regular movies, I wonder?

Bullhorn says, "Think the news was bad. It was just the beginning! Take a look at this. Scenes from the front!"

Well, that got them coming out to gawk. Not.

"OK, OK, I'm kidding. It's outtakes from *The Rescuers* movie. This is the only way you can see them! Come one, come all, this is the screening of a lifetime!" It does look like it could be from the movie. I hope none of the kiddies are out Trick or Treating on this block, because this would scar their minds. "Adults only! R rated!" Now, we're talking. People are pouring out of the houses and Random and the liquor store and the office complexes and Beauty Store. This is exactly what I need to capture and stream to Brandon with this video camera in my left hand. Projector in my right. Yep, we got ourselves a little demonstration, here, ladies. Step right up. Yell for your heroes. Aren't they sexy?

"See what the Rescuers have found in a well. Aww, look, look, her dress is all wet. Just soaked."

That's right. Here the protesters come. Here they come. Terrific. But it could be so better. So much better.

Oh, haha, and now it is! There's that wacky ice cream truck zooming by. A'ziggin and a zaggin' through traffic. Some day, I've got to see her face. I sort of assume it's a woman driving, considering the woman's voice on the music it broadcasts. Oh, up, there she blows. "Tingle single kinkle do, HULLO! haw haw!" I can make out the silhouette of an elbow through the window, honking the horn. The HULLO! Is the horn. Oh man, poor driver. Really? Sounds like it's zooming around Becky's block up ahead and coming back.

It always adds such a surreal atmosphere. The sky is appropriately cracked looking on this street, with the branches spreading out against the lamplit golden-grey fog. The projection of Stan's video compilations will only brush by the dreams of some, the half-memories of others. But some of the neighbors are coming out of their houses, hearing the shrieks. There are some here now that I've made it look like a riot, from other local stations. The competition is fierce. "Hey, hell's! How ya doing'?" More people are joining, to see what the fuss is about.

The projections show the outtakes of the Rescuers beating a baby around the face, then sticking it in a hollowed-out area in rubble. Then, pulling it out, and holding it victoriously in the air, to cheers. As always in their videos, the babies' diapers are clean though they've been supposedly stuck under the destroyed buildings for days.

Then, the Rescuers stuck the baby back into the hole in the debris, and pulled it out again a couple more times until they got it right. Then, the baby was handed to a man who mimed sticking it on his penis, lifting it up and down. The crowd watching is angry. They get it. It's finally over-the-top for them.

Bullhorn says, "We can't just ignore this. The police won't do anything. They're involved."

"Shut up!" calls out the oldest woman in the neighborhood. Hey, Mr. Interrogator, can you hear what other people say, or just me? If I can hear it, can you? I mean, why not. Right?

"What are you talking about?" yelled another. She grabbed it out of my hands and smashed it on the curb. Great, thanks a lot.

I like being able to skate right on by, sliding past bitches.

The ice cream truck almost drove over someone to get to the church.

I like this part that's being projected now. CIA-sponsored "rebel" admitted that he'd been captured and forced by his terrorist commanders to kill civilians in areas protected by the government, the western part of the city, with cannons and mortar. Two of the women were crying out behind the man, as bombs fell toward them, for the president to save them from the evil rebels. The women died in the blast.

I hate to say, most people, even out here in the street, are ignoring me. They're starting to go back in, I guess when they figure out it's not outtakes from an action propaganda flick. This is my first time with a bullhorn. It seems like it would be great. But if people aren't getting into it, it's kind of pathetic. Lots aren't even looking at the projections.

It seems like Becky's style to stay home during something like this. But maybe she'll see me leading this, a hero. Maybe she'll love me for a minute more. She'll wish she'd said yes to another date. Maybe she'll dump her guy, some toad who sits on the sidelines when the revolution is happening all around him. Or maybe he's at home asleep. Haha, I'll bet he is. Snoozin'.

Here's a good projection. Rescuers with guns, walking along waving the terrorist's banners. And here they are standing on a national army corpse, urinating on his mouth while the poor man is yelling because the Rescuer is shooting him. Oops. So much for neutral and unarmed. The bullhorn chant gets them riled up. "That little bit? It's the trailer for the video. This is what's supposed to make people *buy* it. For entertainment purposes." Chant, chant! This feels good, swinging my free arm around, my elbow all bent up, my hand in a fist. Me bending down. Kind of hopping along. I've never done this before, but it seems right for Irish music, or Scottish or something. Jaunty I am.

I hear the sound of the helicopter. Or more than one. Maybe he told his buddies. Maybe the news got wind. Gotta make it look like a real riot. But, gotta get this part out of the way right now, before I'm recorded doing the big thing in my whole life, the big thing I was born for.

And, here goes something! Lobbing the painted rock first. Bam! Crack, bang, shatter, hell yeah! And then all the other rocks in my bag, at the largest stained glass window I've ever seen in my life, on the wall of the church. Facing the crowd I've drawn down this street. Right in front of their faces.

And there they are. Now we see what this is all about. Now, we see. "What the hell are they doing in there?" "WTF?" "Murder!" They're screaming and shouting and pointing. I knew it. They're human. They care.

In the church, with the glass broken out, it's easy to see there are tall curtains hanging all around the edges. On the outside edge, which we're privy to with some of the wall gone, are women in wedding gowns lying in pools of blood. A man is just standing there in shock with a rosy mop and a pail, beside a trail of blood from the other side of the curtain. The curtain is split regularly, and there were men standing next to each split, peering through into the church itself. They turned their heads when the glass broke.

Now that the glass broke, the crowd's getting bigger. I just have to make it a big enough crowd I can get lost in it and escape. People chanting, and now they're paying careful attention to the video I'm projecting. The Rescuers murdering people both on set and on location. It's got to boggle their minds. On one hand, there's fake news. On the other, murder.

Bullhorn says, "What ties together the murder in the church and the fake news, you ask? The murders are snuff movies to make money for the Nevermind. The Nevermind is also behind the Rescuers. Claiming they're humanitarian. But they're just making the little kids more valuable stock in the snuff trade. So they can fund the terrorists! Get'em!"

People look completely confused. But they're ready to be mad about something. Anything. They're ready to throw shit. Here come more rocks! More crashes, and all the glass is broken out farther, and here comes the good part. Perfect. Got to blend in with the crowd, get behind the right people, make sure no one is pointing a phone camera at me. OK, perfect moment to detonate the wee explosives the gang bangers said would knock a hole in a wall. I'm fucking stupid for believing them about how it wouldn't hurt anyone. But they'd be in big trouble if they lied. Right? They always stand on that corner.

BAM! BABAM!

And there they are. More murderers and sickos and their victims inside the church, for all to see. They're like worms squirming. Now we see what this is all about. Now, we see.

And, I got it on Stan's video camera. Surely someone would put this up on YouTube or something. The red velvet adds a lovely touch to murder.

The men around the edges all have something like straws attached to their fingers, which were pointed toward the action on the other side of the curtains when the first rock hit. As I skate along, I see here we have a good break in the curtains. Someone grabbed it when the explosion went off and tore that bit. There he is, rolling around on the floor trying to get up. The red velvet is wrapped around his naked body. Rrrrubenesque, I would say.

All right, got to take off my skates, 'cause we're here, now, we're at the destination, so I'll just stand here and protect the tripod with the projections. Maybe no one will notice it was even me at the front of the line before.

They won't even remember my appearance in a minute, because here I go, crouching down, putting on my Halloween costume. The burn mask and wig I found under the bridge. Wacky, stupid-ass look, that's for sure. Hilarious. And now, the little lady's jacket slipped on over my shirt, and it's complete. Presto chango. Looking as silly as all the other people in the crowd running around in their costumes they were about to wear to parties. This party trumps any others. This one might change the world.

And, right on time, the news helicopters. Thank God they believed me. They're not going to miss this scoop and lose to competing stations. This will rock their views.

The crowd is growing by the second, and I wish you could see this, Interrogator. They're running into the church, over the broken glass and concrete, and grabbing people. They're pulling off their masks. Oh, delight. I don't know them all. But I recognize a few of the guys that were standing at the curtains, believing they're part of some cool vampiric special elite.

Bam. Police chief. Definitely. And it goes without saying, bunch of local police. I've had enough run-ins with them over sleeping. There's that pretty policewoman. I'd hoped she was better than that. I kind of had my eye on her in case Becky didn't work out.

Bam. Judge? Must be, because someone is yelling, "It's the judge! Look, Judge Willard!"

Bam. Some kind of FBI-looking brother.

Bam. People are yelling about some kind of Representative or other.

Man, oh man, are the congregation of this church going to be shockered. They'll never see their minister the same again, now will they? Revered Red in the Face, haha! He wears his costume all the time.

I feel so alive! Like this is the moment God made me for. Like I'm bursting in flames. Or flower petals. Or like I'm a stained-glass window. Like I'm cracking. Seeing through the dark parts in between the colors.

Like that's where Mr. Interrogator lives. In the cracks between the glass. And he's coming to get me. To dress me. To change me. To put me someplace I don't understand. Like when I stashed my stuff by Stan's house and left it there by mistake, and he got me back there to pick it up. When I walk with Mr. Interrogator, down the halls between the cracks, brittle sounds reverberate.

Interrogator says, "I see you're already dressed. But let's get going, get your face washed, your teeth brushed, get you moving along. A little something on your lips. They're looking dry. Here's the water bottle I put in your side pouch."

"I know, I know, they're so much better than me. Oh! I'm burned! Help me! But so what. That's no different from me and Becky. Sure, I haven't been burned on the goddamn face. But I can still feel isolated. I wanted to share my whole life with her. All I got was one date for killing that jerkwad. Was a fantastic kiss, but come on."

"I know. Don't get like that again. You're agreeing with me."

"Why don't you leave me alone? You're the only person I've ever been close to. And I can't even see you. Why won't you ever tell me why you care about me?"

"Because of the things you've just done. Stan. The church. Violence is wrong. But do you care? You've got just the explosive temperament we need to save Becky and change the world." *We?* Who exactly were *we?*

"I do act on my feelings. And I've got powerful ones."

"And no limits as to what steps you'll take. Dave. You can't go back to the bridge, now. If anyone sees you, there's a chance you'll be recognized."

"They won't find me if I wear the right costume. Recyclers are invisible. I got no ID, no record in any phone or email or whatevers."

"Dave. You're done. You've done what you were born for. It's over."

The cracking sounded louder. The crowd is being fired on with rubber bullets by police in riot gear. Do you hear it? You *are* it, my Interrogator! The gray, the gray, it's turning into black. I'm dying? I don't even feel sick. Where do you always take me when you take me away? Do you love me? Does anybody love me?

Chapter Thirty

Hello

Nancy couldn't make it work out in her head. A step was missing. There she was, suddenly awake, and standing up, already dressed, in the middle of a riot in front of Becky's house. Last thing she knew, she'd been *asleep*. She'd been dreaming. Sort of. But now she was upright, in Becky's neighborhood. A woman standing next to her was staring at her. "Are you OK? You've been standing there not moving for a full minute. Are you having a seizure? Do you need help?" Nancy ignored her and moved on along with the crowd. She felt as if she'd just come through a tornado. She recognized that feeling from the past. She'd be sure she'd never have the crazy sensation again, after her escape; the Nevermind Agents weren't there to program her anymore. So, why was this strangeness happening? All her thoughts were bubbling up at once, and they weren't all Nancy's.

Have I split again?

She shook her head. No time to think about it yet.

The ice cream van pulled out from the front of the church and went past her. She noted that even in such sudden circumstances, she'd finally learned to accurately call it an "ice cream van" instead of "truck," which came more naturally. She tried to see in the windows, wondering if the driver was the same person who had thrown the ice cream snowball at her. Then it did an unexpected thing. It stopped ahead, right in front of Becky's apartment, honking the impatient, judgmental, arrogant hag voice, "HelLO!" horn over and over, and waving an arm out the window, beckening.

That seemed too improbable to be true. Nancy held her head. *Am I breaking down? Have I been imagining the ice cream vendor all along? Did I only imagined the rock inside the snowball that he threw at the house? Was it really just kids running along chasing the ice cream truck, playing a prank on me?* Had she lost her mind and fallen into hallucinations, creating a delusion of a rock inside the snowball, with the painting she liked to think of as herself and Becky? She thought about how the rock had disappeared under the bridge. Maybe it had never existed at all.

Nancy kept walking. Becky's face appeared in the window of her apartment, costumed in a gray wig in curlers and a long blue old-lady nightgown. A blond man came up behind Becky, standing straight and tall. He looked wholesome in spite of his pirate costume. Quite the switch from Stan. He put his hand on Becky's shoulder, as they looked out the window. His other arm was in a sling. Nancy hadn't seen him before; she figured she must have met him since Becky went under stronger surveillance and interference. She would have told her about him if he'd been in her life earlier.

"HelLO!" accused the ice cream van. The driver jumped out. Finally, the mystery revealed! It wasn't a woman that matched the recorded Jewish-neighbor voice. It was, startlingly, a wiry man wearing scrubs, a jerky fast-mover, with graying hair and mustache. He waved to Becky and the blond man to come out. How ironic, since Nancy had joked with Becky about how much she wanted to see the ice cream vendor's face. Of *course*, Becky was going to out.

That blond guy would be nuts to let a grieving woman go alone into that chaos alone, to talk to a stranger, for no reason. The church Becky thought she was going to be proposed to for Halloween was splayed open for all to see. Broken glass and pieces of the building littered the ground. Pale, dead women's bodies, in their ripped white wedding gowns, against the blood and velvet. And syringes. Nancy wanted to hug her friend and help her handle it. Becky could have been one of the corpses if someone hadn't killed Stan.

How many more women in queue had been saved that night by whoever shattered the church window?

The Experiencers in the church, with the long red straw-claws still stuck to their fingers, fought awkwardly to hold onto their costumes, which were being torn off by the mob to reveal their ordinary clothing underneath — if they were wearing any. One of the ritual Experiencers was naked, his straw-claws covering his penis, protecting himself against the rabid undressers.

A man's medical jacket was being torn from him, but he was standing by something that didn't look like a costume prop. There were knives, sponges, and blood. Had he been cutting into the women? Some kind of operation? And who was that man stumbling around behind the curtains in a hospital gown? Was that how the gold-diggers were killed at the moment of their ecstasy, releasing the best energies for the people believing themselves to be psychic vampires?

Even though she'd had no officials to turn to that she could trust to bring justice, Nancy felt guilty she hadn't stopped the ritual in the church, herself. There was only so much saving the world one person could do, but she felt weak because she'd abandoned the women to their fate. She loved whoever had broken the facade and exposed the ritual for all to see, and brought it to the attention of the news helicopter that was hovering overhead. The police couldn't pretend innocence — especially the ones who were inside the church trying to suck the life force of the women, or sexually getting off on the snuff. She searched for the leader of the riot but no one was obvious. That was wise. People were passing around a bullhorn, yelling about murder and the Rescuers being a hoax.

POW! Sounds like gunshots. Someone throwing fireworks in the streets.

The ice cream man opened the two doors that constituted the back of the van. Nancy thought she could make out well-worn narrow shelves high along the sides, with little gates around them, to hold in the things she couldn't make out. Toiletries? And something else inside. Was it moving? Was it a big dog living in there, covered up in a blanket? She saw two aluminum cold freezers, but there was too much medical equipment all around it, surely, to be a place where ice cream was kept.

The ice cream man lifted out a wooden ramp. He partially closed the doors; they banged together back and forth, and Nancy peered inside. Had she really seen a picture of an anatomical heart with diagrams all over it, in a scarlet frame, on the van's wall over the freezer? Instead of putting the ramp against the back of the truck, as she expected, he lugged it around to the front of the van. She couldn't see what he was doing any more.

The crowd was wild around her. This wasn't the normal subject matter people got riled up about. It wasn't on the cool list for virtue signaling. This was real. Others looked hesitant, or tried to reign in the few who were nearly on the verge of a dangerous riot. The area around the windows of the church was blown apart. Half-naked men grabbed the curtains to cover themselves, held there by the spontaneous protesters for all to see. The chief of police had been wearing a plague mask, the kind worn by doctors, with the long beaks to keep them from breathing in the disease. This one had a kind of long tubule coming from the beak, no doubt to suck the energy from the gold-diggers. A woman was waving it around.

Nancy flashed on the gold mines in the countries like where the Rescuers worked, apparently enslaving the citizens to dig the gold. Was there a connection with the Gold-Diggers Project? She vaguely remembered hearing it from a woman with a flyer.

No reason to bother walking on the sidewalks any more in that melee. Nancy continued striding toward Becky down the street. Such a sweet woman. Nancy was going to miss her after disappearing. And Becky would never know why her best friend had to leave. She'd be angry for sure, and never know how Nancy had dedicated so much of her life to her.

Arriving police were beginning to stop cars coming into the area from a few blocks away.

The news station that made the announcement earlier had to be going off the charts with that Halloween crime scene. The helicopter pilot must have been made out of adrenalin.

Powerful Experiencers were unmasked inside the church, one after the other. The mayor. The police chief. A judge. The crowd was naturally increasingly riled up after Tom Tellen's revelation about the news station's conniving theatricality. The projections on the walls of the Rescuers took the rioters on a journey into the heart of darkness.

The faces of two people throwing rocks were primal, their aim wild, their strength breaking more windows in the church. Other people were scurrying away from destruction of the crime scene, hunkering down and rushing away from the fireworks a teenage boy was throwing at the asphalt. Nancy wondered if they even knew what they were that angry about, or what was going on. They seemed ready to go overboard into unnecessary violence.

One man looked on, his slack mouth sloppy and registering little. Babies' and children's cries could be heard from the side streets.

One old woman chewing gum calmly looted the bags people set down on the street.

Many people were ready with outrage. They chanted for justice.

The ice cream driver jumped back into the van. He started the engine. Sirens getting louder from all directions. Helicopters dipped down loudly overhead, stirring her wig. Wearing the mask all the time she missed feeling air against her face.

As she neared him, the sign that had been tacked to the back of the van came into focus for her. The print continued getting smaller as it went down. It was speaking to her. She veered away from Becky and stood right behind the van.

BECKY'S FATHER

She bent down to peer at the smaller print as Becky was calling something to her, hugging herself and coming toward her, with the man beside her, his arm around her.

NANCY
YOU BOUGHT
My Daughter.
you
look
different

The van lurched forward, and upward on the ramp. The last, smallest, sentence of his message to her flipped up as she read.

She'd bought *Becky*? How could that *be*? A loud sound came toward her from the back of the van's bed, smooth plastic sliding on a slick surface. The van's back doors pushed open violently, something unidentifiable rushing toward Nancy on a sled, aiming straight for her.

It seemed to be a wad of clothing; that was all she could make out. Bits of arm-like and leg-like, neck-like fabric, and everything going in all directions. But there was long hair flying in the breeze toward her. From something that had somewhat face-like qualities. As if someone were musing over a wood knot and seeing "The Scream's" face in it after it had fallen sideways after being hit by Dali's paints, sliding onto her "shoulder," the chin running down, the length at the end attached to the belly.

Nancy turned her head sideways to look into the crooked face that looked as if it had melted into place.

Nancy's eyes locked into the thing's lower eye as The Blob sped toward her, flying off the ramp as the van drove off the ramp, bucking it upwards. She remembered. It was unmistakable. Those eyes. That face. It was everything.

That was who she'd bought. Not Becky. That was Becky's sister who had been deformed from birth. Becky had been the little girl living downstairs, when Nancy had recruited for the Nevermind. The ice cream man was the father Nancy had convinced to sell The Blob, so long ago, when she was Ageless.

Nancy ripped off the burn mask and wig. She let her face be seen, so she could, with all her might, beam an apology the size of the planet at the Blob.

Becky screamed. Nancy didn't blame her, poor woman. She'd never seen Nancy without those things on before. She'd had no idea how she looked. Nancy's face was not burned at all.

As Nancy arose, the sled slammed into her. The Blob's body pressed up against her, knocking her backward. Nancy regained her footing.

The van stopped on a dime, throwing the sled against her harder. The Blob smashed into her ribs, and Nancy was thrown painfully backward. She struggled to stand. The Blob's father ran around it toward them.

Nancy couldn't hold the sled balanced against her body and the tip of the van's bed for long. The Blob was going to fall.

The van's back doors crashed into them, and they both yelled. The deformed woman was silent.

The woman had grown and developed, with more folds than Nancy remembered. They had both been youngsters when Nancy had last seen her, inhabiting her Angela Ageless personality, in front of a video camera, when she had changed the course of The Blob's life forever. Nancy's heart curled into itself. Her ribs sunk in. She snapped out of it with a fast breath when The woman fell toward the asphalt, head-first. Her arms weren't discernible from her triangular-shaped body; she couldn't protect herself.

Nancy and Becky's father grasped for her, bumping their heads together in the process. The saucer sled pushed back away from her, flipping up to cover the father's chest and face, pushing him backwards as he bowed back at the waist. That movement lifted Nancy's legs backwards in the air, and she nearly fell on top of The Blob.

She regained her footing in time, as the father righted himself and the sled fell to the side. They picked up woman from the sidewalk, dirt and tiny glass shards ground into her face, her nose bleeding, her eyes red and wet. They put her on the sled, lifted her up, and both held her, as she was such an awkward shape. Neither made a move to set her back in the ice cream van. Nancy had the sense that giving her back to him might not be much of an option. But if she didn't, she'd have to find a way to support her the rest of her life. Was this a test? Was that what this was about?

But she couldn't even make a decision about what to do. She had too much on her minds. She was integrating her split personalities at the same time as the mysteries were being solved and new ones presented. This was beyond intense. She felt as if she were a glowing tube of ice. Or was she inside the ice tube? She couldn't tell which it felt like. But her head felt as if it was elongating. The ice suddenly shattered. She looked down from the parts of herself floating from above. They plunged towards the part of her falling out of the tube, smashing on the ground.

The slivers of Nancy's world fell from the sky, cracks of glass, her sense of self, her memories of being scared to pieces. She'd caulked the shards together again in the past. Now, the pieces were flying apart again, only to be set into another pattern. This split had been *her own* doing this time.

Her subconscious had learned the coping mechanism the Nevermind had taught her when traumatizing her beyond what she could handle. Her subconscious had months ago voluntarily begun using the Nevermind's technique of splitting the personality. Ironically, she had created another part of herself, to take a shot at the Nevermind.

She felt her body, her muscles, her blue jeans, her short dyed-brown hair wet from sweat. Her muscles strong from working out more than she ever had before. She'd had an alternate personality who'd also lived under the radar, with a man's capacity for obsession with Becky. The Recycler.

Wait a minute. The rock in the snowball the ice cream man had thrown had disappeared later because Dave took it from her. That rascal! He thought the picture was him and Becky!

Owning the fact that she'd been Dave was like suddenly remembering a dream made of clues. His jealous distrust of Stan. Living and making money untraceably by recycling and paying attention to clues, money which Nancy had found in her pockets. His outburst when discovering the Rescuer's malfeasance. Just the kind of anti-Agent she'd actually needed on her team if she was going to succeed in exposing the Nevermind's social engineering.

She'd gone full Dissociative Identity Disorder. Only one personality was the Recycler. The other alter had been the Interrogator. The Interrogator had made the smooth transitions between the her and Dave, so they didn't figure out the breaks in their timelines. It had debriefed them and silently shared only what was essential to them both, like telling Dave about the ritual at the church at the last minute when his passions were high. The Interrogator had gotten her from one side of the bridge to the other, and in the proper personalities. The Interrogator had dressed and groomed them each properly.

She was even more of an anti-hero than she'd realized.

Nancy's head was in a whirl. So many answers at once. None of it would have ever happened if Becky's father hadn't been the one giving her those anonymous messages. He was surely the one who had sent her to "Befriend Becky Lowensly Bronvonowich." The rock he had thrown at her had broken her into serious action. But if he'd simply told her the facts, it wouldn't have been her journey. He wanted to see what she'd do? That was beautiful. She loved him, and The Blob. No, that sounded too much like Glenda in *The Wizard of Oz*. That was stupid. Maybe he threw it because he hated her. Or because he was hateful.

As it all suddenly came together, electricity rushed along Nancy's spine. The recent events, orchestrated by the ice cream man, could have played out in any number of ways. Had he set it all up for that eye-to-eye moment between Nancy and The Blob?

Was she supposed to apologize to Becky, now? She didn't want to confess her horrible role in her friend's family. She'd have to apologize to the whole world if she got arrested.

Something about the patient woman on the sled that compelled her to respect the nuances of her movements. The woman had learned to communicate by barely moving her body, her face, if she could be truly said to have either one. Nancy wanted to learn the language.

Policemen grabbed teen girls throwing rocks nearby. They struggled to wrench free, yelling, "Fucking Nevermind! Fake news, fake war!"

"Fake heroes!" People were pushing against each other, the police distracted by them. Nancy and the father were jostled by the crowd, and both had to adjust their hold on the sled. Neither could hold her alone. Nancy eyed the closed-up wheelchair in the van.

"Go inside!" gestured Nancy, mouthing words impossible to hear. Becky and the man were in front of Becky's apartment door. But they came over to Nancy instead, ducking when something zoomed over their heads and glass exploded over them. Buck held his hands under The Blob when she started to slip, but watching their faces, he backed away.

What was she supposed to do with Becky's sister? Take care of her forever? Was that was she was being asked to do?

Had the father regretted selling his daughter? How much had he reformed?

Had the father been diligently taking her with him everywhere while he worked to support her, ice cream by ice cream, maybe living on the streets together in the ice cream van? What an incredible story of devotion.

Was his daughter too hard for him to handle and he was trying to give her back to the Nevermind to take care of, or to retire?

But. Did he even sell ice cream?

What was happening? Nancy was so confused she stopped moving and stared at him. She pleaded with her eyes for him to respect her at this moment, to tell her what all this had been about, why he had orchestrated her life, to bring her to befriend Becky. He'd sent the message about the congressman's party. That much was clear.

Had he been the man coaching the woman to give the flyer to Dave? If it hadn't been for Dave going ballistic after hearing what the woman had to say, Nancy would have left the church ritual going on while she got the Rescuers on the news instead. She would not have broken her word she'd given in the blackmail process.

Who knows how many different endings to the story had almost happened by accident? But this was all coming together, somehow. She wanted more than anything to know *how*. And most importantly, why.

The father lifted his knee and put his foot on the back of the van and balanced his side of the sled on his knee. Nancy moved even closer to him, to hold her side of the sled, which was claustrophobically uncomfortable.

He explained, amidst the crowd jumping back from the sound and light of fireworks thrown onto the street, "I got the codes for the Freak Show and the Gold-Digger Project." His convex cheeks twisted below his cheek bone, his jaw nudging sideways briefly, when he used the word "Freak." It didn't seem as easy for him as his gruff voice suggested it might. "I sprung her before the doctor harvested her heart for the Congressman to use."

"Oh!"

"One reason these Freaks get born is because people like my wife and me, well, we were given these vaccines that cause birth defects. We thought we were just getting vaccines for the virus that was going around. But they were caught spraying the virus to make everyone sick. I think the vaccines made us go kind of *off*." He moved his neck forward like a turtle while saying that, and opened his eyes wider. Nancy had been nodding, and wasn't sure if it was polite to agree with him at that point, so she let her head move slowly in ambiguous and flexible directions. One corner of her mouth twitched.

"See, the vaccines deliberately genetically modified our daughter. They do that to people so they have a lower immune system."

"Why?"

"Their immune systems were changed in just the right way to make organs more easily accepted into a host's body. Bone marrow, corneas." He wiggled his eyebrows, then raised them, thrusting his face toward hers.

FACE TRANSPLANTS." His neck whiskers scratched loudly against the collar of his scrubs. He was starting to continue, but Nancy shook her head and he stopped the list.

Nancy asked, "Her heart would have . . ." She struggled to think of how to ask it. "Fit him OK?" The Blob closed her eyes, and tilted back her "head": a slightly moist knobby protrusion that was oblong and pointed at the top.

"Who knows? I guess. I don't transplant them into the bodies. They weren't about to put me through school for all that. I remove them and keep them in here while I drive to where they need to go."

And if he finds pretty kids in the neighborhood, does he stop, and lure them into get in the van for some "ice cream." "You keep the hearts in the ice cream freezer? In your van?"

"Just got to keep the temperature nice and low. Once I turned up the dial and froze a heart by mistake. So, I transfer them to the hospital. Or whatever. But you understand how the ratline works with DieCorp and D/Web/B, and the UN peacekeepers, right?"

"Do you mean about how they go into countries that have been attacked in these cover proxy wars, or maybe after 'natural' disasters. They traffic sex, drugs, arms, enslave them to mine for them."

"Exactly. And the docs go in and give supposedly neutral, unarmed humanitarian aid, right? Hell, they're armed with vaccines. Those vector in a virus to shift the proteins around. See, doing that suppresses the antigens. Then, they test for degrees of Acquired Immunodeficiency Syndrome. They feed'em peanuts with lots of mycotoxins. When they get the combo just right, it makes your organs easier to harvest, just like that! Voila. Then, they use what they learned there and apply it to people living here."

"For stem cells? Vaccines? Sacrifices to the gods, like the Mayans and Aztecs did?"

"You got it. The goal for a lot of these wackos is a kind of spiritual regeneration into higher frequencies. Each transplant takes them up a degree in their secret society. They run the world through blackmail, and that impunity just encourages them in their idea that they're becoming gods, one transplant at a time. Like the Phoenix. You know about that? That's the same god as the Egyptian god, Bennu. A flamingo-god that arises out of Osiris. Now, that's something I'd like to see. Got to be pretty colorful, eh?"

"Tut this is like the forth of July right here. The street's going *off*!" Orange and yellow fireworks. *I always hate it when people shoot those off at night for no good reason. Wakes me up and I can't get back to sleep. Maybe they'll use up their supplies tonight and I'll be able to get some sleep. Some much of that time I thought I was sleeping, I was doing Dave stuff. No wonder I'm exhausted!*

"Those guys using the organs at the church over there, see, it's a cult of Bennu. They have lots of lives with every new organ, and they start over, like being reborn. They say the rituals are drinking the blood of the esoteric Bennu bird. They die under anesthesia, when their hearts are taken out, like Osiris Slain, and they return as Osiris Risen. As soon as they do it, they're beholden to the cult that runs all through the whole network. They have to make their pledges not to rat each other out if they want to be reborn into higher and higher realms each time.

Each time they're given a new organ in a ritual, they're said to inhabit planes that have all these wild names like Triarch and Biarch. And they're given new fancy names, themselves, too. They're inhabiting higher and higher levels. They're mixed alchemically with their victims, so that makes them get more like some kind of esoteric gold. It's all tied up with the Pyramids, and the ruling root race of Atlantian giants. And Theosophy. And Crowley. Well, I'm sure you remember about Giant Jack."

"I sure do."

"Rituals like that draw on the auric substance of the dying person, and the weirdos breathe it in. Drinking blood. Injecting blood. Taking baths in it. Doing magick over the hearts. They've prepped a lot of the victims all their lives to give them occult powers, right up until the time they're killed for transplants. They like the DID victims the best, 'cause their alternate selves supposedly float out of their bodies when they dissociate. They say the auric fragments spread out through the church and the guys behind the curtains draw them in through their straw-claws. So they get to bond in the club by sharing different auric personalities from the same victim. They're called Aura Brothers when they do that."

That was possibly the most amazing thing Nancy had ever heard. And that was saying a lot.

"And we don't know for sure, but there's evidence that they work with the D/Web/B to mix human and animal genes."

"Are they're big on the whole Edgar Cayce business about Atlantis?"

"They are. And they're finding ways to grow organs in people. The donors basically don't have much else to them. Some people have more than two eyes or ears. There are kidney people. Liver people."

"Sick!"

"They literally drop peanuts on the populations. First of course, they've got to make sure they're starving. And they feed them specially formulated peanuts. You know what they've got? Ever heard of aflatoxin? Rice has a lot of it too. Shit gives people cancer. Some people are super allergic to peanuts, and they say vaccines cause that."

"Should we really be talking about this in front of your daughter? I mean, should we —?"

He didn't miss a beat. "Plus, they do, ahem, 'female reproductive health awareness.' Abortions, that is. You think they just throw the fetuses away? That's why they've got a quota."

"Oh!"

"So they give the starving people in those countries genetically modified formulas to eat and they monitor them. And while they're at it, they keep track of all the kidnappings, and, you know, 'excessive civilian casualties.' *Too bad so many people died.* Got it? Creepy, eh?"

"Oh my God!"

The Blob blinked languidly. Nancy thought she felt subtle energy emitting from her, like a glowing aura. She was talking to her with it. Embracing her. Filling her with light. Or was it just her imagination?

"The ratline stuff, it's like eternal return, isn't it? If you have oil companies, natural gas pipelines, or gold mines, you're going to have the whole international situation all set up for trafficking even blood that they mine. Can you imagine being kept in a blood mine? Gives me the willies."

Nancy said, "Same thing they do to bears to collect their bile."

"Poor damn bears. This eternal return deal, hey, it's a perfect concept for all the lives some of these old guys have, one transplant after another."

"I'm not following you." She felt dizzy, and this was insane, holding a woman on a sled in the middle of an incident on the street with projections still running of the Rescuers from the projector in front of the church, and the vampires being arrested. The police were telling bystanders to get out of the crime scene.

If Nancy let go, the woman would fall onto the asphalt. Nancy made a slight move toward lowering her to the ground, but the man held tight, and his daughter started to slide down. Nancy raised it again, still looking him square in the eyes.

"Some of the elites change personality when they get new organs."

"The war zones are like their own multiple personalty farm."

"They get new blood from the kids that have been trained in the occult arts. The ones that are telepathic and clairvoyant, those are the tops. The elites like sucking in life force. It's an addiction. Cocaine is apparently mild in comparison; they like to combine them."

"Believe me, I know about Bennu. I was probably even being prepared to be one of the victims."

"The Congressman's already gone through four Freak hearts. His first one, that wasn't a Freak. Almost killed him. His body rejected it. So after that, he stuck to just Freaks. Just the ones that have been modified to make them better donors. He thinks of them as his saviors, as long as they make sure they damn well know he's their master. Last year, he chose The Blob to be next. *That* was a no! I'm not going murder my girl. I want to be the best father I can."

Nancy couldn't imagine how to answer to that. "Yeah, killing her while she's wearing her wedding dress. Not quite the same as giving your daughter away."

The father looked away, frowning. He looked genuinely anguished. "The Congressman's crazy about The Freaks, I tell you. He said last time I saw him he wanted to be called Lord of the Freaks. He'd be ass-dead if it wasn't for our ratline keeping him alive with the transplants."

"And I tried to get him to be an ally and help me take Stan down!"

Women wearing their wedding gowns were showing up for their proposal videos, and there's police tape around the church. Nancy saw one whisked away by the man with her, and she considered telling the police. What would she say? A couple showed up and he got her to leave when they saw the nastiness? And which policemen were in on the snuff videos? What would should possibly say that wouldn't implicate her?

She was just trying to figure out what was going on. The man talking so candidly with her maybe hadn't regretted selling his daughter and wasn't repentant. Maybe she hadn't caught in a moment of weakness when she'd bought The Blob from him. Maybe he hadn't become a sad, dedicated father selling ice cream. Nancy had felt so guilty about doing that she could hardly stand it. But, then, he *had* apparently been living with his daughter for a year, feeding her instead of letting her be abused.

He'd had the vision several months before to bring her to Becky, most likely to save her. He couldn't help but know what kinds of things Nancy was capable of. But *she'd* left the program entirely, once she realized what they'd made her do. She was having trouble judging him for what he'd done. He looked exhausted. It was all on his face. The tiny movements around his eyes. Subtle movements of his jaw in his bony face. They were working through it second by second.

Had he stayed in the organ harvesting business until this unmasking at the church, so he could stay in the loop and rat them out? He was doing a job someone would have done anyway. Did he stay in the organ harvesting business, or even take the job to begin with, to save Becky? Someone else had to expose it. Someone who had a passion for getting out the truth. Someone like Nancy.

Time was dilated as they stood there holding Becky's sister. Nancy wanted to praise him for saving the woman. She wanted to thank him for giving her life direction, bringing her to a true friendship with his daughter. His blue eyes were so fierce, her throat felt stopped up. She could only swallow hard.

He continued: "The Reverend had signed on to get Becky's heart tonight when Stan proposed. He was really into that, presiding over the Halloween ceremony. He wasn't going to get a transplant, though. For him, the sacrifice is a spiritual thing. He had to settle for one of the other gold-diggers killed tonight instead. I have her heart in the 'freezer' now."

Nancy shuddered. She was so shocked, her fingers tightened around the woman's "hips" and the sled. Her fingers felt like cold claws. She couldn't even blink.

"The Chief of Police's daughter has a heart condition, but she got a transplant last year, a heart that came from a beautiful girl the Rescuers 'saved.'" You might have seen her being pulled out from the rubble on the news. Tom Tellen made a big deal of her. So she sold for a lot. These guys fall head over heels in love with those kids. The Police Chief wanted her heart inside his daughter. You don't want to know why."

The news helicopters had been shining their lights toward the church, but they were moving uncomfortably close to Nancy and the rest of the troupe. They couldn't move away from where they were. The Blob on the sled was heavy in Nancy's hands. She could smell the father's breath.

Once Nancy had gotten the answer, it was almost too much to take in. Every bit of information was coming into her at once, from inside and outside, so many clues and suspicions, unmaskings, and near-deaths. The information seeped into the compartments of herself that her subconscious activist had purposefully sealed itself into Dave and the Interrogator. That was the way to get the distasteful job done more explosively than she ever could have on her own, as only Nancy.

She felt proud, along with everything else flying around inside her, that her splitting of personality had succeeded in one of the most important whistleblowing operations she knew of.

She felt like she was entering inside the hardest decision of all, for all of them. Becky, the blonde, the father, herself, the media. Not to mention "Dave" and "Mr. Interrogator." Where were she and the father supposed to be setting down The Blob at that moment, and what did the chosen placement imply to the rest of their lives?

They looked at each other, panting under the weight. The father certainly wasn't going to thank Nancy. Was he going to kill her? Was he going to entrap her? Maybe she could trust him. Their desires to do the right thing by Becky had orchestrated the takedown of the operation at the church, after all. The father stared intensely at her eyes. She forgot what color hers were, his were so brilliant, and unwavering. It seemed impossible for her eyes to be any other color than his. It was the color of intense.

She had to adjust her arms or they couldn't hold onto the sled and The Blob any more. Nancy looked into The Blob's long-suffering, soulful eyes and said, with all her heart, "I'm sorry. I'm sorry." The always silent Blob blinked her long soft eyelashes slowly, kindly, as if she were looking deep into her, opening her heart, sending something that warmed Nancy's chest, and embracing it all, everything Nancy had done, making her feel as if she were part of the earth and part of the sky. Nancy felt more in that moment than she ever had before in her life. She felt as if she had been reborn.

She turned around to see Becky and the blond man standing behind her in front of the pole, which was decorated with a Halloween scarecrow.

Becky was reading the message on the back of the van. Pausing, concentrating. Her eyes widened and filed with tears. The father's eyes softened. She could see the strange resemblance to his daughter, as if he had been taken out of the freezer and set on the edge of a counter to thaw, and he'd begun to melt over the edge. Becky helped hold the sled, with her sister on it, and awkwardly buried her head in the man's chest. His scrubs puffed out and covered her face, and she came up for air, sobbing.

Glass crashed all around, people throwing bottles from recycling bins.

It was the night of all masks coming off. And it was Halloween on mainstream news.

Finally, Nancy had a nationwide community. She'd created it. People who knew what she knew. She just couldn't let herself be traced. But whatever country she ended up in next, she'd trust her closest friend with the truth next time. She'd learned.

Nancy *couldn't* take care of the woman. Her slavery wasn't even specifically her fault. The woman had been bred for that. Nancy had to disappear. She had to change her appearance and move on to the next adventure right away. She made up her mind. She pushed, and in answer, the father pulled The Blob toward him. Nancy helped lower her to rest against the edge of the van. He bounced a door open while also holding onto the woman, while leaning back and opening a drawer.

He pulled out a thick piece of foam and put it down. They lay Becky's sister onto it. The Blob looked at Nancy with profound forgiveness. Nancy held the little bit of hand that could be disengaged from the amorphous mass and kissed it with reverence, barely able to see it through her tears.

The father put the sled in the back, leaning up against the wheelchair and the ramp. He stood ready to close the doors up and get back in the ice cream mobile and take off. Or, be detained and arrested.

Becky grabbed Nancy and her man, and said, "Let's go in. Let the police sort this out." The crowd was thinning. "If we don't go in now, they won't let us leave. Oh, sorry, this is Buck. Buck — Nancy." Becky's gait showed she was drunk with new information. She had just seen Stan's plan for her, had met her sister, seen her father, and learned about Nancy buying her from their father. She'd also seen Nancy take off her mask for the first time, and Nancy was suddenly Dave, the man she'd gone to dinner with only days before.

Becky asked The Blob if she needed some ice on her head. The woman nodded, which moved her whole body, as it was all connected in the strangest ways, to be one shape with a long, slanted, oblong forehead, without a neck, or limbs, independent of the whole mass.

Nancy and Buck held each other's gazes, and she suspected the truer love she'd wished for Becky might be beginning. He seemed flexed and ready to spring into action if needed, putting himself between them and the crowd. He was listening, watching what was going down. He took a step closer to her. He smiled. "Hello," he said.

That about said it all. Nancy and Buck looked back at Becky's father and sister in the truck. The police were beginning to arrest people and were heading their way. The father waved good-bye to them all.

Nancy had won, leaving Becky's in their father's care, rather than being strapped with her forever, while on the fun. Nancy looked back and forth between them and Becky. Could they really leave Becky's family to their fate? The organ harvester and the saint? She goaded Becky with her eyes.

"Come on," mouthed Becky to them. The father put down the ramp, set out the wheelchair and opened it up. He and Buck lifted Becky's sister onto it. They dashed into her apartment, and closed the curtains to the noisy street.

***

Appreciate This Book?

Nothing matters more to an author, after spending years researching, writing, editing, and promoting a book, than reviews. Reviewing on Amazon would be a *delightful* thing to do. Reviews at Goodreads, magazines, and blogs are also wonderful gifts to the author, whose livelihood relies on her writing career. Help readers interested in the topics covered here, or who might want to learn about them. Help people who love a good story find this series.

Chapter Thirty-One

Author and Series

About the Author

Tantra Bensko grew up in a woodland animal sanctuary in Indiana, maintained ties with the family homestead on Sand Mountain in Alabama, and lived in a variety of locations across the country, including Tallahassee, where she graduated with her English MA, while teaching composition and rhetoric. Then, she taught at Memphis State, and moved on to teaching again as she obtained her MFA from the Writer's Workshop at the University of Iowa. She wrote the series while living in Berkeley, California. She has taught fiction writing online for several years with UCLA Extension Writing Program, teaches regularly at Writers.com, and her own Online Writing Academy, and has taught often at Writers College.

She enjoys dancing, walking where ever she goes, trees, house finches, camping when she gets a chance, laughing with friends and spending time with her son.

She's widely published as a visual artist, and her work was extensively displayed internationally, such as a solo show called Reality Burn!, which traveled for years through the Spanish levant, with openings including speakers and bands. She was the artist on staff at *MKzine*, Art Director at *Mad Hatters Review*, *Times Journal of Photography's* "World Class Photographer," and an international judge of photography and visual arts at BTDesigns.

She was a columnist at *Unlikely Stories*, guest edited *Medulla Review*, put out *Exclusive Magazine*, runs a resource site called

Everything Experimental Writing, and published authors' chapbooks, and anthologies. She's had essays published, such as in *Paranoia Magazine,* and she blogs about social engineering at https://www.minds.com/AgentsoftheNevermind. Magazines of literature, such as *Evergreen Review* and anthologies, such as *Strange Little Girls*, have published over two hundred of her stories, nearly a hundred poems, and numerous essays and publishers, such as ELJ, have put out many of her Literary Fiction books. She has been published in all major and interstitial fiction genres and now is devoted to bringing out her Psychological Suspense series.

About The Agents of the Nevermind Series

Psychological Suspense combines profound, innovative aspects of Literary Fiction with Genre's fast paced, high octane intensity, straightforward language, forward momentum, and tense intrigue and mystery. Psychological Suspense is perfect for entertainment about the antagonists such as media's social engineers, who are informed by military secrecy and toxic corporate lobbyists. The genre is made for exploring eerie and important questions about identity and reality, bewilderment, being tricked and gaslighted, mental aberrations, coping mechanisms, intense mystery and intrigue.

Since our society's behavior is orchestrated using propaganda's illogic, this genre is an appropriate one for exploring larger issues of international politics. Intrigue and mystery are always integral, as the reader finds his way through the maze. Suspense tends to be slower paced than Thrillers, more internalized and focused on what might happen, a building dread of the victims, but can be combined with the Thriller genre by the victimized characters becoming more proactive in creating far-reaching effects in the world, whether for the good or the bad.

This book, and *Glossolalia* are Suspense Thrillers. Often the distinction between the antagonist and the hero is ambiguous, and there may be an anti-hero, someone dangerous and impulsive enough that he's prone to moving the plot forward through the explosions, car chases, fights, last minute struggles, doing what he needs to survive or help others survive in continual life-or-death situations. We often see such conflicted, gritty characters in Noir and Crime.

Reading the books in order is recommended for full enjoyment; *Remember to Recycle* provides a bit of a spoiler for a couple aspects of *Glossolalia*. But they're written to be be enjoyed if read independently. They're Alternate History, because in this series, our world took a turn in the 1980s. The fictional Nevermind is an intelligence agency formed at that time to take care of covert public relations work previously done by the CIA and other organizations, specifically doing public perception management organizations in the US, allied with Britain. They function as theatrical and invasive PR, working with the news stations to con the populace into supporting interventions in other countries, covertly creating coups, using tools like blackmail and mind control. Bell Pottinger and Purpose are real-world examples of the kind of companies they would work with.

The plots imaginatively riff off a pattern of targeting one interchangeable "enemy" foreign leader to the next, with disinformationists justifying interventionism as a cover for resource-grabbing and power mongering, enhancing DOD profits, putting through pipelines, destabilizing areas competing with US supremacy. Outstanding journalists who have spent time in Syria and Turkey analyzing the regime-change-by-proxy-war disinformation agenda, such as Vanessa Beeley, Eva Bartlett, and Sibel Edmonds, inform the international events in this book, as well as Cynthia McKinney, who went to Haiti. However, the plot is entirely fiction, and combines imagination with factuality. I recommend watching the videos of George Webb for more background of the trafficking, and his speculations based on a variety of people sending him information.

The history referred to in the books is true other than that specific to this series in which it veers off into the Alternative History creation of the Nevermind in the 1980's; at that time, some of the fictional characters, including the President of the US, were experimenting with human growth hormone. In fact, the HGH was in wide use at the time. Gigantism in the books was used to promote the actual common Theosophical concept that the British were the true descendants of giants in Atlantis. They were claimed by the spy Madam Blavatsky to be a "superior root race" and thus imperialism was their right. This and other dubious Theosophical concepts are part of the background revealed in the prequel, the last book in the series, *Giant Jack*. The New Age occultism prevalent in the 1980's was based on Theosophy, and in the series, the Nevermind were meant to keep those fires burning bright.

The protagonists are faced with difficult moral choices which they solve as unique, damaged individuals in extreme circumstances. These Spy Thrillers aren't black and white. The Nevermind circulates through protagonists and antagonists, gullibility and deceit. It can't do its dirty work if hackers bypass the compromised legal system and people's gullibility. Still, that way be dragons. Vigilantes doing violent acts are a core part of the Thriller repertoire, but are rarely meant as role models. This is inclusive, nonpartisan fiction. The goal with the series is to entertain everyone with exciting story of how good-natured people navigate such challenges that have been inherent due to human nature throughout history.

Do you love the books? Feel like doing something very helpful and reviewing them on Amazon? That would be fabulous!